SANCTUARY FOUND

PELICAN BAY #2

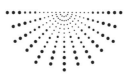

SLOANE KENNEDY

Sanctuary Found is a work of fiction. Names, characters, businesses, places, events and incidents are either the products of the author's imagination or used in a fictitious manner. Any resemblance to actual persons, living or dead, or actual events is purely coincidental.

Copyright © 2018 by Sloane Kennedy

Published in the United States by Sloane Kennedy
All rights reserved. This book or any portion thereof may not be reproduced or used in any manner whatsoever without the express written permission of the publisher except for the use of brief quotations in a book review.

Cover Images: © Wander Aguiar

Cover Design: © Jay Aheer, Simply Defined Art

Copyediting by Courtney Bassett

ISBN-13:
978-1985387010

ISBN-10:
1985387018

SANCTUARY FOUND

Sloane Kennedy

TRADEMARK ACKNOWLEDGEMENTS

The author acknowledges the trademarked status and trademark owners of the following trademarks mentioned in this work of fiction:

Pixar's *Cars*
He-Man
Stradivarius
Fiverr
Google
Thermos
Academy Awards Oscar

ACKNOWLEDGMENTS

Thank you to Claudia, Kylee and Lucy for the helpful feedback and to Courtney for the thorough proofing job!

PROLOGUE

ISAAC

Snow.
So much fucking snow.
Like... *everywhere*.
I held my breath as the car suddenly skidded to the right.

"Are we gonna crash?"

"No, buddy, we're not," I said over my shoulder to my little brother. I didn't dare look at him because I was too busy wrestling with the steering wheel. Weren't you supposed to steer into a skid or some shit like that? Wait, that was for ice, wasn't it? Did that even work in snow?

"Oh," Newt said from the back seat, sounding disappointed. "Lightning McQueen would've crashed and still won the race."

I smiled at that even as I felt my stomach drop out when the car chose that moment to jerk in the other direction.

"You think Lightning would like Minnsopa?"

"Minn*esota*," I corrected. "I'm not sure, buddy. I think as long as he had Mater, Sally, and the rest of the gang with him, he'd like any place."

"'Cause they're his family?" Newt asked.

"Yep." I let out a breath as the car stopped sliding around. Unfortunately, my attention was once again drawn to the sputtering sounds the engine was making. The heat hadn't even bothered to kick in when I'd gotten the car started back at the Grainger place. I had a feeling it was the car's way of telling me to just let her go already so she could cross over to the other side.

The idea of a bunch of old cars frolicking in heaven had me snorting. I doubted Pixar would be making a movie about that anytime soon.

"What?" Newt asked.

"Nothing," I said.

"Where's *our* family?"

All my humor died at the question.

Good question, buddy. But of course, I didn't say that.

"We're each other's family, Newt."

"Just us?" my brother asked. "Shouldn't we have a big family like Lightning?"

Should've, would've, could've, I thought with a sigh. "Families come in all sizes, buddy. Just 'cause it's just us doesn't mean we aren't as cool as Lightning's family, right?"

He was silent for a moment before he said, "Lightning doesn't have a mommy and daddy, either."

I felt my heart drop into my stomach at his words. I was saved from having to say anything when Newt flopped his head back against the seat and groaned, "Are we there yet?"

"Almost," I said. "Look, there's the sign Mrs. Grainger was telling us about." Newt whipped his head around, but his height and all the junk in the back seat made it impossible for him to see. "Lake Hills County Wildlife Rescue and Sanctuary," I read out loud so he wouldn't feel like he'd missed it.

"You think they'll have elephants? And lions? Can you ask if I can ride one of the elephants?"

I laughed. "I don't know if they have elephants, but even if they do, how are you going to get up there?" I asked.

I made the turn onto the road that appeared to be the sanctuary's driveway as Newt began coming up with ideas.

"A ladder?" he asked.

"Hmmm, maybe."

"Your shoulders?"

"Don't think I'm tall enough."

"Maybe you could tell the elephant to lie down so I could get on?"

"I don't speak elephant," I reminded him. He giggled. His laughter always did funny things to me and I selfishly wanted more of it, so I began coming up with outrageous ways for him to get up on the fictional elephant's back. "Parachute? Rocket? Tidal wave?"

The car slogged through the deepening snow, but fortunately didn't do much more than groan and sputter as we made our way along, foot by agonizingly slow foot. After several minutes I was certain the driveway led to nowhere, when the trees cleared a bit. I noticed a couple of people standing by a pickup truck near a nondescript building that didn't look like much of anything. My nerves started to get the better of me as I remembered why we were here.

God, Nolan Grainger was going to fucking hate me.

And that was assuming he didn't try to throw my ass in jail the second he realized who I was.

I needed to make this quick. Get in and get out.

"Buddy, I need you to stay in the car," I said as I pulled in beside the pickup truck. There were two guys next to it and I instantly recognized one of them as Nolan. I'd seen his picture often enough to know him anywhere. Guilt went through me as I realized I was a big reason Nolan was out here in the middle of nowhere in the dead of winter, instead of back in San Francisco or off in some exotic city showing the world how incredibly talented he was.

"But I wanna see the elephants," Newt complained.

My eyes shifted from the two men next to my car to the guy who was closer to the front of it. My belly dropped out at the sight of him.

God, he was a fucking tank.

A tank that looked ready to spit nails.

"No, stay in the car," I murmured to Newt as my eyes met the man's through the windshield.

Okay, I'd definitely need to steer clear of him. Big guys and I just didn't mix. The gay ones only saw me as an easy lay and the straight ones figured why not kill two birds with one stone and beat the shit out of the fag who also looked like a freak. And the not-so-straight ones–they were the worst because they had a tendency to think that the makeup and nail polish I liked to wear meant that there was something besides a dick behind my zipper or that fucking a "girly" guy made them less of a homo.

I resisted the urge to turn the car around and get us out of there. I'd envisioned a quick, harmless encounter with Nolan. I hadn't been expecting He-Man to be at the party. I shifted my gaze from the brick wall to Nolan and the man leaning heavily against him. He looked like a slightly smaller version of He-Man.

Though small wasn't the right word.

He looked like He-Man who hadn't discovered the joy of steroids yet.

God, either way, I was getting my ass kicked.

But I didn't have a choice. The guilt was already crushing me–not only would my mother have been horrified by what I'd done, but how was I supposed to look Newt in the eye and tell him to always do the right thing when I couldn't live by that motto myself?

I forced myself to open the door. My jacket was sitting on the front passenger seat, but I didn't bother grabbing it because I wasn't planning on being here long enough to warrant it. Of course, I'd forgotten we were in the land that the sun could no longer reach.

"Shit, it's cold," I muttered as the icy air blasted my skin. I tucked my hands up under my armpits and then forced a smile to my mouth. But when not one of the three men uttered even a single word of welcome, I let the smile drop off. Holy hell, did they already know who I was? Maybe Nolan's mom had told them I was coming?

No, it was something else.

Whatever was happening, whatever tension was rife in the air, it wasn't about me. I'd clearly interrupted something. I automatically looked to Mr. Brick Wall and saw him staring at me like I'd just stepped out of an alien spaceship.

Judgmental asshole. I wanted to tell him to get his ass out of

Bumfuck, Minnesota sometime and see that the world was full of freaks who were even more out there than me. I was about to tell him as much when a flash of white caught my eye.

I know, right? White in the land of snow? But this white had four legs and scary-looking eyes that latched onto mine as it came around my car.

"Holy fuck, is that a wolf?" I asked as the animal approached me. I wasn't particularly scared because I doubted the men would allow a dangerous animal to be roaming loose.

"Can I see?" Newt called as he opened the back door.

Damn, for a four-year-old, he had excellent hearing. Of course, that only applied when he *wanted* to hear something. When he didn't, well...

"Hey, no, stay in the car," I said to him. "It's too cold out here for you."

"No, it's not," Newt responded. The rusty door squeaked as Newt tried to push it all the way open, so I quickly grabbed and held it so it wouldn't inadvertently swing back on him. I watched as the wolf approached my brother. Newt didn't have a lot of fear when it came to trying new things, so I wasn't particularly worried about him being afraid of the large animal, but I kept an eye on the pair just the same.

"What's his name?" Newt asked.

"Loki," Nolan answered. "What's your name?"

Before I could say Newt's fake name as a reminder for him not to use his real one, he announced, "Newton."

Every time we moved to a new place, I tried to explain to Newt that he needed to remember to use the fake name I'd made up for him, but he always forgot. I knew it was a lot to ask a four-year-old, but it wasn't like Newton was a forgettable name. And Newt and I really needed to be forgettable.

"Can we help you?" Nolan asked after watching Loki and Newt make friends. My brother began tossing snow up into the air for Loki to catch. I was glad I'd had him leave his parka and rain boots on after leaving the Grainger house.

"Um, you're Nolan Grainger," I said, more to buy time than

anything else. I couldn't help but glance at the brick wall again just to make sure he wasn't within reaching distance. Not that I could actually get away from any of them if they chose to try and grab me. Even if Newt had stayed in the car, I still wouldn't have had a chance of escaping the two bigger men. The one next to Nolan had a bandage on his throat, but I doubted it would slow him down if he wanted to detain me. But Brick Wall was my immediate concern, even though he was the farthest one from me.

Because he wouldn't stop looking at me like... like he knew who I was or what I'd done. It was impossible, of course, but that didn't matter to my brain. All I saw was a guy capable of inflicting a lot of pain with little effort.

"I am," Nolan said. "Have we met?"

I shook my head. "Um, no, my name's Blaze."

"No, it's not," Newt interrupted before I could continue. "It's Isaac."

I sighed and said, "Newt, remember what I told you? You're the only one who gets to call me Isaac."

"Sorry," my brother said, though the response was an automated one. It wasn't often that I truly got angry at Newt, so he knew the difference between my exasperated voice and my pissed-off voice.

I returned my attention to Nolan. "Yeah, um, so Blaze is kind of a stage name. I guess you can call me Isaac." Fortunately, we wouldn't be sticking around long enough that it would matter if these guys knew my real name. "Anyway, I have something that belongs to you."

I ignored the urge to hug myself with my arms to ward off the cold and the fear and stepped around Newt and the wolf to go to the trunk of my car. As soon as I pulled the violin case out of the trunk, I heard Nolan gasp and I steeled myself for what was to come.

"It's my violin. What are you doing with it?" Nolan asked as I handed him the case.

I could feel heat tinging my cold cheeks.

Before I could respond, Nolan said, "It's you. You're the one the cops saw on my apartment building's surveillance video. You stole the Stradivarius."

CHAPTER ONE

MADDOX

The kid was a fucking thief.

No surprise there, considering he looked like a hooligan. I mentally shook my head–no, goth was the word they used to describe it. The dark eyeliner, lip piercing, gauges in his ears, painted fingernails–he spelled trouble with a capital T.

I braced myself in case I'd need to grab the kid before he tried to get away. He threw me what had to be his fifth look and I barely hid my smirk.

Yeah, he knew I was onto him.

"Yes and no," Isaac said.

"Stealing's bad," the little boy piped in. "Isaac says so." He dropped down into the snow to play with Loki.

"It is," Isaac responded. "Stand up, buddy, your pants will get wet."

"You said I could play in the snow."

Isaac let out a tired sigh and I felt a sliver of pity go through me. I glanced at his car again and couldn't help but wonder what was going on with the pair. No doubt, from all the shit in the back seat, that they likely had their entire lives packed in the little yellow sedan. "I know I did, but we have to get you some snow pants first, okay?"

He'd have to do more than that. Minnesota winters were brutal.

And the kid needed to find himself some decent outerwear. I took in his purple shirt with a glittery logo on it. His black jeans were so tight they looked painted on. God, the kid was practically a stick figure.

"Okay," Newt said, but didn't get up.

I wondered if the little boy was Isaac's kid, but Isaac seemed way too young. I put him at late teens at best.

"Look," Isaac began, his eyes back on my brother's boyfriend, Nolan. "I took it, but only because Trey said you wouldn't give it back to him. Then I saw the news about you being accused of stealing it."

I didn't know who Trey was or what the two younger men were talking about. My eyes drifted to my brother, Dallas. As focused on the conversation as he was, I could tell he was tired and in pain. I'd learned only this morning that he'd had surgery on his vocal cords about a week earlier.

And I hadn't even heard it from him.

No, I'd had to hear it from a mutual friend who'd asked me to come help out at Dallas's animal sanctuary for the day while my brother was having a follow-up visit with his doctor in Minneapolis. Our friend, Sawyer, was a vet who'd been helping Dallas and Nolan with the sanctuary. But when he'd received an emergency call as part of his on-call veterinarian duties for the state, he'd called me to see if I could come and help out for the day. I'd readily agreed, though I'd known it would piss Dallas off.

Not that I could blame him.

He had a lot of reasons to be pissed at me.

And I deserved every single one.

"You're friends with Trey?" Nolan asked.

"Friends, sure," Isaac answered, his eyes shifting to Newt. "Let's go with that."

I saw Nolan pale and realized why when I understood what Isaac's response meant. No, I still didn't know who Trey was, but from Isaac's answer and Nolan's reaction, I figured Trey was someone Nolan had once been romantically involved with.

From the sounds of it, so had Isaac.

Which meant Isaac was gay or at least bi.

The realization did something funny to my stomach, but I forced the uncomfortable sensation away.

"I shouldn't have taken it, but Trey was pretty convincing, and he paid me a lot to get it back for him. When I realized it was a scam, I thought about going to the cops, but I... I just couldn't." Isaac's eyes went to Newt for a second and I knew why.

And it reinforced my belief that it was just the two of them against the world.

I resisted the urge to interrupt and ask Isaac if that were true–if it was just him and the little boy. I had to remind myself that this kid was trouble. He'd already admitted to being a thief and fucking around with men who were involved with other people... he didn't deserve my pity or concern.

Dallas typed something into his phone and handed it to Isaac. It was hard to watch my brother communicate through the little device. When I'd left town so many years ago, Dallas's mutism had been so new that I hadn't really had a chance to adapt to it. When I'd seen him again a couple of years later, I hadn't been interested in anything he had to say, so it hadn't mattered. I'd only been back a few weeks and had just assumed my brother had eventually gotten his voice back, but I'd been shocked to find that the only way he could communicate with the outside world was through the written word.

And it had gutted me.

Lots of things had gutted me, but that had been one of the hardest things.

Because it was a reminder that my brother hadn't walked away unscathed from the car accident that had taken our mother's life and put our father in a wheelchair for the final years of his life.

"Um, yeah, I sent those recordings to the cops. I started taping Trey when I realized he'd lied to me. I didn't want to go down for that shi–stuff, you know?" Isaac explained.

Before Nolan or Dallas could respond to Isaac, two cars made their way up to the parking lot from the driveway.

The sight of the sheriff didn't particularly bother me, but when my eyes landed on the truck behind it that read *Animal Control* on the door, I stiffened and glanced at my brother. I was momentarily distracted when Isaac suddenly reached down and grabbed a very quiet Newt and picked him up. To my surprise, Isaac stepped toward me. Newt was wrapped around him like a vine.

I heard Isaac whisper something to Newt that sounded suspiciously like, "Don't worry, buddy, I won't let them take you," but I couldn't be sure. The little boy nodded his head and then tucked his face against Isaac's neck. I *did* hear what he whispered to Isaac.

I love you, Isaac.

I recognized the sheriff as he made his way toward us. His name was Curtis Tulley and he'd been the sheriff of Pelican Bay for years. We'd actually been on good terms with him when we'd been kids because he'd been our father's best friend.

But that had all changed after the accident.

I could practically feel the hatred seeping off Sheriff Tulley as he approached Dallas and Nolan.

"Mr. Grainger, Mr. Kent," he said, nodding his head slightly. The contempt was dripping from his voice and I knew why.

He blamed Dallas for our father's death.

We all had.

But the conversation I'd been having with Dallas and Nolan right before Isaac's arrival had planted a seed in my mind that was sprouting and growing like the most invasive of plants. My father had been the one to break it to me that Dallas had been drinking the night of the accident that had killed our mother. He'd said both he and our mother had begged Dallas to hand over the keys. When he wouldn't, they'd gotten in the car with him so they could try and stop him. It had ended in disaster.

Dallas's betrayal had ripped a hole in me so wide I hadn't been able to breathe after I'd been given that piece of information. As kids, my brother and I had made a pact that we'd never so much as even touch a drop of alcohol if there was even a remote chance we'd be driving. After spending so many years trying to keep our alcoholic parents from killing themselves or others by driving drunk, it had made sense to vow that it was a trap we'd never fall into.

So to learn Dallas had broken that pact had felt like the ultimate betrayal and I'd punished him gravely for it.

Only now I was starting to fear that I'd gotten it wrong.

Really, *really* wrong.

The sheriff spied me, and I could tell he was surprised to see me. "Didn't know you were back in town, son."

I'd always disliked the man because he'd been a blatant suck-up around my father, but around everybody else he looked down on them like they were nothing. The man was a self-righteous prick.

"I'm not," I responded. Sheriff Tulley's lips pulled tight for a moment, then his gaze shifted to Isaac and Newt.

I had no clue why I did it, but I moved closer to the pair so that I was partially blocking them from the sheriff's view. The grizzled man looked back at Dallas and I felt my hackles go up because I knew whatever was coming wouldn't be good.

"Mr. Kent, we've received several complaints about your business. This serves as notice that a public forum has been scheduled for tomorrow night to address those concerns and what steps will be taken to shut you down, since this place is clearly a threat to the residents of Pelican Bay." He handed Dallas a piece of paper. My brother, clearly angry, opened and scanned it, then started to type a message on his phone.

But the fucker didn't even give Dallas a chance to respond before he continued with, "We've also received a complaint that your wolf viciously attacked a resident who was in the area recently."

"That's a lie," Nolan cut in, which earned him a sharp look from the sheriff. He didn't respond to Nolan and instead handed my brother another piece of paper.

"This is an order authorizing me to remove the animal from the premises for quarantine purposes and to determine what action should be taken to make sure he can't hurt anyone else," the sheriff said, not bothering to try and hide the smirk on his face.

Before Dallas or Nolan could even respond, the animal control officer appeared and looped a snare around Loki's neck. The wolf hybrid was startled by the action and jumped back when the noose tightened around his neck. My brother let out a strangled shout and began rushing the sheriff. Nolan tried to stop him but wasn't strong enough. I was already moving forward and reached Dallas before he got to the sheriff. I grabbed my brother by the arms and held him as gently as I could while still keeping him from moving any closer to the officer, who had his hand on the butt of his holstered gun.

"Don't," I said firmly. I might not have been around my little brother much in the past ten years, but I knew what that look of determination in his eyes meant. I'd also seen for myself what the wolf hybrid meant to him.

"Dallas," Nolan said as he grabbed my brother's face to force him to look at him. "Please, don't. We'll get Loki back, but not like this, okay?"

"Dallas," I said softly and waited until he looked at me. "It's what he wants," I whispered so only he and Nolan could hear me. It was the absolute truth. From the moment Sheriff Tulley had learned Dallas had been driving the car that had put my father in a wheelchair and my mother in the ground, the man had wanted vengeance. My father had begged him to officially call the accident just that and leave out any mention of Dallas having been drunk. But in private, the sheriff had railed at my father that Dallas should spend the rest of his life behind bars. I hadn't really understood his anger until my father had told me Dallas had been drinking.

Then I'd shared his rage, though I hadn't wanted my brother to end up in jail.

But I'd pursued my own form of vengeance when I'd tried to keep Dallas from inheriting part of our family's money after our dad died two years later.

Guilt tore through me as I silently pleaded with my brother to heed my warning. His eyes went to the sheriff, then the wolf hybrid who was struggling violently against the man trying to drag him to the animal control truck.

Dallas gave me a quick nod and I released him. He motioned something to the sheriff and while I couldn't figure out what he wanted, Nolan did because he said, "He wants to put Loki in the truck himself, Sheriff. Please, it will go easier on everyone if Dallas does it."

The prick of a sheriff waited several long beats before he finally nodded. Dallas hurried to the animal, who instantly calmed at his appearance. Something deep inside of me ripped open as I watched my brother fondly hug the large animal after placing him in the truck. I wanted to tear Sheriff Tulley limb from limb for what he was doing. I quickly looked over my shoulder to make sure Isaac and Newt were okay. Isaac was visibly upset, and I could hear Newt crying and saying Loki's name. Isaac was trying to calm the little boy with quiet words and by rubbing his hand in circles on Newt's back.

I forced myself to return my attention to Dallas. It wasn't until the sheriff and the animal control officer left that my brother showed the first sign of cracking. Neither Nolan nor I managed to reach Dallas before he dropped to his knees in the snow.

"Dallas," Nolan called in a panic as he grabbed my brother's face.

My brother's eyes were just dead space.

"Let's get him inside," I said. I put my arm around Dallas's waist and hauled him to his feet, then practically dragged him to the truck.

"Is he okay?" Isaac asked, his voice ripe with fear.

"Follow us to the house," I said.

I didn't know why, but I knew it wasn't time to say goodbye to the pair just yet. I held Isaac's gaze until he nodded because I wanted him to understand that I hadn't been asking, I'd been telling.

I got Dallas settled in the front seat as Nolan got behind the wheel.

"Get in," Nolan said as he motioned to the back seat. I felt my body instantly break out into a cold sweat and my throat threatened to close up.

"No, I'll meet you at the house."

Fortunately, Nolan didn't seem to be interested in questioning my decision to take the footpath to the house. I quickly shut the door and hurried across the expansive property. I got to the house just seconds after the cars did.

I was pleased to see that Isaac had done what I'd said.

I reached Dallas's side of the truck before Nolan and helped my brother out of the vehicle. He stumbled against me, but luckily, he didn't fall. Nolan went around to his other side and put his arm around Dallas's waist.

"Just a little longer, Dallas," I said softly as Nolan and I worked to maneuver Dallas's big body toward the front door. "Just a little longer and then you can lie down, okay, buddy?"

"We'll get Loki back, baby," Nolan said. As we got Dallas up to the bedroom, Nolan continued to talk to him, but my brother didn't really react. I knew it was likely the mix of stress, exhaustion, and pain pills he was probably on that were causing him to zone out.

Once Dallas was sitting on the edge of the bed and Nolan began working his coat off, I turned to leave.

"Can you ask Isaac to stick around for a bit?" Nolan asked. I turned to look at him. He was focused on Dallas but kept shooting me glances. "Tell him to make himself at home."

I nodded. I wasn't at all surprised he wasn't extending the same offer to me. I certainly didn't deserve it. I spared my brother another glance, then left the room, pulling the door closed behind me.

I returned downstairs and found Isaac and Newt sitting at the small kitchen table, their coats still on. Newt was swinging his legs back and forth beneath the table as he and his brother played some kind of game with their hands. I almost smiled when I realized what it was.

"One, two, three, four, I declare a thumb war," Isaac said. As soon as he said the last word, the pair began dueling it out with their thumbs. Neither of them noticed me, so I was free to watch their interaction. A smile split Isaac's mouth as Newt managed to pin his thumb down.

"Oh no!" Isaac cried in mock fear.

"I've got you," Newt declared. I nearly laughed because Newt was holding onto Isaac's thumb with both his hands, a clear violation of the rules.

Both of them dissolved into a fit of giggles after Isaac declared Newt the winner. They were about to start another round when Isaac looked up and spotted me. The amusement slipped from his expression and was replaced with one of wariness and uncertainty.

I tried to tell myself that was a good thing, but I didn't like the little twinge of guilt that landed in my belly.

Isaac climbed to his feet and subtly placed himself between me and Newt. I wanted to laugh at that. One, because what exactly did he think I was going to do? And two, if I *had* wanted to do something, a scrawny teenager wasn't going to be able to stop me.

"Is he all right?" Isaac asked.

"He's fine," I said as I stalked toward them.

The kid paled a little and stepped back but didn't move away from the little boy. If anything, he moved closer.

I practically towered over him. I guessed I had at least five inches on him and outweighed him by a good fifty pounds. "Nolan wants you to stay."

Isaac swallowed hard and nodded but didn't say anything. Up close, I could see his eyes were a startling shade of dark blue with what looked like flecks of gold and green in them.

Makeup aside, they were... pretty. And actually, the heavy liner surrounding his eyes kind of made them even more intense.

It occurred to me that in order to see his eyes that close up, I had to be standing really close to him.

Really, *really* close.

I was.

When had that happened?

I took a step back and let my gaze travel over his face. His skin was pale and I didn't even see a hint of facial hair.

It was another reminder of how young he was.

His hair was thick and so dark it looked blue under the light. And then I realized it looked blue because there actually was some blue it. It was subtle, but it was there.

"You're one of those goth kids, aren't you?" I asked.

Isaac looked startled. "What?"

I let my eyes sweep his body and felt an unpleasant sensation stroke through my system.

Okay, not *entirely* unpleasant.

"You're into all that heavy metal death shit," I said.

"Oooh, he said a bad word," Newt whispered. "You gotta do what Isaac says now."

"What?" I asked.

"No, he doesn't," Isaac said at the same time.

"I gotta give up Lightning when I do it." The little boy whipped out a red toy car from his pocket. "And I can't get him back for fifteen whole minutes," Newt declared, his eyes going big.

"Is that right?" I asked as I turned my attention to Isaac. A shiver of awareness went through me when Isaac's tongue darted out to wet his lips and I found myself once again stepping closer to him. "You gonna punish me now, Isaac?" I asked, dropping my voice just a bit.

I expected him to cower, or at least look away. But he held my gaze and I saw a subtle shift in his expression. Suddenly, he was the one pressing forward, and I found myself practically nose to nose with him.

He smelled like lemons.

Why the fuck was I noticing *that* about him?

"I don't particularly like wasting my time trying to teach lessons to guys like you."

"Guys like me?"

His eyes slid up and down my body.

"You're one of those dumb jocks, right?"

"What?" I asked, completely caught off guard.

"The muscles, the intimidation, the inability to speak more than a few syllables at a time…" he practically purred. "I mean, that's what we're doing here, right? I'm the weird, freaky goth guy because I wear black and like to use a bit of eyeliner now and again, and you're the brainless jock who can't string more than a few words together and expects everyone to fall at your feet because you're big and built and gorgeous."

His hand actually came up to stroke over my chest and I felt his touch everywhere.

Yeah, *everywhere*.

"Newt, what's our rule about letting people hurt us with words?" Isaac asked as he held my gaze.

"It don't count if they don't know our middle names," Newt declared.

"*Doesn't* count, and you're exactly right, Newt." Isaac dropped his hand and stepped back. "People like that just aren't worth our time, are they?"

"Nope."

"'Cause if they don't care enough to know our middle names..." Isaac began.

"...they don't care enough to be nice," Newt finished.

I couldn't help but feel a weird sense of pride. Not many people had the balls to stand up to me. This kid had done it with very little hesitation *and* made a teaching moment out of it.

I forced myself to move back and give both of them a little more breathing room. "Nolan said to make yourself at home," I said, then turned to head for the door. I didn't like all the shit going through my head at the moment and there was only one thing that would help ward it off.

I needed to move.

And just keep moving.

"Is there anything I can do?" Isaac called. "For Nolan, I mean?"

"Yeah," I said without looking at him. "Don't steal anything."

CHAPTER TWO

ISAAC

Don't *steal anything.*
What a monumental asshole.
You're actually surprised by this?
"No," I said to my inner voice as I wrapped my arms around myself and hurried to the car to get our stuff. I shouldn't be accepting Nolan's offer to spend the night, but truth was, the idea of driving around the snowy roads in the backwoods of Minnesota in the dead of night in a car that was on its last legs scared the hell out of me. The idea that Nolan's generosity could be some kind of trap filtered through my head, but I dismissed it. Newt and I had already been at the house for the better part of an hour, part of which Nolan had spent in the upstairs bedroom with his boyfriend. If he'd wanted to call the cops, he could've done it then and they would have arrived by now.

So while I wasn't keen on hanging around the guy I'd stolen from, especially after all the shit I'd admitted to him about my connection to his ex, Trey, I knew that Newt and I didn't have a lot of options. I didn't have enough money to spend on a motel if I wanted to have cash for a place when we got to New York, and since it was way too cold to sleep in the car, accepting Nolan's offer was the smart way to go. I'd just make sure Newt and I were on the road first thing in the morning. And I had to admit, the idea of sleeping in a bed appealed to me, not to mention Newt could use the normalcy of sleeping in a warm house for a change. There were only so many times I could turn sleeping in the car or in a tent in the woods into a fun adventure, especially when the temperature dropped so low.

Anger went through me at my own stupidity. I'd been in such a hurry to flee our apartment in San Francisco that I'd somehow managed to drop my stash of cash when I'd been packing the car. We hadn't been wealthy by any means, but I'd done a lot of disgusting shit for that money.

Our *moving on* money.

I'd eventually remembered the money, of course.

Yeah, about ten hours after the fact. We'd just crossed into Utah and had stopped at a cheap motel for the night. It'd been all I could do not to cry when I'd reached into my pocket only to find the wad of cash gone and realizing I'd likely dropped it on the street outside of our shitty apartment building while I'd been getting my car keys out. The mix of fear and despair had been crushing as the reality of what I was doing had hit me all at once–dragging my little brother across the country with nothing more than a few hundred bucks in my wallet and all our worldly possessions stuffed into our crappy rattrap of a car. It wasn't like it was a new thing for us, but at least the last couple of times we'd done it, I'd had a little bit of extra cash on me.

After trying to plead my case to the motel owner that I'd clean rooms in the morning in exchange for a night's stay, he'd made me a much uglier offer. One I'd actually considered for about thirty seconds, since it wasn't like he'd been asking for something I hadn't given up before. But I hadn't been about to leave Newt in the car for the few minutes it would have taken the guy to use me and toss me aside.

So I'd ended up finding a spot near a small lake that had been private enough that Newt and I had made an adventure out of it, including a fire over which we'd roasted hot dogs and marshmallows before snuggling up in a single sleeping bag in the back seat of the car.

The second and third nights had been worse, because the weather had turned considerably less accommodating the farther north we'd headed. Last night I'd had to leave the car running most of the night to ward off the subzero temperatures in North Dakota.

So yeah, spending a night in a house where I could actually sleep would be a good thing. It would make it that much easier to get back to normal tomorrow. Hopefully, I'd manage to get us closer to Chicago and the temperature would be a little less frigid. And the second we got to New York, I'd make use of the money that remained and find a decent motel along with someone trustworthy to watch Newt and I'd go out and earn us enough cash to last us a while. Maybe I'd even rent us a house soon.

With a back yard.

And a dog for Newt.

I flinched as I thought about how many dicks I'd have to suck or take up the ass to manage something like that. Maybe not as many as a hooker walking the streets, but I'd stopped considering what I was doing classy about a hundred fucks ago. Didn't matter that I called myself an escort. It was time to call a spade a spade.

No matter how much money it cost for some guy to bend me over a piece of furniture or whether there was carpet rather than cement beneath my knees when I got down on them, I was still just one thing.

A whore.

At least the brick wall didn't know *that* about me. If he did, it sure would have been a lot harder to get in his face like I had. But I *had* gotten the satisfaction of catching him off guard. No, poking the beast hadn't been my finest moment, but I hadn't been about to let the condescending prick set that kind of example for Newt. Maybe I couldn't give my brother the biggest house or fancy toys and gadgets, but I'd be damned if he would ever allow someone to see him as *less*.

And that started by making sure I didn't let anyone treat *me* that way.

Even if I hadn't been trying to be someone my brother could look up to, I still wouldn't have let Maddox the Dick's treatment of me slide. I'd gotten enough of that shit from Gary, thank you very much.

And I'd been doing swimmingly until Maddox the Asshat had tossed that last line over his shoulder.

Don't steal anything.

"Dick," I muttered as I reached the car and opened the back door.

"You always talk to yourself like that?"

I jumped at the sound of the deep voice and immediately hit my head on the doorframe. "Ow, fudge!" I cried out as I grabbed my head and turned around. "What the ever-loving heck?" I bit out when I saw Maddox standing not five feet behind me.

"Fudge? Heck? Are you for real?" he drawled as he moved closer to me. A flood lamp attached to the front of the house illuminated his hard features. Not surprisingly, there was no smile to accompany his words.

"Jesus," I snapped as I rubbed the knot that was already forming on my head.

"So is calling out to the lord a punishable offense or not?" he asked as he stepped into my personal space. I realized with dismay that I hadn't moved quickly enough to keep him from caging me between the open car door and his body. A vision of the many times I'd be calling out to God and Jesus and any other deities who were willing to listen as this man's big body moved over mine had me swallowing hard. I drew in a breath and reminded myself that I knew how to deal with guys like him.

"Depends on who's doing the punishing," I said, injecting a huskiness into my voice that I knew guys liked.

Well, the not-so-straight ones, anyway. But it would serve a purpose in this case too. I let my fingers slide down my cheek and then slowly along the column of my throat. It was kind of a girly move, but it rarely failed me.

But of course, nothing about today was going my way, so why should this be any different?

Maddox held my gaze as he planted a big hand on the car next to my head.

"That shit really work with guys?" he asked.

"Does this?" I asked as I motioned to his big body. "What? Am I supposed to be trembling in fear? Should I be asking you what you want or begging you not to hurt me?" I asked. "Please, I've eaten pricks like you for breakfast," I said with false bravado. It was true, I'd dealt with my fair share of different kinds of assholes, some who'd even managed to scare the hell out of me, but I'd always been able to find their weak spot pretty quickly. Usually it was just a matter of trying to tailor my temperament to match theirs. Most wanted compliant or sweet or coy. A few of them had wanted kinkier shit. It was only on the rarest of occasions I ran into men who were only interested in inflicting pain and terror, no matter what version of me I gave them. Fortunately, I'd learned early on how to spot those guys and steer clear of them.

To prove my point, I turned around and bent over so I could grab the duffel bag from the far side of the back seat. I was pretty much putting on a show for Maddox as I wiggled my ass while pretending to struggle to reach the bag, but that was the entire point. He already thought I was a thief. Add in slutty, over-the-top fag and I'd have him on his way in no time.

Or so I thought.

But when my ass brushed his body, he didn't move back. So I waited for him to grab me and grind his dick against me, but he didn't do that either. I snagged the bag and forced myself to turn around.

"Quite the show," he said.

"Bite me," I responded before I could stop myself.

"Now what would your kid think of that?" Maddox asked as he studied me.

My kid?

Huh?

"Was your football helmet on too tight in college, Mr. All-American? Newt's my brother, not my son."

Maddox held my gaze for a moment. His eyes seemed to slip to my mouth for a second, but the move was so brief, I was sure I'd imagined it.

"Thought you were a little young to have a kid," he observed.

"Yeah, and a little too gay," I added, though I wasn't sure why I needed to point that out, since he clearly knew what I was.

"Figured him calling you by your first name was some kind of newfangled new age thing."

"Newfangled?" I said. "Um, I hate to break it to you, Grandpa, no one says *shi*-stuff like that anymore. Unless I ended up back in time in addition to the middle of nowhere," I added. I wasn't sure where the jab at his age was coming from, since I figured him to be around thirty, but I held my tongue.

Maddox sighed, then suddenly reached for me. I couldn't help but shrink back, and I regretted it immediately because something flashed in his eyes.

Fuck.

Now he'd go for my metaphorical jugular for sure.

Since I had no place to go, I had few choices when he wrapped his fingers around my arm. Yeah, I could scream, but what would that accomplish? He'd slap his hand over my mouth before I managed to even get the first sound out.

"Relax," he said, his voice surprisingly soft. "I just want to make sure you didn't hurt yourself when you hit your head."

When you caused me to hit my head was what I wanted to say, but what I actually said was, "I'm fine."

"Uh-huh."

He drew me forward just a little, then closed his hands over my cheeks to tilt my head down.

"What's with the blue?" he asked.

I knew he was referring to my hair, so I retorted, "What's with having no hair?"

I actually kind of liked his hair. It wasn't completely shorn, but he definitely favored the military style haircut. It occurred to me that's probably what he was. He had the bearing of a soldier. I'd noticed a silver chain around his throat earlier when we'd been practically nose to nose in the kitchen, but I hadn't given the jewelry much thought. But I was definitely a little more than curious to know if it wasn't actual jewelry, but dog tags. "Can't even tell what color yours is," I added, like that would somehow make him look like the weird one instead of me.

"It's dark, like Dallas's."

I winced when his fingers pressed against the bump on my head. "You guys do look alike," I mused. "Except the eyes. His are…"

"What?" Maddox asked. "His are what?"

He pulled back so I could see his face. I didn't need to see the color of his eyes to know they were an intense green that reminded me of the evergreen trees that dotted the woods around us. "Kinder," I finally said, though I wasn't sure why I'd chosen to be so honest. What the hell was wrong with my mouth tonight?

"Can't argue with that," he said. "I don't see any blood."

Thank god.

Not the blood part, though that was good news, but because it meant he'd finally stop touching me and back away.

Of course, he didn't.

"Well, I should go inside," I said. "Newt is waiting for me."

Jesus, now I was actually lying? Since when had I become such a coward? If I wanted to leave, all I had to do was tell him so.

I was about to do that when Maddox once again caged me against the car before saying, "So what exactly are you running from… Blaze?"

CHAPTER THREE

MADDOX

Even though it was dark out and the floodlight didn't show me as much as I wanted, I had no doubt the already pale Isaac went even paler. He made the mistake of dropping his eyes briefly before lifting them again to meet mine. He jutted his chin out and said, "No idea what you're talking about."

"What's with all the shit in your back seat?" I asked.

"What? You've never seen a messy car?"

"Your car passed messy about a thousand miles ago," I responded. "You were with Nolan's ex, right? That means you lived in San Francisco."

"That's a lot of information you have on your brother's boyfriend there, He-Man. You got a little man-crush on him, or you looking to add overprotective asshole to your list of titles?"

I knew he was deflecting and while I had no intention of taking the bait, I couldn't help but press just a little closer to him and drop my voice. "Did I just hear an actual swear word come out of your mouth?" I dropped my gaze to his plump lips.

Plump?

Huh?

I fought back the uncomfortable sensation that flooded my belly and tried to tell myself my dick was hardening in my pants because it'd been months since I'd gotten laid. It certainly didn't have anything to do with wondering how plump those lips would look when his mouth was open.

Wide open.

"Does that mean I get to punish you now?" I asked as I forced myself to look at his eyes again. They widened for a moment and then he opened his mouth to say something. I was surprised when he snapped it shut again. It seemed unlike him not to have a comeback and I found that it kind of irritated me.

Though I didn't really know why.

I put some space between us and said, "I have a phone and Google." I met his eyes. "And believe me, the last thing my brother wants or needs is my protection," I added, though I wasn't really sure why. "So again, what are you running from?"

"Newt and I have friends in New York we're going to stay with. Sorry if that's not exciting enough. You know, with me being a thief and all. But it is what it is."

I studied him for a moment. "So, being considered a thief bothers you?" I asked.

"What?" he asked in surprise.

"I called you a goth, not a thief," I pointed out.

"You told me not to steal anything," he responded, then seemed to realize what he'd said. "Are we done here?" he said. "Not really interested in playing twenty questions with a goon who probably can only count to twenty-one when he's naked."

The jab reeked of desperation to change the subject and I felt a little pang of regret for having gotten him to such a state that he felt the need to do so. I preferred it when he stood toe to toe with me, but he hadn't managed to even look me in the eye with the last comment. As I studied him, he shivered, but I knew it wasn't because of me. The nice thing would have been just to let him go in the house and drop the whole thing.

But we'd already established I wasn't nice.

I shrugged my coat off and closed my hand around his upper arm enough to pull him forward. Then I settled the heavy parka around his slim shoulders. He looked at me in surprise.

"Relax," I said. "Just don't want you turning into a popsicle while we do this."

"Do what?" he asked. "Unless you're thinking about trying a rainbow flag on for size, we're done here. And if that's what you want, you're kind of shooting yourself in the foot by bundling me up in layers." He leaned forward just a bit and said, "I'll let you in on a little secret, straight boy. We gay guys might have a few less clothes that need to come off for the deed, but there's still a couple of important ones that you gotta figure out how to work." He glanced down at my pants briefly, and I was supremely glad it was too dark for him to see the bulge there. "Then again, opposable thumbs that can handle a button and zipper *are* kind of necessary."

I felt a smile threatening to tug at the edge of my mouth, but I managed to quell it. As interesting as it was to spar with Isaac, I had more important things that needed dealing with. "So, *Blaze*, why the stage name? You an actor?"

"Yeah, Meryl Streep asked to borrow my Oscar so she could polish it up for me real nice."

"Do you even understand the concept of giving a straight answer?" I asked with a sigh.

"I don't understand the concept of *straight*, so..."

What had been somewhat amusing a moment ago was turning irritating, so I used my body to force Isaac back against the car. His only choice was to either hold himself still or actually end up falling into the back seat.

"Stop testing me," I said coolly.

He had the sense not to respond this time, though I could see the comeback was right on his lips.

His still-too-fucking-plump lips.

"Who are you?" I asked. "What's got you running halfway across the country in the dead of winter in a car that you'd be lucky to get five more minutes out of? And with a kid, no less. Do you have any idea what could happen to you if you got stuck in a ditch somewhere on one of the remote roads out here? What could happen to Newt?"

"Hey!" Isaac suddenly exploded as he shoved me hard. "Don't you say shit about that! I take good care of Newt. I make sure he gets everything he needs, even if—"

"Even if what?" I asked when he suddenly snapped his mouth shut.

But he remained stubbornly silent and then turned his face away from me. The fire was once again gone and that pissed me off to no end.

"Are we finished here?" he asked.

No.

"Yeah," I said after a moment and stepped back. "We're finished."

Duffel bag in hand, Isaac shoved past me, not bothering to close the car door. My coat looked huge on him as he hurried back to the house, his shoulders stiff and his spine straight.

Just a little too straight.

Like he was trying too hard to prove how unaffected he was.

I waited until he was inside and then closed the back door. I opened the driver's side door and reached in to pop the car's hood. It took just minutes to remove the sparkplugs I wanted. I quickly dropped the hood and then walked toward the house. The kitchen was empty when I entered, but I saw my coat lying on the floor, like it had been shrugged off and forgotten.

It was undoubtedly Isaac's way of sending me a message. I went to the refrigerator and stashed the sparkplugs in the butter dish, knowing Dallas would eventually find them. Hopefully he'd understand the significance of it. Since our alcoholic parents had had a penchant for driving drunk, as Dallas and I had gotten older, we'd come up with a plan to remove the sparkplugs from our parents' cars whenever they started losing themselves in the first bottle of alcohol. We'd store the sparkplugs in the butter dish in the fridge and return them to the vehicles the next morning when we knew our parents were sober enough to drive. It'd been our way of protecting both them and innocent people from their alcohol-induced stupidity.

Since there weren't any concerns with Isaac being a drunk, my hope was finding the sparkplugs would at least cause Dallas to question why they were in the refrigerator in the first place. He wouldn't necessarily keep Isaac and Newt around simply because *I* thought that was what needed to happen, but maybe he'd pause long enough to see what I saw.

I closed the fridge and reached down to scoop up my jacket when I heard footsteps on the stairwell. I hated the little flurry of excitement in my belly at the thought of sparring with Isaac again, but it was Nolan who turned the corner and entered the kitchen a moment later. He jumped when he saw me, and I saw him glance at my chest.

Well, not my chest exactly, but the arms I had crossed over my chest. It was just a natural part of my stance, but to him, I supposed it did look somewhat combative and intimidating.

If he only knew what it would take these days to send me to my knees quaking in fear...

"Sorry," I murmured. "You shouldn't let him leave. He's in trouble."

Surprisingly, Nolan seemed to know exactly who I was talking about. "Did he tell you that?"

"Didn't need to," I said. I wasn't really interested in explaining my instincts when it came to Isaac and his cute little brother, because I couldn't even make sense of them myself. So I decided to take advantage of the few moments of privacy I had with my brother's boyfriend. I didn't know why it mattered so much that I say anything, but it did.

"Dallas gave up believing our parents would change, but I guess I never did. That's why I didn't even think to question our father when he said Dallas was driving. Dallas never even denied it."

I was coming to acknowledge that I'd made a terrible mistake in trusting my father. But that meant accepting my own father had not only lied to me, he'd betrayed his own flesh and blood in the process. And I'd somehow made things even worse for Dallas because his earlier reaction of shock and hurt couldn't have been faked. He'd clearly been stunned to learn our father had told me Dallas had been the one drinking and he'd insisted on driving, despite both our parents trying to stop him.

Which meant one of my parents had been driving that car...

I couldn't even process that yet, so I focused on Nolan, who was watching me curiously. "I didn't think our father was capable of a betrayal like that. But I guess I never thought I was capable of saying what I said to my own brother." I felt bile rise in my throat as I thought about all the times I'd practically ordered my lawyer to make sure Dallas didn't get even one cent of his inheritance from our parents' estate. "I didn't mean it, but it doesn't matter. I said it and I let the shame of what I did afterward keep me from telling him how wrong it was."

"You tried to keep him from getting his half of the inheritance. You let him face this vindictive town by himself for years. The one person he should have been able to count on and you weren't there."

Nolan's words cut into me like glass, but I deserved them. And I was glad he didn't pull his punches. My brother had chosen himself a valiant protector in the small-framed violinist.

"Yes," I agreed, because what else could I say? I'd done everything Nolan had accused me of. And that didn't even include all the internal things I'd had to do to cut Dallas out of my life. Shame curled through me as I turned to go. But my limbs seemed to stop of their own accord. I kept my eyes down–a move wholly unusual for someone like me–and said, "Will you tell him something for me?"

I didn't expect an answer because I didn't deserve one, so I continued with, "Tell him... tell him I have his back."

And with that, I left the house and hurried across the property. It was pitch-dark outside and cold as fuck, but those things made it a little easier to catch my breath and calm my raging nerves. I pulled out my phone as I cut across the property to begin the walk home. I found the number I wanted and dialed.

"Alex, it's me, Maddox," I said.

"Hey, Maddox, when did you get back into town?" my friend said. Alex Miller was someone I'd gone to school with. He also happened to be Sheriff Tulley's deputy.

I didn't answer him. Instead I said, "I need a favor."

"Sure, what do you need?"

I pulled in a deep breath and said, "Can you get me the pictures from the accident, specifically of the car?"

Alex hesitated for a beat, then said, "Um, sure." There was a hint of something in his voice, but I didn't have the energy to decipher it.

"I need it tonight," I said. "And I need to talk to you about something else. Can you meet me at my house?"

"Uh... yeah, your house as in—"

"Raven's Wing," I cut in. God, I just hated that name. Leave it to my parents to not only build a completely out of place Victorian-era mansion on a bluff overlooking the small town of Pelican Bay, they had to go and give it a name that sounded like it belonged in an Edgar Allan Poe tale. "I'll be there by nine," I said as I glanced at the clock on the phone. "Will that be too late for you?"

"No, not at all. I'll still be on shift, though, so I may have to take a call."

"That's fine," I said. In a town like Pelican Bay, I highly doubted there'd be a lot of calls that time of night. The snow had started to fall again, so most residents knew enough to stay home and wait until the plows made their way around town, and that wouldn't happen until morning.

At least Isaac and little Newt weren't going anywhere.

I cursed myself for letting the weird-looking and utterly annoying Isaac back in my head, even for a moment.

"I'll see you then," I said to Alex, then hung up. My legs burned as I trudged through the thickening snow, but I welcomed the discomfort. It would have been easier to walk along the road, but I wasn't looking for easy. I had a lot of shit rolling around in my head and right now, I didn't want to deal with any of it. If the only way to escape it was to push other parts of my body to their limit, so be it. And if I did have to think about something, it sure as shit couldn't be how deeply I'd betrayed my brother or the unexpected feelings his cute little new houseguest had stirred in me.

At least with Dallas, I could do what I should have done all along–have his back. But with Isaac... well, that just needed to die a quick death. Despite the innate need to know what troubles Isaac was dealing with, I was starting to wonder if I hadn't made a serious mistake in manipulating the situation so he was forced to stick around. In truth, part of me really, really wanted him gone by morning. It was a coward's move, but I sent my eyes heavenward and willed the snow to stop so it would be one less obstacle for Isaac if he did manage to figure out the thing with his car and headed out at first light.

But the snow grew heavier, not lighter, and I couldn't help but laugh that fate wasn't going to give me a break on this one.

Yeah, so what else is new?

CHAPTER FOUR

ISAAC

"Fuck, fuck, fuck," I whispered to myself as I covered my face with my hands in the hopes the move would somehow stave off the tears that were threatening. I was pretty good about not swearing, even when Newt wasn't around, but when things were really bad, my brain didn't try to mince words, even the curses.

And things were pretty fucking bad.

I was sitting sideways in the driver's seat of my car with my feet flat on the ground, staring at the expansive property laid out before me. I could see dozens and dozens of enclosures, but none were close enough for me to make out what was in them, despite the snow having stopped a couple of hours earlier.

I'd been ecstatic to wake up this morning to only a few flurries here and there, but my hopes for making a speedy escape before Nolan and Dallas could get up had died a quick death when I'd rushed out to the car to get it started so it would be nice and warm by the time I got Newt dressed and our few belongings packed up. But as soon as I'd turned the key over, the car had sputtered several times, but never actually started.

I'd tried over and over, feeling my stomach sink with every desperate turn of the key, but it had been the same thing each time.

When I'd returned to the house, Dallas had offered to take a look at the car. I'd still held out hope he could work some magic, even if it was with something as simple as duct tape and a toothpick, anything to get us to the next big city... but when I'd come downstairs, he'd merely shook his head and typed out a message that he'd need to take a more in-depth look at it. His comment had been followed by an invitation for me and Newt to stay with him and Nolan as long as we needed to until he could get the car fixed.

Newt had been ecstatic and had begged to see all the animals and ride the elephants. I'd barely managed to thank the man and accept his generous offer, because inside I'd wanted to die.

It was just par for the course, I supposed.

Nothing had gone right since we'd left San Francisco.

Although, if I was being honest, things hadn't exactly been going right before then, either.

Long before then.

I sighed and ran my fingers through my hair, then began mentally counting up how much money I had left. There was no way I'd have enough to pay to fix the car. I pulled out my phone and pulled up the local online ads using one of the bigger-name general classified ads sites that included a section for guys looking for "dates." I felt a mix of relief and dread when I saw that although most of the ads were looking for guys closer to one of the larger cities, a handful mentioned towns I'd seen on our way to Pelican Bay. Which meant I could post my own ad offering my "services" and hopefully find someone local. If I was really lucky, I could find a place nearby that I could walk to, since I wasn't willing to get into a car with a date.

But what to do with Newt?

I glanced at the farmhouse behind me.

Nolan and Dallas had been incredibly generous to let me and Newt spend the night with them, especially after what I'd done to Nolan. And fuck if it hadn't been incredible to sleep in a real bed rather than a sleeping bag. But could I really push my luck by asking them to babysit Newt for me for a few hours?

Did I even want to?

They seemed kind and good with kids—hell, I'd even walked in on them playing cars with Newt this morning. But what if they questioned Newt while I was gone? And as much as Newt knew we couldn't trust strangers, his natural inclination was to find the good in people, and he'd warmed up to Dallas and Nolan pretty quickly. It wouldn't take much for them to get him to tell them things they didn't need to know.

But what choice did I have?

I needed money.

Period.

My belly rolled uncomfortably as I pulled up the map on my phone and searched out a motel that was within walking distance but wasn't too skeevy. Once I found one, I quickly typed out an ad and included a picture of myself. I submitted it before I could change my mind. Part of me hoped nothing would come of it, but the other part of me was afraid what would happen if nothing did.

"Isaac, I got to see a bear!" I heard Newt shout, and I looked up to see him hurrying toward me. Dallas and Nolan were walking behind him, hand in hand. I felt a pang of envy go through me. Not only because of how they were clinging to each other, but the way they were smiling at Newt.

Like he was their kid or something.

Tears stung the backs of my eyes as I imagined Newt in a world like this. Where he'd have no worries and he'd have people who could give him not only what he needed, but what he wanted too. But instead, he was being dragged all over the country by someone who couldn't guarantee him anything and had to sell his own ass just to give him the basics.

You had no choice.

I wanted to scoff at the inner voice. I'd had a choice. I'd just been a selfish dick who'd believed Newt was better off with me than anyone else.

I glanced at the shit in the back seat.

"Better off, right," I whispered.

"Isaac, he was bigger than Kenai!" Newt shouted as he came

barreling at me. I smiled at the reference to *Brother Bear*, one of Newt's favorite movies after the *Cars* ones.

"Oh yeah?" I said as I caught him in my arms when he reached me. I gave him a good squish and said, "Do you think he's really a boy like Kenai was?"

"Nuh-uh," Newt said with a shake of his head. "He's a real bear. Dallas said so."

Newt suddenly leaned in and whispered, "Dallas can't talk but Nolan knows what he's trying to say. But you gotta look at Dallas, even if Nolan's talking, 'cause it's 'olite."

"Polite," I said with a smile. "I'll remember." I was so proud of my brother and the compassion he inherently showed others. As much as I tried to make sure he knew his manners, his goodness came from deep inside him. On the one hand, it sometimes made him more sensitive to things, which could work against him, but I wouldn't have changed it. It was a quality he shared with our mother, and while I'd watched people take advantage of her over the years, I'd vowed I'd never let anyone do that to Newt, no matter what. If I had my way, he'd never have some asshole telling him he needed to toughen up or take things like a man.

"Isaac," Newt said as he grabbed each side of my face, a move he only did when he was deeply serious.

Well, as deeply serious as any four-year-old could be.

"I gotta save Loki, 'kay?" he said.

"I understand, Newt, but there's nothing we—"

"Nu-huh, there is," he interrupted. "We's gotta talk to the people tonight."

"We *have to* talk," I amended. "What people?"

"I'm sorry, Isaac, it seems Newt overheard me and Dallas talking about the hearing in town tonight. The one where we're going to try to get Loki back," Nolan explained. "But you guys don't need to go," he quickly added. "You're welcome to stay here at the house."

The reminder that we were stuck here just made my stomach hurt even more, but I jumped on the offer and said, "If you're sure."

It wasn't that I didn't want to help these men get their pet back, it was that I *couldn't*. We'd already had a close call by coming into such close contact with the sheriff yesterday. It'd been one of the first times since we'd left Boston that we'd interacted with any kind of law enforcement agent, and instead of just pretending like we had every right to be in Pelican Bay, Newt and I had both panicked and called even more attention to ourselves. I could only hope that Nolan and Dallas had assumed it was because of my role in taking his violin.

"No!" Newt said as he began shaking his head.

"Newt—" I said, sensing the mother of all temper tantrums kicking in, but he surprised me by keeping his voice low and surprisingly calm.

"I gotta help Loki, Isaac. They took him away from his family," he said softly. It was the words he didn't speak that made my heart hurt.

On the one hand, I didn't want to go anywhere near town, and especially into a situation where we'd stick out like the sore thumbs we were, but on the other, Newt didn't often ask me for much.

"I gotta tell the mean people what a nice dog Loki is. They'll believe me, Isaac, 'cause it's the truth. And we always gotta tell the truth."

I wanted to laugh at that because it was a lesson I was always reinforcing with Newt, despite the fact that our whole lives were pretty much one big lie. I studied my little brother for a long time. As the person who'd pretty much raised him from birth, it was both humbling and overwhelming to see him becoming this actual little person with emotions and beliefs. And despite all he'd been through, he still had such a good heart, and in spite of everything, his trust in others wasn't completely destroyed yet...

I shook my head because I couldn't trifle with that. It would change him into someone he was never meant to be.

Newt must have mistaken my shaking head as my answer because he suddenly looked crestfallen, so I quickly said, "You know what, Newt, you are absolutely right."

He paused for a moment, then a big smile split his lips. "I am?"

I tickled his stomach. "You absolutely are. I'm so proud of you for being brave enough to tell the truth about Loki."

As trusting as my brother instinctively was of people, he'd had to learn in the past year that he needed to go against his nature and not trust every person he met. So for him to be willing to get up in front of a room full of strangers would be easy for him in some ways but frightening in others. I needed to make sure we were cautious, but that he could also have this moment to let a little of himself shine through.

I looked up at Nolan and Dallas as I pulled Newt into my arms for a quick squeeze. "We'd love to come with you, if you don't mind giving us a ride."

"Of course," Nolan said. Dallas typed something on his phone and handed it to me.

You guys are welcome to stay with us as long as you like, Isaac.

"Thank you," I said as I handed the phone back to him. "I think we'll have to impose on your hospitality one more night, but hopefully by tomorrow I can get someone out here to fix the car."

I felt my phone buzz in my pocket and fought the urge to check it. On the one hand, I really, really needed it to be a response to my ad, but on the other, that was the last thing I wanted.

Dallas and Nolan exchanged a quick look between them, but I didn't understand what it meant. Dallas typed something again.

I'll look at your car again tomorrow. Maybe I can get it running once the cold snap eases a bit.

If the whole state of Minnesota suddenly burst into flame, I doubted it would change the outlook on my car, but I nodded anyway and said, "Yeah, thanks."

The fact was that if I could meet a couple guys at the motel in a span of a few hours, I could earn enough in one afternoon to buy another cheap-ass car that would at least get us to Chicago. Chicago wasn't New York, but we could get sucked up by that city just as easily as the Big Apple.

"How about some lunch?" Nolan asked. "Newt, you look like a peanut butter and jelly kind of man to me. Just like this guy," Nolan said as he motioned to Dallas.

"Grape jelly?" Newt asked.

Dallas nodded and then held out his hand. I swallowed hard when Newt automatically took it.

Yeah, he *needed* to trust just so damn bad.

"He's an amazing kid, Isaac," Nolan said as we watched the very tall Dallas lead the very small Newt up to the house.

"He is," I agreed. "How's Dallas feeling?" I asked.

Nolan nodded slightly. "Hanging in there. He'll be better when we get Loki back and get this town off our ass for good."

His bitterness surprised me. There was clearly a history between the pair and Pelican Bay that went beyond a few freaked-out citizens trying to take their pet away and close their center down. I wanted to ask him about it, but reality intruded right before I opened my mouth.

He and I weren't friends. Yes, he'd been kind to me and didn't seem to be holding a grudge over the fact that I'd both stolen from him *and* slept with the man he'd considered his boyfriend, but even if I could trust that he was being genuine when it came to not wanting revenge for all that stuff, I couldn't do something stupid and start to think of him as something more. He was just a kindhearted soul feeling sorry for me and my kid brother and that was it. At most, we could repay that kindness by offering support at the meeting tonight.

So I kept my mouth shut and politely nodded and then followed him back to the house when he offered to reheat the lasagna from last night for lunch.

By the time we sat down around the table with Dallas, Nolan, and Newt talking about the most recent *Cars* movie, my phone had buzzed for a third time and the food in my belly soured.

Yeah, in twenty-four hours we'd be able to get the hell out of this place for sure.

No matter what the cost, either in dollars… or in what was left of my soul.

From the moment Newt and I walked into the town hall meeting, I was sure someone was going to point at us and tell us we didn't belong. And yeah, I definitely got my fair share of curious looks, but that was nothing new. But no one seemed focused on us for more than a second as soon as Dallas and Nolan walked hand in hand down the aisle toward the small group of people seated at a long conference table at the front of the room. They were all stern-looking older people and something in my gut said this wasn't going to go well. I saw the sheriff in the corner and while I normally would have been scared to death to even be in the same room with the man, he barely seemed to even notice anyone but Dallas.

Jesus, what was the guy's damage with Dallas? I mean, Dallas seemed like the nicest guy in the world and yet the sheriff looked ready to spit nails.

The guy in the center of the table used a gavel to get everyone's attention and as people settled down, I saw Nolan's mother just a few seats in from the row closest to me and Newt where we were standing along the wall in the packed room. She waved at us and we quickly waved back. She'd seemed nice enough when I'd met her the previous day, but there was something about the way she'd talked about Nolan when she'd been giving me instructions on how to find the sanctuary that had made me think not all was well between the two.

It took a few seconds for the room to fall silent and for the guy to announce the issue that was up for discussion. I ignored some of the back and forth between the council members and focused on Nolan and Dallas, who were holding hands. For a couple where one of them wasn't able to speak, I'd never seen two people communicate with one another more. I'd never even conceived that you could have that kind of connection with another person where words weren't required.

I was once again envious, so I forced myself to focus on the conversation. One of the council members had said something the sheriff clearly hadn't liked because the pissed-off-looking cop got all red and said, "How I do my job is none of your business."

God, the guy sounded just like Gary.

I felt my muscles tense up at even the mere thought of the man who'd made my life a living hell, but fortunately, a commotion at the entrance to the room distracted me. I felt my insides bounce around with anticipation as I spotted Maddox standing in the doorway.

"It is when you cover up crimes," he announced.

The whole crowd turned to look at him, but I followed Maddox's gaze to the front of the room where Dallas and Nolan were standing. Whereas Dallas had been ramrod straight before, I saw him hunched over now. His free hand appeared to come up to wipe at his eyes, but the move was fleeting. But something told me I was witnessing something really profound, so I ignored everything but the two brothers. With his hand still tucked in Nolan's, Dallas turned so he could look at his brother.

And that was when I saw the proof that something big was happening between the two men. It was there in Dallas's eyes for everyone to see.

Relief mixed with disbelief mixed with something... more.

I turned to look at Maddox because I was just completely shocked he could bring out such a response in another human being, considering what a dick he was most of the time. But I was surprised to find not an arrogant know-it-all standing there, but a tense and very unsure-looking man who, for once, didn't look entirely forbidding and unapproachable.

There was still a certain stiffness to him, but it seemed to be more like he was waiting to see how he'd be received. And was he...

I looked closer because I couldn't be sure what I was seeing.

He was... sweating.

Did that mean he was *nervous*?

How was that possible? Guys like him didn't get nervous, did they?

I wasn't paying attention to what Maddox was saying, but I was surprised when he made a move to open the door behind him. Moments later, Loki entered the room.

Completely loose, no leash in sight.

The animal ran straight for Dallas as the sheriff yelled. I actually saw the man go for his gun and was about to call out a warning when another voice said, "Don't even think about it, Sheriff."

Another cop was standing next to Maddox. Several people began talking at once, so I tuned them out and let my eyes drift back to Maddox's. I flinched, and not in a bad way, when his green eyes met mine.

God, it just wasn't fair that someone so beautiful was also a dick.

Oh, and straight.

There was another person behind Maddox who I didn't recognize. He was gorgeous, though not quite as striking as Maddox. But unlike the walking wall, the other guy had an easygoing way about him. He wasn't exactly smiling, but he was so relaxed that it actually put me at ease. Like he somehow knew everything would be okay.

Maddox patted Dallas's shoulder as he walked past and stopped in the front of the room, along with the cop and the good-looking man. The head of the committee gave Maddox permission to address the room. Maddox called Loki to him, then to my surprise, he found me and Newt. His gaze zeroed in on my little brother.

"Newt, do you think you can help me with something?"

When just about everyone turned to look at us, I couldn't help but jump a little. It was basically one of my worst nightmares come to life. I *absolutely* did not want these people to notice us. Newt seemed unfazed and only had eyes for Maddox.

"Are you still mad, Mad?" he asked as he scrutinized the big man at the front of the room.

For once, Maddox looked completely taken aback. Several people laughed. Maddox finally relaxed and actually smiled.

He smiled.

Like with his lips and everything.

Okay, so maybe Pelican Bay really was the entryway to the underworld, because it seemed like hell had just frozen over.

"No, I'm not," Maddox responded, his voice a low purr that had my dick taking notice.

Yeah, right, like it hadn't jumped to attention the second the man had walked into the room. Newt turned to me and said, "I gotta go help Loki, 'kay?"

His voice was so matter-of-fact, I felt my chest swell with pride. There was no hesitation whatsoever, either in approaching a man who had frightened him just yesterday, or in the fact that he was about to do something completely unknown and in front of a roomful of strangers.

To Newt, he was just protecting his new friend, Loki.

I ruffled his hair and with a thick voice said, "Go get 'em, kiddo."

Newt turned on his heel and walked straight to Maddox. He threw his arms around Loki's neck, which caused a few people in the crowd to make some tsking sounds, but otherwise the room was so silent, you could hear a pin drop.

I listened to Maddox explain to the crowd that Loki had been removed from Dallas's care because he'd bitten a passerby. To my surprise, he asked the cop next to him, a man named Miller, if he thought the accusation that Loki bit someone was true. I waited for the man to deny it, but my stomach dropped out when he said, "Yes, I do."

Gasps erupted, and my gaze shifted to a very shaken-looking Nolan and Dallas.

Miller continued without being prompted.

"*Three weeks ago,* when the man helped Jimmy Cornell and another man break into the center and attack a bear that lives on the property."

There was only one bear at the sanctuary–the one Newt was so enamored with.

Gentry.

I'd seen the huge animal myself when Nolan had taken me on a tour of the place when Dallas had been lying down earlier in the day. The animal had been restlessly pacing one side of his enclosure and I'd instantly felt sorry for him. It wasn't until Nolan had explained that the bear had recently been through a trauma that I'd realized the behavior wasn't normal for the animal. To know several men had purposefully attacked the animal broke my heart.

I watched the back and forth between Sheriff Tulley and his deputy, along with one of the council members. From what I was able to take in, the man Loki had bitten during the attack on Gentry had been pressured into filing a complaint against the wolf hybrid, giving the sheriff cause to remove the animal. However, the man hadn't been an innocent passerby but one of Gentry's assailants. The whole thing had been an elaborate scheme the sheriff had come up with, along with one of Gentry's other attackers.

The council member, Jeb, managed to quiet the room down after a minute, and that was when Maddox motioned to the good-looking man next to him. "Can you tell everyone who you are, please?"

"My name is Sawyer Brower. I'm a vet specializing in the care of large animals and wildlife. I treated Gentry, the bear who lives on Dallas's property, after he was shot repeatedly with a BB gun and burned with cattle prods."

Several people in the crowd gasped as Sawyer described the nature of the bear's wounds. I'd seen some of the still-healing injuries myself on the traumatized animal, though I hadn't realized what they'd been from.

God, humans really could be sick fucks.

"You've been working around Loki, right?" Maddox asked Sawyer.

"I have. For a couple of weeks now."

I noticed my brother and Loki were both on the floor and Newt was playing with the animal's ears.

I listened as Maddox went on to ask Sawyer about the behavior of wolves and whether or not Loki acted more like a dog or a wolf. But it didn't become clear to me what my brother's role in all this was until Maddox asked, "Wolves have a high prey drive, don't they? They'll pursue things that are smaller or weaker than them and kill them, correct?"

"Correct," Sawyer said. I swallowed hard. There was no doubt an animal of Loki's size could kill a child like Newt with one bite. The animal hadn't even shown the slightest bit of aggression toward my brother, but if Maddox was going to do what I thought he was going to do, it would change the game entirely.

I felt myself tense up as Maddox looked at Dallas and said, "Dallas, do you trust Loki? Do you trust him with this boy's life?"

I managed to keep my mouth shut at the ominous question, but I felt like I was going to be sick as Maddox's eyes met mine after Dallas nodded. I knew what he was going to ask me long before he did.

"Do you trust me not to let anything happen to your brother?"

I wanted to do a million things in that moment, including googling anything and everything I could about wolf hybrids, ask Sawyer a gazillion questions about Loki specifically, and most importantly, grab Newt and hightail it out of there. I knew I could say no and that would be the end of it.

I knew that.

No one would judge me for it, either. I mean, was I really supposed to put the animal's life above my brother's?

I opened my mouth to ask that very question, but when my eyes met Maddox's green ones and they softened just the tiniest bit, I knew that he knew what he was asking of me. And I also knew if he had any other way of saving his brother's beloved pet, he'd have done it.

But more than anything, I knew, just knew, he wouldn't let anything happen to Newt.

Don't ask me how I knew that last part, because I was clueless.

Completely and utterly clueless.

But the same instinct that'd had me sidling closer to Maddox the day before when the sheriff had pulled into the sanctuary's driveway was the same instinct that had me nodding my head. For his part, Newt hadn't even seemed to notice that the discussion revolved around him.

I watched nervously as Maddox knelt down by Newt and explained to the little boy that he was supposed to run to me as fast as he could, and that Loki would chase him, but to not be scared. I almost smiled when Newt looked at Maddox with what could only be classified as a *duh* expression and then said, "I'm not scared. Loki likes me."

I barely had time to hold my breath before Newt jumped to his feet and raced toward me. Loki jumped up after him and caught up to him in a few strides. I heard people gasp as the big animal reached the little boy, but he didn't do anything more than run beside him for the final steps it took to get to me.

Relief slammed into me as Newt wrapped his arms around me. *See?* his eyes seemed to say. I patted his head and then he was gone again, running back to Maddox as ordered.

I sucked in a deep breath as Maddox asked the committee to let Dallas take his pet home and they readily agreed. I thought that was the end of it, but when Jeb ordered the deputy to look into the sheriff's conduct, more chaos erupted, and the truth came spilling out faster than I could make sense of.

It was a painstaking process to piece together that at some point in the past, Dallas had been accused of driving drunk and causing an accident that had killed his and Maddox's mother and left their father in a wheelchair. From everything I was hearing, Dallas's own father had pointed the finger at his son as the driver when, in fact, it had been Dallas and Maddox's mother who'd been driving the car. Sheriff Tulley had somehow covered up the truth that would have exonerated Dallas even after his father died a couple of years later, and the entire town had been allowed to believe the lie. I didn't really understand the impact of why the whole town seemed so invested in the drama, but one thing was clear.

Dallas had spent his entire adult life being blamed for an accident that hadn't been his fault and the town had persecuted him for it.

Once Maddox had told everyone the truth of what had happened, the entire room began talking at once, including the sheriff who was screaming at his deputy and the council members. I couldn't keep up with things and was about to call Newt to me so we could wait outside when my eyes fell on Maddox.

He was standing stock-still in the same spot he'd been in, but there was something different about him. Sweat was dripping down his face and his hands were clenched into fists. His blank eyes were staring at nothing in particular.

It was like he was just... gone.

A moment later, his eyes slid shut completely. And when Jeb

suddenly began pounding his gavel to get the room's attention, things completely changed. Every time the gavel struck the wood block, Maddox jumped. His hands were fisted so hard the knuckles were bloodless. A few people had gotten up to go talk to Dallas and every time they brushed past Maddox, his entire body got tighter and tighter.

Like a rubber band that would snap at any second.

I was moving before I could even consider what I was doing.

I didn't know what was wrong, but there was nothing natural about the man's behavior. Not for him, not for anyone.

I carefully stepped over Loki and Newt as I made my way to Maddox.

"Maddox," I called, but there was just too much noise for him to hear me. I practically yelled his name as I put my hands on his face, hoping to God he wouldn't instinctively lash out at me. I had a feeling the man was having some kind of flashback or a panic attack, but I had no clue how you were supposed to approach someone in that state.

What I did know was that I needed to get him out of there.

Maddox's frantic eyes landed on mine, then began darting around. Every time someone bumped him, or the gavel would hit the wood block, Maddox drew closer to the edge.

And I was terrified of what would happen when he gave up the last of the self-control he seemed to be clinging to.

"Maddox, look at me!" I demanded.

"Isaac?" Newt asked worriedly. "What's wrong with Mad?" he whispered.

I could tell he was scared. His fingers were buried in Loki's fur and the animal began to whine. But as badly as I wanted to comfort my brother, I knew Maddox needed me more.

"Maddox, eyes on me," I practically snarled. My tone must have registered with the man because his gaze snapped to mine.

"That's good," I said softly as I held his gaze. I reached down to wrap my hand around his fist. "We're leaving," I explained.

I made sure it wasn't a request.

I swore he nodded at me, but I couldn't be sure. I walked backward several steps, maintaining the eye contact with him. I noticed Loki and Newt following, which I was grateful for, because I didn't want to take my attention off Maddox long enough to call to Newt.

It seemed to take forever to clear the room and every time someone got too close to Maddox, I was terrified I'd lose the hold I had on him, both physically and metaphorically. But he seemed as desperate to cling to me as I needed him to. I wasn't satisfied with just getting him to the hallway, since it was still noisy outside the room. But once the doors closed behind us, I did drop my eyes from him and turned so I could walk ahead of him rather than backward. I managed to get us out a side door and then headed toward the parking lot where Dallas's truck was parked. The air was cold, but thankfully, it wasn't snowing.

I maneuvered Maddox so the bed of the truck was at his back in case he needed the extra support. At some point, he'd closed his fingers around my hand instead of the other way around. His grip was hard, but not painful.

He began gulping in one lungful of air after another as he started to come back to himself. I used my free hand to rub his upper arm. The muscles there were still tight with tension.

"Try to slow your breathing," I told him. Every once in a while, Newt would have really bad dreams that left him breathless. Maddox's behavior reminded me of that–it was like he was still stuck in that state of trying to figure out what was real and what wasn't.

"Here, Mad," Newt whispered as he shoved his Lightning car into Maddox's now-lax hand. I could tell my brother was scared. Not of Maddox, but of the situation. I pulled Newt against my side and ran my fingers through his hair.

"He's okay, Newt. He was just having a bad dream," I said. "Like you do, sometimes."

"But he wasn't sleeping," Newt said quietly as he wrapped his arms around my waist.

"I know, buddy. But sometimes grown-ups get different kinds of nightmares than kids."

Newt seemed to accept the explanation. To Maddox, who'd become more alert, Newt said, "Isaac helps me get rid of the monsters, too. He's really good at that."

Maddox's eyes went from Newt to me. "I can see that," he said softly. His voice sounded shaky, but he seemed looser than before.

"Are you... are you okay?" I asked. "Can I get you something? Some water or something? I can go back in there—"

I pointed to the building, but Maddox quickly said, "No, I'm okay. Thanks." He shifted awkwardly back and forth, then straightened. "I need to be going."

"What?" I asked in surprise. "Don't you want to wait for your brother?"

He didn't answer me. Instead, he said to Newt, "Thank you for what you did for Loki in there, Newt. You were really brave."

Newt beamed at the compliment. "You're welcome, Mad."

I wasn't sure, but Maddox seemed to briefly smile at the nickname. When his eyes shifted to me, I felt my insides drop out. Now that the initial concern had passed, that *thing* was there again. That constant flicker beneath my skin that told me this man was dangerous to me.

But not in the normal way.

No, in a whole other way that wasn't entirely unwelcome.

Maddox held my gaze for a moment, then he turned and walked away. He didn't head for any of the cars parked in the lot. Instead, he walked toward the back of the property. I'd seen that section of the building when we'd arrived and there was no parking lot back there. I hadn't seen any cars parked on the street, either.

So where was he going?

Rather than return inside, Newt and I stayed by the truck while he regaled me with the story of how he'd saved Loki, as if I hadn't been there to witness the whole thing. While we waited for the others, a few people approached us, but their interest was in Loki. I watched as my little brother explained to people how gentle Loki was and that they could pet him if they wanted. By the time Dallas, Nolan, and Sawyer came out, Newt had become a self-proclaimed expert on wolves.

Dallas frantically began typing on his phone when they reached us, but I put my hand over his phone to stop him, because I knew what he wanted to know.

"He left," I said. I pointed to the back of the building. "That way."

"What? On foot?" Sawyer asked.

I nodded.

"Weird," the vet murmured.

"Why is that weird?" Nolan asked.

"Because he got a ride here with Deputy Miller. I just assumed he'd leave with him."

I hadn't seen the deputy leave, but with the two police vehicles still parked in the lot, I had to assume the deputy was inside with the council members. Probably still being yelled at by Sheriff Tulley.

God, I hoped the jerk got what was coming to him.

"Okay, maybe he's back at the center," Nolan read from Dallas's phone. To Sawyer, Nolan said, "Do you need a ride?"

Sawyer shook his head. "No, I've got my car. I've got an injured deer I want to check on over in Greene County. I'll see you guys tomorrow."

We said our goodbyes and piled into Dallas's truck. I tried to listen in on Newt's retelling of the evening's events, but I was too distracted. As we pulled out of the parking lot and turned right and drove past the back of the town hall building, my eyes fell on the single set of footprints marring the perfectly fallen snow. I kept my eyes out for Maddox the entire drive back to the center, but I knew he wouldn't be there.

And I was right.

But the question that kept me up most of the night long after Newt had fallen asleep next to me was, where the hell was he?

Right after that came another question that equally had no answer.

Why do I care so much?

CHAPTER FIVE

MADDOX

There was something about the sound of snow crunching beneath my boots that soothed me in a way that little else could. It was different than when you were walking on sand. Even walking in the deepest snow felt easier than walking on uneven sand.

Of course, that probably had more to do with the fact that walking on snow meant the likelihood of coming under sniper fire was unlikely. I supposed that feeling would have been different if my unit had been tasked to follow our enemy into the mountainous regions of the Middle East where snow was more common. So, there was *that* particular silver lining in coming back to Pelican Bay.

Because it was about as different from the hot, dry desert that had become my home... and my hell... for the past several years as you could get.

It was an odd thing to feel so rudderless. Growing up with parents who never seemed to have a plan meant that was all I'd ever wanted to have.

Graduate West Point.

Serve my country in active combat.

Work my way up the ranks to general with a post that preferably kept me as far from Pelican Bay as possible.

But all that had changed when I'd learned of the accident that had taken my mother's life, left my father paralyzed from the waist down, and put my little brother in a coma that would take him a full month to recover from.

I could still remember the sounds of the machines surrounding his motionless body as I'd sat by his bedside day after day waiting for him to wake up. I'd begged, bargained, and cursed him more times than I could count, all in the hopes he'd just all of a sudden open his eyes, see me staring at him, and give me some sign that he was back and he was there to stay. I hadn't cared what condition he'd been left in, I'd vowed to take care of him no matter what.

And then one day my wish had come true and Dallas had opened his eyes. There'd been no recognition in them for the few seconds he'd managed to keep them open, but as they'd drifted shut and I'd told him I was going to be right there by his side when he woke up again, he'd squeezed my hand just a little. And that was when I'd known everything would be okay.

Only it hadn't been.

And I hadn't kept my silent promise to him and God that I'd always take care of him if he would just wake up–not once I'd learned the truth about what he'd done.

I'd broken the promise I'd made to him when we'd been children, too.

Because I'd never had his back again after that. I'd merely walked out of his life, leaving him to care for our disabled father, and I'd never looked back. Not until after our father had died two years later. And then I'd been a man on a mission.

I'd let all the rage and hatred and betrayal mix into this dark, ugly thing inside of me that I'd never been able to let go. Instead of just walking away from Dallas again, I'd needed him to hurt like I hurt, so I'd used one of the few weapons I had against him.

Our parents' inheritance.

Which, in hindsight, had been utterly ridiculous because Dallas had never been enamored of the money, not like our parents had been. Yes, like me, he'd enjoyed the things like getting a new car when we were old enough to drive and being handed a stack of money if there was ever something in particular that we wanted, but he'd never really flaunted the fact that we were so much more well-off than the kids we went to school with. Even when we'd moved to Pelican Bay and our parents built the atrocious house overlooking town, Dallas hadn't advertised the fact that he came from money. His focus had been baseball, baseball, baseball.

Like me, his plan had been to get out of Pelican Bay and away from our parents all along. And just like me, his entire life had changed in an instant when fate had finally caught up to our parents and their incessant need to drink. But unlike me, Dallas hadn't had a way out anymore after the accident. He'd been abandoned and betrayed by those who should have been watching out for him. His career had been left in ruins, and the town that had once adored him had turned on him instead. All the support that should have gone to Dallas had been showered on me instead.

I'd become that "poor Kent boy" who'd lost his family and Dallas had become a whole host of other things.

Killer.

Disappointment.

Freak.

I hadn't stuck around at the time to know those were the titles that had been cast upon my brother after the "truth" had come out, but I'd learned them easily enough in the few weeks I'd been back in town. Up until last night, whenever I'd run into someone I knew, they'd *tsk-tsk* and tell me what a shame what had happened to me was.

I'd become the saint and Dallas the villain and our parents had been the martyrs.

And it had all been a big fucking lie.

One I'd perpetuated.

I shook my head as the perpetual nausea in my belly grew. If I'd only heard Dallas out...

Even if he hadn't told me the truth when I'd confronted him, if I'd looked hard enough, I would have seen it in his eyes. I would have known there was no way he could have done what our father had said that he had. But I hadn't been able to get past the sense of betrayal that he'd done the one thing he'd promised me he'd never do–that *we'd promised each other* we'd never do–drive drunk.

I hadn't known which of my parents had been driving the car when Alex Miller had finally shown up at my house the night Loki had been taken away. But one look at the pictures of the smashed-up vehicle and I'd known.

It'd been my mother.

She'd been considerably shorter than my father and from the position of both the steering wheel and the front seat, I'd known she was the one driving. Not that it had really mattered–if the situation had been reversed and our mother had asked Dallas to protect the memory of our father, he'd have done it.

Because it was like I'd said at the meeting the night before.

Dallas protects those he loves.

While I let them down.

I sighed and scanned my surroundings. I'd been walking for a good three hours and while I wasn't too far from the sanctuary, I had no plans to go there. I was relieved I'd managed to get my brother his beloved pet back the night before and that the town finally knew the truth about him, but I wasn't foolish enough to believe that had earned me any kind of pass with Dallas.

I didn't want one.

Just like in Mosul, I'd made the wrong call and others had paid for it.

There were just some things that no amount of being sorry for could fix.

The reminder had me pulling out my phone. I searched out the number I wanted, but not surprisingly, there was no answer when I dialed it.

Fuck, I knew what that meant.

I waited for the voicemail to pick up and said, "You better call me back, asshole. Because if you don't, it means I have to get my ass on a bus and come down there to check on you. And you know what kind of mood that's going to put me in."

I hung up and waited. Sure enough, not three minutes later, my phone rang. I didn't look at the caller ID because even if I hadn't just called him, Jett was the only guy I talked to anymore.

"I'm fine," Jett snapped before I could even say hello.

I doubted he was fine. It'd been less than three months since the man's entire life had changed.

Or, as he saw it... ended.

"You going to PT?" I asked.

"You going to the head shrink?" he responded.

I sighed and said, "Just get your ass up here, Jett. I'll send a fucking private jet for you."

The old Jett would have laughed and called me a pretty, rich white boy or spewed some crap about how my kind didn't belong on his kind's side of the tracks. This Jett didn't do anything other than whisper, "I'm tired, Maddox. You just caught me going to bed."

More like I was catching him still in bed.

Despite being his commanding officer and growing up in two very different worlds, Jett was the closest thing I had to a best friend. The product of a black mother and white father, Jett had been fighting battles long before he and I had become roommates at West Point. While I'd been a shoo-in because of my father's powerful connections, Jett had had to fight tooth and nail for his chance to be accepted into the elite program, specifically the ever-important nomination that was a requirement to even be considered for admission. While I'd practically had my pick of senators to provide the nomination, Jett had had to struggle to even get noticed long enough by his state's local senator to be considered for a nomination.

But he'd done it.

And once he'd gotten to West Point, he'd made it clear to the world that even though his mixed race may have played some role in being accepted to the diversity-loving academy, he knew he deserved to be there and he'd worked just as hard, if not harder, than the rest of us.

Jett and I'd had big plans for the future, and they'd all come to a screeching halt one hot day a few months earlier when I'd gone with the intelligence I'd been given, rather than my gut.

Ten men had paid for the oversight. Jett and I were the only ones who'd survived the roadside bomb and subsequent ambush that my commanding officer had assured me wouldn't be there.

"My grandma's calling me," Jett added. It wasn't like I'd actually thought he'd take me up on my offer anyway. God knew I'd made it enough times after we'd been discharged.

"Yeah, okay," I said. "Call me later."

We both knew he wouldn't.

He didn't even bother to agree or say goodbye. He just hung up. Despite Jett's repeated reassurances that he didn't blame me for anything, I knew there had to be a part of him that did. And even if there wasn't, just looking at me would be enough to remind him of everything he'd lost.

Because while we'd both been diagnosed with PTSD, at least I still had my legs and could literally walk away from the truth.

Jett, not so much.

I tucked my phone back into my pocket and drew in several deep breaths to try and calm myself. My legs burned from the hours I'd been walking, but not enough to make the lead weight in my chest go away.

I also couldn't stop thinking about those moments where my secret had been exposed for the world to see.

Fortunately, "the world" had been too busy going crazy over the fact that Dallas had been so grievously misjudged and maligned.

But my near panic attack hadn't gone completely unnoticed.

A fact I was both unhappy about, and thankful for.

Unhappy because somehow having Isaac to have been the one who'd not only recognized I was in trouble, but gotten me out of that room, was like a punch to the gut, though I didn't know why. But I was also thankful because I'd been on the verge of completely losing it–something I'd only done once before that'd had dire consequences. Since then, I'd learned to recognize my symptoms more readily, and more importantly, I did all I could to avoid them. The people hadn't been too much of an issue the night before, though being around crowds wasn't my favorite thing in the world.

No, it'd been the gavel.

I hadn't been expecting it. I still couldn't believe I'd managed to hold out as long as I had when that thing had started its banging, but there was no doubt in my mind that it'd been Isaac's voice and his gentle touch that'd kept me from completely losing it. While I hadn't been so far gone that I'd believed my life was in danger, I'd hung onto Isaac like it had been.

Because I never would have gotten out of that room without him.

At least not of my own volition and without hurting someone.

I wanted to laugh at what those townspeople who kept talking to me like I was some hero would have thought after I'd ripped that room to shreds, believing I was back in the desert and Jett was screaming in agony as he called my name and pounded the end of his M240 machine gun against the roof of the overturned Humvee.

I wondered if Isaac had told Dallas or if Dallas had noticed for himself. I'd been too out of it to see if my brother had seen my reaction to the events that had occurred after the council had dismissed the case against him.

Didn't matter.

I'd done what I'd come here to do. I'd never expected Dallas to actually forgive me or give me a second chance at being his brother. He was in a good place, better than I could have even hoped for. It was time for me to move on.

Maybe I'd head down to Oklahoma and check on Jett in person. I had enough money that there was no need to work anytime soon, so maybe I'd just explore the country a bit. Any place that didn't have too many people in it would work for me. Maybe I could even convince Jett to come with me.

Yeah, because he's so eager to talk to you on the phone. Of course the next step is being cooped up in a car with you for hours at a time.

God, my inner voice was a sarcastic asshole.

I automatically smiled as Newt's voice rang in my ear, calling me out for the swear word. But my humor died as I considered whose job it would be to "punish" me for the oversight.

God, Isaac's touch had been so soft the night before.

Soft, but still firm.

Such an odd contradiction.

He was such a contradiction. Such a unique mix of strength and vulnerability. I wanted to know what made him tick, but I didn't know *why* I wanted to know that.

I mentally shook myself. Didn't matter. I needed to focus on the next steps, and not the weird kid who wore makeup and smelled like lemons. With that thought in mind, I raised my head with the intention of crossing the road so I could turn around and walk home while still facing oncoming traffic. But when my eyes caught on a familiar truck parked outside the Sleep-EZ motel across the street, I paused.

The motel had been around forever and wasn't known for its stellar accommodations. It was basically just a cheap place for truckers who were forced to travel the backroads instead of the interstate for one reason or another. Occasionally, tourists would stay at the place, but only if everything else in Pelican Bay and the surrounding towns was sold out.

So what the hell was Dallas doing there?

I supposed it could be Nolan.

Or both.

But still, the place was a dump. Even on the off chance they needed some alone time, there were far better places to go.

Realizing it was none of my business, I was about to continue on my way when I saw a man hurrying to the door the truck was parked in front of. He knocked a couple of times and then nervously looked around him. I wasn't close enough for him to notice me or for me to make out his features, but he was clearly on edge. The door opened and he disappeared inside.

My brain said to leave it alone, but my gut had me striding forward.

What if Nolan was cheating on my brother? I mean, Nolan was a sweet guy, but no way in hell was I letting him use my brother like that. And if on the off chance it was Dallas? Well, I'd kick his ass too, because he had an amazing thing going with Nolan.

I trotted across the two-lane highway and reached the door within a couple of minutes. There was only one other car parked in the lot and it was right next to the truck.

I didn't even bother to knock on the door, because I wasn't interested in making my presence known. I figured it would save a lot of time if I caught my brother or his lover in the act and didn't have to listen to excuses that the whole thing wasn't what it looked like. I could get around to kicking the stranger out much faster that way and asking Dallas or Nolan, whichever one of them it was, what the hell they were thinking.

It took practically nothing to use my shoulder to break the door. The damn thing was so flimsy it almost seemed like a waste to leave some cash behind to pay the motel owner for breaking it. Both the door and the frame were so rotted through, he could probably use tape to put the damn thing back together and have it be more secure than it'd been.

Despite how easy it'd been to break the door down, it made a lot of noise, so I had no trouble finding the two occupants of the darkened room the second the sunlight filtered through the open door.

And I recognized them both.

But it wasn't the man I'd seen coming into the room that interested me. It was the man kneeling at his feet that I had my eyes on.

"What the—" the standing man sputtered, his eyes going wide with shock as he suddenly reached down to try and grab the pants that were currently at his ankles. "Oh, God!" he whispered.

I knew who he was right away. His name was Arthur Tomlinson and he'd been Pelican Bay's librarian for years. I felt sick as I watched him yank up his pants and try to get them closed. I didn't miss the fact that his small but very hard dick was shiny with moisture.

Bile rose in my throat as my eyes went to Isaac who hadn't moved, even after Arthur had shoved him out of the way to reach his pants.

"I'm sorry!" Arthur shouted. "Please, I'm sorry!" he said. "Don't tell my wife!"

There was a wad of cash on the bed that Arthur actually tried to grab, but when his beady eyes met mine, his mouth opened into what looked like a silent scream and he only managed to snag a few of the bills, then he was darting past me and out the door, the sun glistening off his wedding ring and the buckle of the belt holding up his still half-undone pants.

Isaac didn't move for several seconds. When he did, it was only to get up off the floor. My gut clenched when he wiped the back of his hand over his mouth.

In my mind, I understood what I'd walked in on, but in my heart, I didn't want to believe it.

Isaac glanced at the cash, then went to the bathroom. It was the kind where the sink was outside the actual bathroom. I saw him reach for a toothbrush and a small tube of toothpaste. Besides the strip of condoms and bottle of lube on the nightstand, they were the only other items in the room that didn't already belong there.

I felt like I was going to be sick.

Isaac calmly brushed his teeth, never once looking over his shoulder at me. When he was done, he turned around and leaned back against the vanity, then pulled out his phone.

"You mind?" he said as he nodded toward the still-open door. "Since you just cost me a client, I need to book another one. And my next one should be here in a few, so you should go."

I wasn't sure if it was his lackadaisical attitude or the talk about more clients that had me slamming the door shut and striding toward him. I snatched the phone from him and slammed it down on the countertop behind him. "Are you fucking kidding me right now?"

If I hadn't been so close to him, I would have missed the fine tremor running throughout his entire frame. He might have been pretending to be unfazed, but he sure as shit wasn't. His makeup was heavier than usual, and his mouth was stained bright red with heavy lipstick.

No doubt the same color was on some part of Arthur Tomlinson's dick right now.

Rage tore through me as I snatched a tissue from the dispenser on the vanity and wiped at the lipstick, mindful of the small hoop piercing in his lower lip. I tried to keep my touch gentle, but inside I was battling the urge to find Arthur and rip him limb from limb.

The red color was somewhat smeared, but mostly gone. I threw the tissue aside and stepped back.

"Feel better?" Isaac asked dully. "Because it won't undo what you saw."

"Why?" I asked, because that was the only word I could get out.

"What difference does it make?" he asked. "It's what you wanted, right?"

"What are you talking about?"

"You knew I was shit from the moment you saw me. A thief, a troublemaker, a fag... why should whore be such a stretch? Now you can run to your brother and tell him you knew it all along. Don't worry, Newt and I will be gone by tonight." He nodded at the door again. "Now, unless you want to stay and watch, which will cost you by the way, you need to go."

When he went to reach for his phone, I grabbed it and threw it across the room. I stormed toward the door but stopped abruptly when a man pushed open the broken door.

"Blaze?" he asked in confusion.

"Yeah, here," Isaac called. "Come on in. My *friend* here was just leaving."

"Oh, okay, cool man," the guy said, then he actually started entering the room. I grabbed him by the shirt collar and propelled him backward so hard and so fast that when I released him just outside the room, he stumbled backward and hit the front of Dallas's truck. When he opened his mouth to protest, I glared at him. Then he took off like a bat out of hell.

I slammed the door shut and used a side chair to prop beneath the knob to keep the door closed.

"You asshole!" Isaac screamed as he came up behind me and shoved me hard. "I needed that trick to pay for my fucking car so Newt and I can get the hell away from this town!"

He didn't say *and you*, but I suspected he wanted to.

But I was still stuck on what he did say.

Jesus fucking Christ.

He'd done this because of his car?

Pure fury went through me and I wanted to rip the room apart. "You foolish—" I began, and then shook my head. Because as fucked up as all this was, it wasn't actually his fault. And that just made my anger so much worse. Never in a million years would I have thought my decision would have such an ugly consequence, but it had. An image of Isaac's pretty mouth wrapped around that old fuck Tomlinson's dick went through my head and before I could stop myself, I slammed my fist into the wall and yelled, "I fucking tampered with your car so you couldn't leave!"

CHAPTER SIX

ISAAC

I was still reeling from both Maddox's discovery and his show of temper, so his words didn't register at first. In fact, I'd just grabbed ahold of the wrist of the hand he'd put through the wall to check the bloodied knuckles when my brain began to process what he'd said.

"What?" I whispered in disbelief a solid fifteen seconds later. "You did what?"

"Jesus, I just wanted you to stick around long enough so if you wanted to ask for help you could, or so that you could see that you could trust Dallas and Nolan... fuck!" he snapped. I released my hold on him and he immediately began pacing.

Humiliation coursed through me as I realized what I'd almost done because of his actions. I felt the telltale sting of tears, but I forced them back. I hadn't cried in a really long time and hell if I'd give him the satisfaction of seeing me do that.

"Get out," I whispered.

"Isaac, I'm sorry—"

"Get out!" I screamed. "You don't get to say those words to me! You had no right!"

"I know, I shouldn't—"

I ignored him and snatched Dallas's car keys off the small table in the room. I didn't bother with the condoms or any of the other shit that was part of my "toolkit."

But when I tried to storm past Maddox, he grabbed my arm. "Don't touch me!" I shouted, hating the panic that began to take over me.

"Please, Isaac, just listen—"

"Dallas," I spit out. "He was in on it, wasn't he? He looked at my car yesterday. Kept putting me off about it today! Did you guys laugh about it behind my back? Was all this some stupid, fucked-up way to get back at me?"

"No!" Maddox said. "Jesus Christ, no!" He ran his free hand through his shorn hair. "God, even if that was true, which it isn't, do you think we'd do that to you after what you did last night? For Dallas?" His voice softened just a little as his eyes held mine. "For me?"

God help me, between his voice and his striking eyes, it was like being sucked into the eye of a storm. Hell was raging all around me, but all I felt was this momentary weird sense of calm.

"I didn't do anything last night," I murmured.

He actually pulled me a little closer to him. "Yes, you did," he said so softly I almost didn't hear him. "Fuck, Isaac, I'm so sorry." He shook his head. "If I'd thought even for a second it would drive you to this…" His hand tightened on my arm momentarily, then gentled. Then, to my disbelief, his fingers came up to wipe at some of the remaining lipstick on my mouth, but his touch was soft. "I want to kill him for doing that to you."

His voice was so low it sounded scary, and I knew he was talking about my trick. I couldn't make any sense of this. The guy didn't like me and he sure as shit wasn't gay, but the way he was touching me and his anger, it almost seemed like he was… jealous.

I knew that wasn't possible, so it had to be the guilt he was feeling.

"I didn't do anything to that guy," I suddenly blurted out, though I had no idea why. I didn't owe Maddox any kind of explanation. No, he hadn't forced me to do any of this, but the reality was that I *had* only done it because of my car. I would have done it eventually in some other city, though, so it didn't seem fair to make it sound like it was solely on him. "I touched him, but that was it. Only long enough to get the condom on."

Jesus, Isaac, shut the fuck up.

"But you brushed your teeth," Maddox blurted.

I felt my cheeks heat. "Yeah, well, whenever I, um, am… *working*… I brush my teeth before and after, no matter what."

Oh God, I needed to stop talking. Why the hell did he need to know that I hated what I did so much that it made bile rise into the back of my throat *every single time*?

Maddox looked horrified, but to my surprise, he didn't pull away. In fact, he stepped even closer to me and I instinctively moved back.

But there was no place to go.

The wall was hard at my back as Maddox studied me like a bug under a microscope. His eyes were… dear god, they were on my mouth. His fingers were still there too.

Why was he touching me? Why wasn't he telling me what a disgusting freak I was for selling my body?

Why the hell was I not moving?

This man was the only reason I was in this shit hole. He was the reason I'd lied to Dallas and Nolan when I'd asked if they could watch Newt for me while I walked to the store to buy Newt some snow pants and better winter gear. Hell, they'd even offered to let me borrow Dallas's truck. I'd whittled down the half-dozen responses I'd gotten to my online ad to find a few guys who hadn't appeared particularly dangerous and had been willing to pay my normal rates. Then I'd had to steel myself to meet them and let them use me in the vilest of ways, all because of this man.

This man who was still touching my mouth.

What the hell was happening?

"I like the other stuff," Maddox said softly as the rough pad of his finger trailed along my lower lip, dragging briefly over my piercing that was just to the left of the middle of my lip. My cock wasn't the only part of my body responding. I couldn't stop the little tremors that began swimming through my body.

"What other stuff?" I managed to ask.

God, he really needed to stop touching me.

So why wasn't I telling him that?

"The shiny stuff." He shook his head. "The red, it isn't… you," he said on a quiet sigh.

What?

What?

Was he seriously upset by the lipstick, but he liked the clear gloss I typically wore?

Jesus, what was happening here?

"The lipstick was his," I suddenly said. "The guy," I said, motioning toward the door with just my eyes. "He wanted me to wear it. He brought it with him."

What the hell are you doing, Isaac?

Hell if I knew. But now that I'd opened my mouth, it was like I couldn't shut it again. It was like Maddox had found the secret door to Narnia the second he'd touched my lip because it was all just spilling out.

"Every guy's got his kinks, you know. Some like to tie you up, others want you to say certain stuff…"

Maddox's jaw hardened, and his eyes turned flinty.

Shut up, Isaac.

But I couldn't. It was like I was in some kind of trance and the only way I'd escape it was if he looked away. And he seemed in no hurry to do so.

"It's gloss," I sputtered as I reached into my pocket and pulled out my tube of gloss. "The stuff I normally wear. It's just clear gloss." I held the tube between my fingers awkwardly as I said, "It's hydrating… winter weather leaves them kind of chapped."

God, Maddox had beautiful lips. Nothing rough about those babies.

"Put it on."

I was in the midst of sliding the tube back into my pocket when the softly spoken order came through.

And it *was* an order.

"What?" I choked out as I lifted my eyes from his mouth.

His big thumb was still sliding back and forth along my lower lip. He gave the flesh just the tiniest of tugs and I was sure I came in my pants a little bit.

"Put it on," Maddox repeated.

I tried to remember everything that was wrong with the situation, but something about the way he said the words and the way he held my gaze while doing it sent me to a place I'd only ever allowed myself to go in my most secret of fantasies. My whole body grew warm and relaxed, even though I was also completely turned on. I tried to remind myself that even if Maddox had somehow gotten caught up in some weird bi-curious moment, it wasn't real. I had the kind of features that could pass for more feminine than masculine at times, and that was all this was.

So why was I considering this? Why was I reaching for the cap of the gloss with one hand instead of using that hand to shove Maddox away from me? Why wasn't I laying into him about manipulating me by messing with my car? Why was I even still here? I should be back at the sanctuary ripping Dallas and Nolan a new one and demanding Dallas fix my car while I got Newt bundled in the back of it.

I knew the answer to all those questions. I was just too afraid to admit it.

It should have been the easiest, fastest thing to do. Slap some of the gloss on and go.

But something about having this moment, about having Maddox watching me like he was, even though I didn't really understand why he was doing it, all of it had me taking my time as I lifted the wand to my lips. The little cotton tip was so light and soft that I almost wished it was Maddox's finger spreading the gloss around my lower lip. His fingers had retreated to my chin and his eyes were fastened on my mouth.

I took my time working the gloss over my lower lip and through the slight opening of the hoop, something I didn't need a mirror for. When I slowly pursed my lips together to spread the gloss from the lower lip to the upper one, I swore I heard Maddox suck in a breath.

His own lips parted just a little and then his forefinger was coming up to gently touch my lips, like he was fascinated with the gloss... or them.

"How old are you, Isaac?" he whispered.

The way he asked it, it was like he was holding his breath while waiting for the answer.

Why?

Would the answer give him the permission he seemed to want? Was my age really the only thing he was worried about? Surely the fact that I had a dick between my legs should have been more of a problem for him.

Unless I was wrong.

God, did I *want* to be wrong?

I pulled in a breath and caught a scent of his aftershave. It was cool with a hint of spice and something uniquely... *him*.

Fuck, yeah, I wanted to be wrong about him. Hell, even if I was right and he was straight as an arrow, I was totally fine if he wanted to pretend I was someone other than who I was. Normally I'd charge a guy a pretty penny to pretend I was a woman and act all contrite when I was "caught." But this wasn't some twisted fantasy. And that alone should have had me pulling away from him.

Instead, I leaned forward just a little, more so that I could get another whiff of him, because I wasn't quite tall enough to subtly put my lips closer to his. If I wanted to do that, I'd have to actually get up on my tiptoes and that kind of movement might break the spell.

"Twenty-one," I said, just as I brought up my left hand to rest on his side. God, even that part of him felt rock-hard. This man could crush me so easily.

But God, what would it feel like to have his weight pressing me into a mattress, or holding me up against a wall? Like the wall right at my back.

I was so lost in the idea of Maddox's big hands holding my ass open as he fucked into me while he pressed me up against a wall as my legs wrapped around his waist, that it took me a moment to realize he'd stepped back a little and dropped his hand from my lips.

I sighed.

So we weren't even going to get to the part where my dick was a problem. He'd heard twenty-one and had come to the same conclusion so many others did.

That I was just a kid.

If there was anything I hated more than being defined by my looks or sexuality, it was my damn age. The asshole had no clue what I'd done in those twenty-one years.

Well, good. His ignorance was going to save us both a world of humiliation and hurt.

"You're unbelievable," I said as I shoved him away from me and pushed past him.

"Don't blame Dallas for this," Maddox called.

I shook my head and laughed. "No, of course not," I sniped. "You guys get to lie and manipulate but I'm just a thief and a whore, so what does it matter, right?" I bit out. I searched out my cell phone, then went to the bathroom and grabbed my toothbrush and toothpaste followed by the condoms and lube and stuffed them into the small paper bag I'd used to bring them into the room. Fuck if I was going to waste a penny to replace them just to save myself a little more embarrassment.

I mean, was that even possible anymore? Not only had Maddox tricked me with my car and seen me on my knees for a complete stranger, but he'd just played me like a finely tuned instrument.

And I'd let him do it.

I saw a couple of crumpled bills on the bedspread—they were what the john had left behind. It made me sick to reach for the thirty bucks, but cash was cash.

"I'll take care of the door," Maddox said as I went to walk past him. I forced my eyes up and pinned him with what I hoped was a stony glare.

"Are you fucking kidding me?" I asked.

Did he actually believe I'd even consider paying for the damage *he'd* caused?

He had the decency to look sheepish, but he didn't say anything. But when I tried to move past him, he thrust his hand out.

But not to grab me.

I stared in disbelief at the wad of bills in his hand and I felt something inside of me die.

Because I knew what the money was for. Maybe if it'd just been charity, I could have smiled politely and declined, but knowing it was charity that was meant to replace the money he'd both forced me to go in search of in the first place *and* cost me by interfering in my business was just too much. I held there a moment as I stared at the money and watched a droplet of moisture hit the green dye of the top bill.

God, he'd really done it.

He'd made me fucking cry.

I let out a harsh laugh. All the shit I'd been through in the past year, all the fear, all the doubt, and *this* was what was finally going to break me?

Him?

I didn't say anything as I moved past him, ignoring the money. I was reaching for the chair to remove it from where it was propped against the door when he softly said, "Isaac."

I didn't dare turn to look at him. Even if that was what I should have done.

"Don't leave, Isaac. No matter what you think of me, you're safe here. Dallas can help you... he *will* help you."

My body felt cold and hollow as I got the door open and walked through it. The drive back to the sanctuary took minutes, but it felt like hours. I was shaking like a leaf by the time I pulled into the main driveway, and the emptiness had once again given way to fury. Tears of rage kept slipping down my cheeks and I angrily wiped them away as I made my way up the narrow driveway. I was forced to pull over to the side of the road when a car came from the opposite direction. Once it passed, I continued on my way. I had to do the move all over again a moment later for another car. When I finally managed to reach the parking area, I was surprised to find it packed full of cars.

People were milling around the door leading into the sanctuary's office and I saw others heading down the path toward the different enclosures.

What the hell was happening?

I had to park the truck behind another car. I wiped at my face as I reminded myself I had just two goals I needed to accomplish.

Make Dallas fix my car and get Newt and get out.

My nerves felt brittle as I pushed past the people waiting outside the office. A few grumbled at me, but I ignored them. The office itself was jam-packed, but it wasn't hard to find Nolan. He was searching through a tall filing cabinet. My anger was like a living thing beneath my skin, but he seemed too frazzled to notice.

"Oh, hey, how did it go?" he asked. "Did you find any snow pants?"

"Where's Dallas?" I asked abruptly.

He paused for a moment, probably caught off guard by my tone, but when a lady handed him a small piece of paper, he turned his attention to it, then nodded and thanked her. He began rifling through the cabinet again as he spoke. "Um, I sent him to go lie down for a bit. He wasn't doing well with all" –he pointed to the people around us who were chatting amongst themselves– "this."

Nolan suddenly dropped his head against the cabinet and I felt a momentary pang of guilt for how tired he looked. His eyes met mine. He kept his voice low as he said, "People just keep showing up and we just weren't expecting that. I guess after last night, they're either curious or want to apologize or whatever. Dallas is still recovering so he wasn't feeling well to begin with…"

I couldn't help but feel sorry for him, but I steeled myself to ignore the pity. Yes, Nolan had been kind to me considering all I'd done, but he'd also lied to me. I'd trusted him to watch out for Newt and he'd lied to me.

"Where's Newt?" I asked.

"Isaac, come see!" I heard Newt call. I turned to see him sitting in the far corner of the office. He was surrounded by a couple of people, so I couldn't really see him. I hurried to him, intent on grabbing him and telling him we were leaving, but when I got to where he was, I came to a stop at the sight that greeted me.

Because he was covered in kittens.

Literally covered in kittens.

There was one in his hands, two curled up in his lap, and even one on his shoulder. Several more were walking all around the little cordoned-off corner that someone, Nolan probably, had created out of some boxes and various pieces of office furniture. Loki was snuggled up next to Newt with his head on Newt's thigh, and there was a kitten between the wolf hybrid's big paws and another climbing along his back.

It had to be one of the cutest scenes I'd ever witnessed.

"And this one is Mater," Newt said to a woman as he carefully held up the kitten in his hands. The woman took it from him.

"Whatcha doing, buddy?" I asked as I knelt down by the barrier keeping the kittens on Newt's side.

"I'm the cat per," he announced.

"The what?" I asked with a laugh. Something in my chest eased at the sight of my brother's broad smile.

"The kitties tell me their secrets, so Nolan says I'm the cat per since I can talk to them."

I chuckled. "Do you mean, the Cat Whisperer?"

"Yeah, that's what I said." Newt dropped his hand to Loki's head. "Nolan says people wanna take the kitties home with them, but I gotta say it's okay because I know them best."

I didn't really understand what my brother was talking about, but just seeing him look so at home made some of my anger recede. "Have you been spending a lot of time with the kittens?" I asked.

Newt nodded. "I helped feed them. And the big cats too. Nolan asked me to name them. This one's Sally and this one's Chick…"

I listened and watched as Newt spouted off the name of each kitten.

"And know what else?"

"What?" I asked dutifully.

"Nolan taught me to play something for Gentry! 'Cause it makes him feel safe. He says I'm real good."

"You are really good," Nolan said from behind me, then he was kneeling next to me. "Twinkle, Twinkle, Little Star is Gentry's favorite and I don't play it anywhere near as good as you," Nolan said as he reached out to poke my brother in the belly with a pretend tickle.

Newt practically beamed. My eyes caught on Nolan's fingers… specifically his nails. They were painted a mix of bright pink and orange. I recognized my brother's handiwork and couldn't help but smile. "I see you've been to Newt's Nifty Nails."

Nolan glanced at his nails and chuckled. "You should see Dallas's," he said. He faked a frown and said, "He got a mani *and* a pedi."

"I promise to do your toes tonight," Newt said. "Any color you want."

I laughed. "Wow, you must be special. He never lets me pick the colors," I said as I showed off my multi-colored nails. Newt wasn't coordinated enough to polish only the nail, so my fingers usually ended up covered in color, but I kept nail polish remover on hand so I could clean the color off my skin afterward, leaving just the nails polished. Nolan's fingers practically looked like they'd been dipped in the polish, but I didn't see any evidence he'd tried to pick or scrub the color off. Some men might have been willing to indulge a small child when it came to something like letting them color their nails, but they would have cleaned it off right away. And the majority certainly wouldn't have been seen in public with nail polish.

I wondered why Nolan hadn't removed the polish. And it sounded like maybe Dallas hadn't either.

"Your brother is quite the talented young man," Nolan said. "Multi-talented," he added. "He's the best manicurist I've ever been to by far," he said with a grin as he waved his fingers around. "I've never seen anyone who could talk so well to the guys." He motioned to the kittens, then his gaze shifted to me. "And he's got a great ear for music. Truly."

I could tell he was being serious about that last part.

"You taught him music?" I asked as the last of the anger from my encounter with Maddox faded away.

"I played his vlin," Newt announced. "Wha's a curist?" he asked Nolan.

"Manicurist. It's someone who does people's nails. And you didn't just play my violin, you practically made it sing," Nolan responded. He glanced at me and said, "I had to help him hold it because it's too big for him, but he worked the bow and did the chords by himself. If it's something you want him to pursue while you guys are here, I could probably find him a violin that would fit him and show him a few things." Nolan said the last words so eagerly, I couldn't help but get caught up in his excitement.

But then the reality of our situation crashed down on me. Not only could I not afford a violin, Newt and I weren't staying here, damn it. These people had lied to me.

"Mr. Grainger," I heard someone call, and I turned to see a woman motioning to Nolan.

"Be right there," he said with a smile, but when he turned around again to face Newt, his expression fell.

"What?" I asked.

He blew out a breath and kept his voice low so the people around us wouldn't hear. "Some of these people want to adopt animals, but I don't know the first thing about how to make that happen. But it's something Dallas really wants… he's got so many that are ready for forever homes and have been waiting years, but no one ever even came to check them out, and now…" He paused and looked around the crowded room. "And now they won't stop coming and part of me just wants to tell them to go so it can just be him and me again, you know?"

Despite his words, I knew he wasn't including me and Newt in the statement. I'd gotten the sense that both Nolan and Dallas hadn't been the most popular of guys in their small town. Since I'd always been known as a freak myself, I understood how easy and comfortable it was to live that role twenty-four seven. I couldn't imagine what it was like for both men to suddenly be thrust into the spotlight like they'd been. If it hadn't been for the animals, I suspected they would have just holed up in their house or something.

"Sawyer volunteered to show people around outside because otherwise they'd be wandering around on their own, but he doesn't know enough about this stuff either, and I want Dallas to rest because he's still recovering from the surgery…"

Nolan's hushed voice began to crack, so I put my hand on his arm. "Okay, let's start with the basics. Do you know if there's an application the people need to fill out to be considered as a potential adopter?"

"That's what I was trying to find," he said as he looked over his shoulder at the filing cabinet. "But I keep getting interrupted…"

"How about this," I said. "I'll start writing down names and figuring out which people are here because they're looking for pets versus which just want to connect with you and Dallas. I'll see if I can't get those people to agree to come back in a few days when Dallas is feeling better. That way we'll just have the potential adopting families here and we can collect their information and find out what kinds of pets they're looking for. I'm guessing you'll want time to review applications to determine if people are good candidates before you start sending pets home with them, right?"

Nolan nodded. "Dallas knows the animals the best. He'd want to make sure each one is going to the right forever family."

"Okay, if you can't find an application form, I'll just type something out real quick on your computer" –I motioned to the older model desktop on the desk behind me– "and we'll get people to start filling them out. The fact is, if the people are really serious about wanting to give the animals good homes, they'll be patient enough to return for scheduled appointments so they can have some one-on-one time with them. You know what I mean?"

"Right," Nolan said softly. "You're right. I should have thought of that." He chewed on his lower lip for a moment before saying, "I don't know the first thing about this *sh*-stuff."

I glanced at Newt, who was smiling knowingly. I shook my head at him, then tweaked his nose. "What are you smiling at?" I asked.

"Nothin'," he said with a grin.

"Really?" I asked, sending him a fake frown.

"He almost said a bad word," Newt whispered.

"But he didn't," I said. I saw Nolan was watching us both with a hidden smile.

"If he does, I know how you can punish him," Newt said, lowering his voice.

"Oh yeah, how?"

He made a big deal of curling his finger toward me. I leaned across the barrier and let him whisper his idea into my ear and automatically laughed. God, I just loved this kid.

"Oh no, what?" Nolan asked, his eyes going wide. "You gotta tell me," he said to Newt. "So I can make sure I don't say one."

Newt eyed me, and I nodded. It was Nolan's turn to get a finger crooked at him. When he heard his potential punishment, he let out a dramatic sigh and clutched his hands over his heart. "No, you can't take away the pedicure!" he said to Newt. "Dallas will never let me hear the end of it!"

My brother laughed and said, "Okay, you gotta be good then."

"I will, I swear it," Nolan vowed as he put up his hand like he was making a Boy Scout pledge.

"Excuse me," the woman holding the kitten Newt had given her said as she knelt down next to us. "Is Mater a good cuddler?"

"Okay, Cat Whisperer, you're on," Nolan said to Newt.

Newt winked at him, then said to the woman in all seriousness, "Yes, he is. But he cuddles even better when he's got Chick with him." My brother proceeded to sell the woman on the merits of adopting two kittens as Nolan and I stood.

"Isaac, if you could help me out for a little while, I'd be really grateful," Nolan said. "I know it's a lot to ask—"

"You didn't ask, I offered," I reminded him. I knew what I was doing was stupid, considering the lies this man and his boyfriend had told me, but unlike with Maddox, I didn't get the sense he was being disingenuous. And the reality was, he needed help. "Let's get to work," I said. "The sooner we get done, the closer some of your animals are to finding their forever homes."

Nolan nodded and returned to the cabinet to search through it. I turned to check in on Newt to tell him the plan, but he was deep in conversation with the woman discussing why three kittens was even better than two, so I left him to it. I rifled around the desk for a legal pad and pen, then began working my way through the small crowd of people inside the office. It was a good two hours before the crowd dissipated.

Darkness was just starting to fall when I looked up from where I'd been entering the names of potential adopters into a spreadsheet on the computer so their information would be easier to sort through when the time came. My eyes fell on Dallas and Nolan who were standing just outside the office door. They had their arms around each other and were just holding onto one another. I glanced over at Newt, who'd fallen asleep against Loki's side. The kittens were tucked up against Newt's little body.

It wasn't until Nolan softly called my name that I realized I'd been lost in a daydream about how badly I wanted every day to be like this for Newt. Where it wasn't about anything but him just being a kid.

I startled, then shook my head and said, "Sorry." Dallas and Nolan both smiled in understanding. My eyes dropped to Dallas's hand. His nails were painted neon green with little globs of pink all over them, which probably were supposed to have been polka dots.

It was on the tip of my tongue to lay into both men about lying about my car, but when Dallas handed me his phone so I could read his message, I merely said, "Sure, you can talk to me about something," and handed it back to him.

It was Nolan who outlined their idea, and admittedly, the job offer caught me off guard. While my plan had been to help them for the day, what they were offering was something more long-term. Nolan made it clear it could be for as long or as short as I wanted, and while I knew there was no way I could accept, I found myself wondering what it would be like if I could. I had no doubt the job offer was made out of pity and in an attempt to get me to stick around for a bit, since both men seemed to have the same thoughts as Maddox–that Newt and I were in trouble and needed help.

They weren't wrong about the first part, but I had no interest in the second part. And since Nolan knew I was an escort and had likely told Dallas as much, I suspected the money they were offering, which was overly generous, had a lot to do with them not wanting me to be forced to sell my body. When I'd been talking to Nolan the night I'd arrived about the fact that I was an escort and not a prostitute–a point of difference that really didn't exist, especially not when it came to me–I knew I hadn't been fooling him, despite my supposed lack of shame about the matter. But while my pride was telling me to reject the offer, the mere thought of how close I was to needing to find some more clients like the john with the lipstick was making me ill.

"Can I think about it?" I finally asked.

"Of course," Nolan said. There was an awkward silence between us, then Dallas stepped over the barrier and began picking up the kittens and handing them to Nolan, presumably so the pair could take them back down to the building they lived in. "Do you need help with him?" Nolan asked as he motioned to Newt.

"No," I said. "I've got him."

I watched as Dallas collected the last kitten. Before he straightened, I watched him run his fingers gently over Newt's temple. Both men stared at my brother for a moment before Dallas stepped back over the barrier. They headed for the door, but Dallas suddenly stopped and turned to face me. His hands were full of kittens so he maneuvered them so they were tucked against his chest, then looked pointedly at Nolan and made a motion with his hand. I didn't get what he meant but Nolan seemed to because he said to me, "He'll look at your car in a bit. We just need to feed the animals first." Nolan hesitated, then said, "But you know you're more than welcome to stay another night, right? It's supposed to get really cold tonight."

The reminder about my car should have angered me, but surprisingly it didn't.

I didn't really know why.

I glanced at Newt. Another night in a warm bed wouldn't hurt. "Thank you, we'd appreciate that. And tomorrow is fine for my car."

Both men seemed relieved and quickly said their goodbyes. I finished what I was doing and saved the file on the computer, then got up and went to collect Newt. He barely stirred when I picked him up. Loki licked my face when I bent down to lift Newt and I couldn't help but smile.

"Loki," Newt murmured as I lifted him.

"He's here, buddy," I said.

The wolf hybrid jumped up to follow us. I stopped at Dallas's truck long enough to grab the lunch bag I'd left tucked behind the front seat and then carried Newt along the path toward the house. His mouth was pressed up against my neck and his little arms were wrapped around me super tight.

"Isaac," he said softly, still half asleep.

"Yeah, buddy?"

"I miss Mommy."

It wasn't unusual for Newt to mention our mom out of the blue like that, but it still killed me every time he did it.

"I know you do, buddy. Me too."

"Isaac?"

"Yeah?"

"You think she's lonely in heaven?"

"No, I think she's got lots of friends with her."

"Animals too?"

"Definitely animals," I said. "And plants and bugs and rainbows."

"And angels?"

"*Lots* of angels."

He sighed, and I'd thought he'd fallen back asleep at first.

"Isaac?"

"Yeah?"

"Can we stay here till we gotta get lost again? It's nice here."

"It is?" I asked.

"Uh-huh."

"Don't you want to go see New York? Check out the Statue of Liberty? Climb up to the top of the tallest buildings so you can see if you can touch the sun?"

He was quiet for a moment. "Can Nolan and Dallas and Loki and Gentry and Mad come?"

"You want all of them to come? Even mad Mad?" I asked as nerves skittered through my belly at the mere thought of Maddox.

Newt nodded against my neck. "I think he's family."

"You mean part of Dallas's family?" I asked. "He is. He's Dallas's brother."

"Like you and me are brothers?"

"Exactly," I said.

"Then yeah, he's gotta come. He's family, even if he's mad. 'Cause he's not mean, right?"

I heard the fear in Newt's voice and I knew the cause of it. "No, buddy, he's not mean. None of them are mean."

"Like *him*," Newt whispered, his voice so low I barely heard it.

"Right, not like *him*," I reassured him. "And remember what I said about him?"

"He can't find us when we're lost."

"Right," I agreed and hugged him tighter.

Newt sighed after a moment and his head lolled against my neck, proof he was drifting off again. "If Loki and Dallas and Nolan and Gentry and Mad get lost with us, can they be our family?" he asked tiredly.

I felt a new round of tears threaten at his faint question. If only life worked like that. I didn't answer him and he didn't seem to be expecting me to. But just as I reached the house, I slowed, then stopped. I dropped my cheek to the top of his head.

"Newt," I whispered.

He made an unintelligible sound, so I wasn't sure if he was actually awake or not.

"Newt, do you want to stay here for a while? With Loki and Dallas and Nolan and Gentry and Mad?"

He didn't answer, and I wasn't sure if I was happy or sad about that. But just as I reached the steps that led up to the door, Newt's lips moved against my neck. I couldn't actually hear his answer, but it didn't matter because the nod against my neck was answer enough.

"Okay, buddy," I said as I pressed another kiss to the top of his head. "We'll stay." A mix of fear and relief went through me and I instinctively qualified my answer so I wouldn't let myself be too overly comfortable with it, because that would be a very dangerous thing indeed.

So I added "for now" and waited for the nerves in my belly to ease.

But they didn't... and I didn't know if that was a good thing or not.

My gut was telling me it was probably a good thing. Because being relaxed meant making mistakes.

And I couldn't afford to make any mistakes.

Not again.

Because I wouldn't be the only one who paid for them.

CHAPTER SEVEN

MADDOX

I'd made him cry.

I'd humiliated him, confused him, and then made him cry.

I downed another swallow of whiskey from the bottle in my hand before refilling my glass and setting the bottle by my feet, and I waited for the warm liquid to take away the pain I'd seen in Isaac's eyes.

He was a prostitute.

He let men use his body for money.

What if that was only who he *used* to be? What if my actions had forced him to go back to that life? Fuck, why hadn't I just talked to Dallas or Nolan about my suspicions that Isaac and Newt were in trouble and let them handle it? Surely, they could have found a way to help the young man without putting him in a position where he had to let random guys fuck him for cash.

The liquor soured in my belly and I fought the urge to throw up. I dropped my head back against the seat cushion of the armchair I was sitting in. My head hurt, but I knew the knocking sound I was hearing wasn't from the throbbing in my brain.

I didn't bother getting up because I knew Dallas would find me pretty easily. Despite the size of the sprawling mansion, I heard footsteps closing in on my location within a minute. Of course, I'd made it pretty easy by choosing only one section of the house to call home. I hadn't even bothered with turning on the heat for the huge house. The massive fireplace in the living room was enough to keep me warm.

God, my brother looked good. Tired, but good. The last time it'd been just me and him, he'd been in the hospital, his body battered and broken and lifeless. I could tell he still suffered some lingering issues from the accident besides his voice, because he walked with a slight limp. But otherwise he looked strong and healthy. I couldn't wait to hear him talk again. Even if it wasn't his old voice, maybe just hearing him talk would let me pretend the events of ten years ago hadn't happened.

Yeah, right.

Even if I could have sold myself on that story, I'd have to be sticking around in order to hear him talk and that just wasn't going to happen. I needed to get the fuck out of Pelican Bay.

Dallas's eyes met mine briefly before he studied the area around the fireplace. My sleeping bag in front of it, all the cloth-draped furnishings moved to the far walls of the room, and the various empty bottles of liquor on the floor near my bedroll.

"Took you long enough, little brother," I said softly.

He came around to face me and handed me his phone. There was a message already typed out on it so instead of taking it from him, I just leaned forward and read it.

Thank you for what you did for Loki... for me.

"Don't thank me," I said as I leaned back in the chair. "All I did was tell the truth. It was long overdue."

I knew the conversation wasn't over, so I let my eyes drift to the roaring fire as Dallas typed. It just hurt too much to look at him. I wondered when I'd become *that* guy. The one who acted before thinking. The one who preferred action to logic.

As a kid, I'd used reason to approach difficult things. But somewhere along the line reason hadn't had the answers I'd wanted. Like there'd been no logical reason our parents would spend their days playing the role of bible-loving, morally perfect community leaders and their nights losing themselves in the lure of alcohol and drugs. No amount of reasoning had changed their behavior, so Dallas and I had been forced to adapt to it.

Like with the sparkplugs.

That change had carried through to the army, but fortunately my instincts had still been my strongest ally in those situations. But with Dallas and Isaac, I'd leapt to conclusions which'd had ugly consequences.

What do you want from me?

I read Dallas's message and felt something inside of me tear open. A million answers came to mind, but they were selfish ones and pretty much all ran along the lines of, *I want you back.*

But I didn't say that.

Instead, I said, "I want you to have the life you should have had ten years ago. I want to go back to that moment and do what I should have done."

What should you have done?

"Told you how fucking glad I was that I hadn't lost you too," I said. I managed to quell the pain until my insides felt numb and empty. I just needed to make it a little longer and Dallas would leave, and I could lose myself in a bottle. Tomorrow I'd get on the road again and head for Oklahoma. The idea of getting on a crowded bus threatened to have all the alcohol I'd consumed come back up, so I drew in a breath and reminded myself that I had two perfectly good legs that could get me to Oklahoma. Yeah, it'd take a hell of a lot longer and be cold as hell, but that was actually a good thing.

"Did the kid and his brother leave?" I asked. I knew Isaac technically wasn't a kid, but he had one of those faces that could pass for a teenager's.

Except the eyes.

He had old eyes.

Like he'd seen too much already in his young life. I'd seen more than my share of eyes like that in the military.

No, he's working at the center for a little while. Nice trick with his car.

I nearly threw up right then and there, but I managed to keep my emotions buried. I had a strong feeling that for whatever reason, Isaac hadn't laid into my brother about the car, or surely Dallas would have said something by now. And if the young man was working at the sanctuary...

"Little fool doesn't know what's good for him," I said with a dismissive wave of my hand like I didn't care what Isaac did or didn't do. But inside, my nerves were skittering all over the place. If he'd taken a job with Dallas, did that mean he was staying for a while? Had he told Dallas and Nolan what kind of trouble he was dealing with? Would he be able to earn enough money so he'd never have to let a sick fuck like Tomlinson touch him again?

Dallas handing me his phone was a good distraction from my thoughts.

What happened to you the night of the meeting, Maddox?

"I would have thought it would be obvious to you," I said. It'd been two nights since the meeting, but it felt like it'd just happened. Of course, most nights were like that if I didn't have the buzz of alcohol to stave off the nightmares.

PTSD?

I searched out my glass of whiskey and downed what remained in the glass. "Textbook case," I said as I turned my attention toward the fire. God, there'd been fire everywhere that day. "Roadside bomb in Mosul. Overturned Humvee, heavy fire, six of my men killed instantly. Three more didn't last long enough to be evac'd. One guy got out besides me. I'm fucked up in the head, he's got no legs. Purple Heart medals for both of us. Textbook," I said bitterly.

Is that why you don't drive?

I couldn't help but look at him in surprise. "How did you know?"

Just a guess. What are your plans?

I needed to tell him I was heading out the next day, but for some reason, the words got caught in my throat. He caught me off guard when he lowered himself to the floor.

I'd like to tell you about my plans. But I want to start by telling you something that someone I love very much and who I once hurt very badly told me not long ago.

I read the message and nodded. It didn't take a genius to know he was talking about Nolan. Even without saying the man's name, he positively shone when he mentioned the person he loved so very much. I used the several minutes it took him to type out his message to study him. Dallas had always been so different from me. Much more easygoing but driven as hell. But he'd also had a harder time with the demands our parents had put on both of us to be perfect–to always present that perfect outer image.

It'd been especially tough after he'd realized he was gay. I'd noticed a change in his behavior early on when he was around fourteen–he'd stopped talking to me and he'd almost seemed afraid to even be in the same room with me. There'd always been this odd look of a mix between fear and need in his expression whenever he looked at me. I'd finally managed to pry the truth out of him one day when he'd been fifteen and I'd been nineteen. He'd been so certain I'd turn away from him when he'd told me he was gay when, in truth, it hadn't bothered me in the least. But I'd been heartbroken that there'd been enough of a fissure in our relationship for him to even think I'd abandon him because of something like that. It'd taken months to prove that I loved him no matter what and that, unlike our parents, he hadn't needed to buy my love by being some perfect version of himself.

Of course, he *had* eventually accepted that I'd always have his back and I loved him unconditionally.

But like everyone else in his life, I hadn't kept my promise to him. My love hadn't been unconditional. I'd chosen a vow we'd made to one another over everything else. Even if Dallas had done what my father had said and betrayed me by driving drunk, it hadn't warranted my response. Yes, I would have had the right to be angry, but I should have made it clear I hated the crime, not the man.

Because just like I'd promised him that day as he'd wept in my arms and told me that he liked boys instead of girls, I'd never stopped loving my brother. But I may as well have. The things I'd said and done were crueler even than what our father had done to him.

I let my eyes linger over Dallas as he typed easily into the phone. I missed his voice. But I liked seeing how expressive his eyes were as he typed. I saw lots of the little things I'd never really appreciated when he'd been able to speak.

After a few minutes, Dallas handed me the phone and I tried to mentally prepare myself for the words of anger and hate I so deserved.

But I realized pretty quickly that wasn't the intent of his message.

We're not the same people we were back then, Maddox. And I believe that if you could change things, you would. I would, too. I would have told you the truth then and there, and I would have made sure you believed me instead of letting you walk away. Because you were the most important person in my life. But I chose to let you believe a lie because inside I was still that little kid who wanted to please his parents. It was a lot easier to live that lie than accept the truth. My hope is that you don't do what I did and start to believe that you deserved what happened to you. My hope is that you don't relive that day and wonder if there was something you could have or should have done differently. My hope is that you will accept that I forgive you for the things you said and did back then. My hope is that we can one day be brothers again. My hope is that you forgive yourself because I really want back the person who's always had my back.

Emotion clogged my throat as I kept waiting for the hatred to shine through, but it wasn't there. I found myself nodding along with the line he said about how much easier it was to live with a lie than accept the truth. But when I got to the part where he said he wanted me to accept that he'd forgiven me and wanted to be brothers again, I felt the tears stinging the backs of my eyes and I automatically wiped at them.

When I was finished, I read the damn thing a second time, just to make sure I hadn't been reading things that weren't there. It was just too good to be true. It was like those rare moments in my nightmares where I'd be waking up to the sound of explosions with pain searing my body. I'd hear the pounding over and over, but when I crawled around the overturned Humvee, Jett wasn't lying pinned beneath the vehicle and calling my name as he pounded the butt of his machine gun on the vehicle to get my attention. He was simply standing on his own two legs, impatiently tapping the roof of the vehicle as he told me to get a move on because we were headed home. Our entire unit was standing behind him agreeing with him.

In my weakest moments, I craved those rare altered memories more than I wanted to admit. But they were few and far between and were starting to become more and more unbearable than the actual memory, because they left me with this god-awful hope that scared the hell out of me.

The same hope I was feeling now as Dallas extended a metaphorical hand to me.

I couldn't take it, though.

Because I didn't deserve it.

I couldn't let him come to see me as the big brother he needed when I wasn't even close to being that anymore. He needed someone strong to always have his back, but I'd barely managed to make it through that town hall meeting in one piece. He'd have been horrified if I'd lost control and destroyed that room like I'd destroyed the wing of the military hospital in Germany when I'd learned that Jett had tried to take his own life not one day after his legs had been amputated below the knee.

He was asking for a brother back who no longer existed.

Dallas suddenly began to stand, and I realized it was because I'd been quiet for too long. I reached out to grab his arm before he could get up. As badly as I *should* let him go, I couldn't. But I didn't want to admit why, especially to him. I barely wanted to admit it to myself. He might *want* his brother back, but what if I was the one who *needed* mine back? What if Dallas was the one thing that could keep me from going down that rabbit hole of self-destruction that always seemed to be on the edge of my mind, along with the screams and pleas of my dying comrades?

"You said you wanted to tell me about your plans," I said.

Dallas relaxed and settled back onto the floor.

He typed another message to me, which caught me almost as off guard as the previous one.

Do you need a job?

It was just after eight in the morning when I cut across the back part of the sanctuary's property. It'd been just over twelve hours since I'd seen Dallas and accepted his offer to continue to help around the sanctuary. We'd argued briefly about the money part of the job, but I'd found a quick way to end the discussion when I'd told him what to do with my earnings. He'd undoubtedly been surprised by the request but hadn't argued. After all, he knew I didn't need the money. I'd barely touched my half of the inheritance in the years I'd been in the military. I'd tried giving some of it to Jett, but that hadn't gone over well, and when I'd nearly lost him over the issue, I'd been forced to let it go.

So technically, I was a very rich man.

But hell if the idea of slogging through knee-deep snow and bone-chilling temperatures for several hours to get to a job where I cleaned up animal shit and fixed broken fencing didn't sound like the best damn thing in the world.

My body felt comfortably loose and warmed up despite the cold as I made my way past the dog enclosure and along the path between the livestock area and the bear enclosure. I could hear music playing and knew it was likely Nolan playing his early morning serenade for Gentry, the tormented bear. But the beautiful strings piece was just ending, and I was sorry I'd missed it. My plan was to head to the office to check in with Dallas, but I stopped when I heard the music start up again.

It took me a moment to realize what the song was, and I had no doubt it wasn't Nolan who was playing it.

I turned to go down the little path that led to Gentry's enclosure and came to a stop when I saw a slim body standing at the end of the path.

Isaac.

His back was to me, so I had a second to take him fully in. He was wearing the same black skinny jeans he seemed to favor. A heavy twill coat was settled on his shoulders. It looked too big for him, so I figured it was probably Dallas's.

Meaning whatever jacket Isaac owned, if he even owned one, was too thin for the elements.

His hands were tucked into his pockets. He wasn't wearing a hat, so I could see his black-blue hair catching the glint of the early morning sun. Every once in a while, he'd lift a hand to brush his hair out of his face. My eyes caught on the large gauges in his ears. God, he was such an odd individual. I'd seen people like him from afar, but up close, all the things about him that should have weirded me out just… *worked*.

And why was that even a thing for me?

That they worked?

Why was I even noticing something like that?

My thoughts drifted to that moment in the motel when I'd ordered him to put on the lip gloss. I'd tried to tell myself it was just to take the attention away from the remnants of the red lipstick that had lingered on his skin, but it was utter bullshit. I'd managed to get rid of all the hated red. I'd just wanted to… fuck, I didn't know what I'd wanted.

I wasn't gay.

I knew that.

I wasn't bi either. Jett had kissed me once when we were cadets at West Point. We'd been on break and had gone to a bar for his twenty-first birthday. He'd gotten pretty hammered and before I'd even realized it, he'd called me hot and then he'd kissed me.

I'd actually kissed him back for a few seconds, but I hadn't felt anything in particular. It'd been fine, but there'd been no sparks, no tightening in my belly, and my dick hadn't particularly perked up, not like it usually did with women.

Usually, but not always.

I'd always passed off my lack of interest in sex as just a byproduct of being busy and focused on my career. Yes, there'd been some girls in high school and later some women here and there, but they'd all been take-it-or-leave-it kind of things. Not having a raging libido just hadn't been something I'd been overly concerned about.

With Jett, I'd gently ended the kiss and taken him home. Fortunately, he'd been too drunk to make another pass at me or even remember it the following day.

But as I stood watching Isaac, I couldn't help but remember that my libido had been working just fine at the motel. And yes, Isaac could most definitely be called beautiful, despite his odd look, and he had some features that seemed more feminine than masculine, but there was nothing in my mind that saw him as a woman. I had no illusions about what was behind the zipper of his skinny jeans.

The idea that I might be attracted to him seemed ludicrous to me, but I also wasn't going to make excuses for it. I'd lived my entire life taking things as they came. My parents had thrived on labels and appearances and expectations while using drugs and alcohol to hide from everything that had been real in their lives.

Whatever this *thing* with Isaac was, it was irrelevant.

I moved until I was standing just behind him. I expected him to respond to my presence, but he seemed not to notice me, and I figured it was because all his attention was on Newt and Nolan where they were standing near Gentry's enclosure. The enclosure had two fences, and usually Nolan played along the inner fence for the bear. But today he was outside both fences and I suspected it was because of Newt. Although Gentry hadn't shown any kind of aggression that I'd ever seen, putting a child anywhere near him would have been irresponsible to say the least, even with adult supervision and a fence separating them.

Nolan was helping Newt hold the violin as Newt carefully moved his little fingers over the appropriate chords and then moved the bow along the strings. The song was played painstakingly slow, but the notes were clear, and I recognized the song for what it was.

Twinkle, Twinkle, Little Star.

The song lasted a good two minutes and I was surprised to see that Gentry had lain down at the far end of the enclosure and was watching Nolan and Newt. Usually, the traumatized animal was pacing the length of the fence. Sawyer had explained to me that the attack on the animal by Jimmy Cornell and his friends had left the formerly abused bear with new physical and mental wounds, and it would take a long time for the animal to heal from them.

I watched Isaac as Isaac watched Newt. From my position, I couldn't see his face, but his failure to stay still told me he was going through something. I watched as he put his arms around his body as if trying to give himself a hug. I actually found myself moving closer to him before I caught myself.

What was it about the young man that made it seem like he was always just barely hanging on? With the way he'd laid into me at the motel, there was nothing weak about him.

Well, not true.

He'd cried when I'd handed him the money that had been meant to cover the cash he'd lost. I had no clue what he charged to let guys use him, but there'd been more than a thousand dollars in that wad of cash. I would have gladly given him more if it meant he never had to even think about getting on his knees for the likes of Arthur Tomlinson again.

But all I'd done was hurt him even more.

"Didya see?" Newt suddenly shouted as he practically shoved the violin at Nolan and began racing up the path toward Isaac.

"I saw!" Isaac responded. I could hear the pride in his voice.

Newt stopped after just a couple of feet when his eyes landed on me. I hated the wariness that came over him. Isaac turned around and let out a gasp when he saw me not even a foot behind him.

"Jeepers creepers," he yelled as he clutched his chest.

I nearly smiled at the ridiculous anti-swear word.

"Sorry," I offered. My eyes roamed over Isaac's body. His coat was unbuttoned, so I saw that his shirt was a hot pink color and had a unicorn farting rainbows on it. There was a bright purple glittery scarf wrapped around his throat. He was wearing eyeliner again, but this time it was a deep shade of purple. And the gloss was there, making his lips look full and very kissable.

God, what was happening to me? Was it really going to be this over-the-top, weird, outrageous, vulnerable-but-oh-so-strong kid who was going to finally get my body to wake up and act like the horny teenager my mother had tried to accuse me of being, but that I'd never actually been?

Newt appeared at Isaac's side and wrapped his arms protectively around his brother's waist. His blue eyes, which were so like Isaac's, pinned mine. "Don't say mean things to my brother, Mad," Newt said, his finger coming up to wave in my direction. "Or I'll tell your mommy on you."

Isaac's hands dropped to Newt's head. "It's fine, Newt, he's not going to."

"You can't be in the family if you're mean," Newt declared.

I had no idea what he was talking about, but clearly, I'd made an impression with the boy. And a legitimate one.

"Hey," Isaac said as he knelt down in front of Newt. "He's not going to be mean to me."

"Yes, he is. He made you cry."

I startled at that. Had Isaac actually told him that?

But Isaac seemed equally surprised. "What? No, he didn't," Isaac said.

Newt began to nod, and to my horror, tears began sliding down his face. "Uh-huh, he did. Last night."

"Hey, hey," Isaac said, his voice full of worry when he lifted Newt into his arms. Newt wrapped his arms and legs around his brother. "What are you talking about?"

"You told him to stay away from you. Then you started to cry. I tried to wake you…"

Understanding dawned as Isaac's eyes met mine and I felt like the lowest form of human life on the planet.

"Buddy, look at me," Isaac said. Nolan had made his way to us after putting the violin in his case and I could see the concern in his eyes.

Newt looked at his brother through watery eyes and let out a little hiccup.

"I was having a bad dream last night, wasn't I?"

Newt nodded. "And you cried."

"Remember how our dreams sometimes get things mixed up?" Isaac asked. "And that the things that happen in dreams didn't actually happen in real life?"

"Like the time I dreamed Lightning drove to our house in Frisco."

"San Francisco, right," Isaac said. "And you ran down to the street in your pajamas to talk to him and it was still just our same boring car out there?"

Newt nodded morosely.

"Well, that's what I did last night. I was remembering things that didn't happen and mixing stuff up in my mind. Maddox didn't make me cry and I didn't tell him to stay away from me."

Isaac was lying through his teeth because I'd done all those things and worse. I felt Nolan's eyes on me and could practically hear the wheels spinning in his head.

"He didn't?" Newt asked, sounding unsure.

Isaac shook his head. "It was just a dumb dream, okay? And he's not going to be mean to me or to you, and you know why?"

"Why?"

"Because Loki will eat him if he does," Nolan cut in. His hard eyes were on me, so his warning was clear. And I didn't blame him in the least.

"Not Loki," I said, trying to make my voice sound terrified as I laid pleading eyes on Newt. He watched me suspiciously and then said, "Gentry too. Gentry likes me and Isaac."

"Gentry's a smart bear," I said. "Ok, Gentry, too. But just don't… just don't sic you-know-who on me," I whispered as I pretended to look fearfully around me.

"Who?" Newt asked.

I shook my head violently. "Oh, no, I can't tell you that."

"Dallas!" Newt guessed.

I shook my head.

"The dogs?"

Another shake.

It went on and on like that for several seconds with Nolan and

Isaac finally chiming in to "help" Newt guess. The little boy was finally smiling, but my guilt was a heavy, dead weight in my belly.

Dallas appeared a moment later and stopped at Nolan's side, his arm automatically going around the slimmer man's waist. He seemed confused as to what was happening at first, until Nolan leaned up and whispered in his ear. Dallas's eyes settled on me and I didn't miss the condemnation there. I had no idea if Isaac had told them about what had transpired between us at the motel, but Dallas clearly was as protective of Newt as Isaac and Nolan were. I saw him get his phone out and pull up something on the screen, then he gave Newt's little sleeve a tug. I'd noticed the night before that my brother's fingernails were covered in bright green and pink nail polish, but it appeared that Nolan's were too, but just in different colors.

The little group huddled together as they all looked at Dallas's phone screen and whispered amongst themselves. All I cared about was the smile I saw on Newt's face and the spark in his eyes when he triumphantly looked at me.

"I know who it is," he said with a big grin.

"No, you don't," I whispered.

"Yes, I do," the little boy said proudly. "It's Jerry!"

"No!" I cried right before I covered my mouth with my hand. I made a show of putting my folded hands against Newt's knee. "Please, Newt, I'll never be mean again, I swear it. Just don't feed me to Jerry the Ornery Zebra."

Newt didn't manage to make it through my plea before he began giggling. Everyone else seemed to relax, and while I knew I had a lot of damage control to do with both Isaac and his brother, for the moment, I felt like we were back on even footing. At least the little boy didn't look like he was going to burst into tears again.

"Okay, so we're good?" Isaac asked as he gave Newt a squeeze.

"Nuh-uh, you gotta do the thing," he said.

"No, we don't," Isaac said.

"What thing?" Nolan asked at the same time.

To Nolan, Newt said, "They gotta hug. When me and Isaac have a fight, we always gotta say sorry and hug. It's the rules."

"No, it's fine—"

"I agree with Newt," I cut in, interrupting Isaac. I held the younger man's gaze and said, "Rules are rules, after all."

I could tell the last thing Isaac wanted was to touch me, but I wasn't about to lose this opportunity. "But first, I think I have to say something to Newt because Newt is your brother and by being mean to you, I was being mean to Newt. Because brothers are that close, aren't they, Newt?" I asked, though I glanced at Dallas while I said the last part.

"Yep," Newt said, as if what I'd said was exactly what he'd been thinking. He made Isaac put him down and then waited expectantly. I reached into my pocket and pulled out the toy car he'd given me two nights earlier at the town council meeting. I knelt down, not caring about the snow, then carefully pressed the car into his hand.

"Thank you for letting me borrow Lightning. He made me feel much better," I said before wrapping my arms around the little boy's body.

"I'm so sorry I hurt Isaac's feelings, Newt," I said loud enough so everyone could hear. "And yours too," I added. I gave him a gentle squeeze, then kept my voice low so only he would hear. "And I promise, I'll never make him cry again."

Newt squeezed me hard. When I released him and leaned back, he followed me and put his hand to his mouth as he whispered something into my ear that nearly broke my heart. I managed to nod. "I won't, buddy. I promise," I said as I hugged him again. Newt stepped back and leaned against Nolan's leg. I rose, keeping my eyes on Isaac.

I could tell he wanted to be anywhere else but there at that moment. Part of me wanted to let him off the hook, but it was the voice that was still ringing in my ears–Newt's voice–that had me closing the distance between us and drawing the slim young man into my arms.

Please don't let him hurt Isaac and me anymore.

CHAPTER EIGHT

ISAAC

Who knew a damn teaching moment was about to come back and bite me in the ass? I'd made the rule about me and Newt needing to hug it out after every fight one time after we'd gone to bed upset with each other and he'd shown up beside my bed in tears, terrified I was going to leave him behind because I hated him.

I was still reeling from the fact that I'd been crying in my sleep and had apparently said Maddox's name. I'd spent the last twenty-four hours convincing myself the man meant nothing to me and that I was completely over the events that had unfolded in the motel. But clearly, my subconscious wasn't ready to throw in the towel.

I watched as Newt whispered something to Maddox and shivered at Maddox's response. I assumed it was him promising not to hurt me again.

I wanted to tell him that wouldn't be a problem because I was staying the hell out of his way, no matter what it took. That should be easy enough to do, since Newt and I wouldn't be staying more than a week or so—just enough to make a few extra bucks to make it easier to get to the next big city. We'd hunker down in Minneapolis or Chicago for the rest of the winter and then get to New York by springtime.

Dallas had "miraculously" fixed my car this morning after I'd finally agreed that Newt and I would stay on for a little while. Right after I'd made the announcement, Nolan had informed me that Maddox had agreed to help out around the sanctuary, so Dallas could continue to recover from his surgery. It hadn't exactly been the best news, but I figured it would be easy enough to stay out of the man's way. He'd probably be just as eager to stay out of mine.

Well, that'd been my thinking up until two seconds ago.

I held my breath as Maddox stepped forward until our bodies were practically touching.

Go for the straight-guy-pat-me-on-the-back-during-a-half-hug thing.

I repeated the mantra a few times, but to my shock, Maddox's arms slowly wrapped around me. I automatically put my hands up at his waist to steady myself and felt the coolness of his leather belt beneath my palms.

Why the hell wasn't his coat buttoned? I needed as many layers between our bodies as possible, damn it.

I waited for the hug to end as I stood there stiffly, but Maddox didn't seem to be in any kind of hurry and my traitorous body began to react to the contact. His mouth ghosted over the skin just in front of my ear so gently that it almost felt like he'd kissed me there. It was the side of my head that the others wouldn't have been able to see.

His lips hovered there as he whispered, "I'm so sorry, Isaac. So fucking sorry."

I was glad he kept his voice low because Newt definitely would have picked up on the swear word.

But the way Maddox had said it sounded so pained, it was like it wasn't even a swear word. It was like it was the only word that he could have used to make me understand he meant what he'd said. His big body felt so warm and strong against mine, that I found myself sinking into the embrace, despite my intentions. And then my hands, God, my hands slid all the way along his sides to his back and then drifted up his spine–*beneath* his damn jacket. His muscles were hot and firm beneath my touch.

I needed to stop.

We'd already hugged for way longer than was necessary.

But when he whispered, "Please, forgive me, Isaac," I barely stifled a cry as something inside of me burst.

Like some kind of ugly, festering wound that I'd been trying to ignore my whole life.

I pressed my mouth against the spot where his throat met his shoulder and used his hot skin as a way to muffle the sound. He was so big that I felt completely enveloped. Newt was gone. Dallas and Nolan too. There were no animals or trees. It was only warm, not freezing cold. And as excited as my dick was, my heart was the part of my body that finally felt like it was home for the first time in a really long while.

Maddox was the one to come to his senses first. Although he probably wasn't coming to his senses so much as just ending the hug like a normal person. It was all I could do to force myself to let go of him. I couldn't risk looking at him, so I glanced at Nolan as I reached down to take Newt's hand. "Should we get going?"

The plan was for me to spend the day in the office going through some of the applications that had continued to trickle in while Newt continued to play with the kittens, as well as some of the older cats. Nolan had said it would help some of the older cats who got along with the kittens to start interacting with people more in the hopes they'd be adopted out as quickly as the babies. Neither Dallas nor Nolan had any issue with bringing the cats and kittens up to the office so I could keep an eye on Newt while he babysat the cats.

I didn't wait for Nolan to answer as I pushed past Maddox and headed for the building that housed the cats. It took about twenty minutes to get Newt settled in his spot with the kittens. We let the older cats roam the entire office but put up a baby gate on the inside of the door frame to keep them from running out when someone opened the office door. Fortunately, most of the lookie-loo types had stopped showing up in masses in the three days since the truth about Dallas had come out. But there were still people showing up now and then. I'd had a chance to meet Sawyer briefly the day before, but he'd been called to a zoo in the south somewhere to consult on an injured bear, so he wasn't expected back for a few days. It was with that thought in mind that Newt and I locked up the kittens in the large crate for their nap and then moved the few larger cats back down to the building they were housed in without waiting for Dallas and Nolan to do it at lunch time. Newt and I walked to the main house, and after giving him a simple lunch of soup and a peanut butter and jelly sandwich, he went down for his nap without argument.

I used the time to clean up the kitchen and make some more sandwiches along with some coffee that I put in several insulated Thermoses. My hope was to find all three men together, but fortune only favored the brave and I ended up finding Dallas and Nolan working together in the livestock area. I had no clue where Maddox was and didn't care, either.

Liar.

I walked into the barn and found Nolan and Dallas cleaning the stalls. Well, Dallas was cleaning them, and Nolan was clearly trying to stop him by stepping into the man's path every time he tried to enter one of the stalls.

"Please, Dallas, just let me finish up here and go lie down for a bit."

Dallas shook his head and put his hand over the bandage on his throat as he rasped something that sounded like, "Fine."

I cleared my throat to get their attention.

Both men looked up.

"I made some sandwiches," I offered. "I've got some coffee, too."

Both men seemed to relax for the moment as Nolan waved me forward and Dallas cleaned off the top of what looked like some kind of grain bin. I handed them each a couple of sandwiches which were in plastic bags. "I made sure the bread was fresh," I said to Dallas. "I know you need to keep eating softer foods for a bit yet."

Dallas nodded and smiled.

"How are things going in the office?" Nolan asked as both men began eating.

"Good," I said. "Quieter today."

I chuckled when both men looked relieved.

"You know, if you want me to help out here with anything, just let me know," I said. "I'm stronger than I look. And Newt can help out with stuff too, as long as someone's keeping an eye on him."

I could see both men were trying to come up with reasons to say no to me, so I cut them off before they could respond. "Please don't make me a charity case," I said softly. "Because if that's what I am, then Newt and I should just go—"

"No!" Nolan said as Dallas made a weird sound in his throat. "Sorry," Nolan murmured. "You're right. It's just that Dallas and I both know how physically exhausting the work can be…"

"All the more reason to let me help," I said. "I'm not saying I'm going to be able to do it all, but surely there are some tasks that don't require brute strength."

"How about tomorrow I show you and Newt how to clean up around these guys?" Nolan said as he motioned to the various livestock in the stalls.

"Great," I said. "Speaking of brutes, any idea where your brother is?" I asked as I looked to Dallas. "I made him some sandwiches… you know, so he won't eat unsuspecting children or villagers who happen by."

Dallas and Nolan both laughed, but Dallas's had a rasping quality to it. Dallas took out his phone. I liked that even though Nolan probably already knew the answer, he let Dallas tell me.

He's fixing the fence on the mountain lion enclosure.

"Do you want me to take it to him?" Nolan asked carefully. No doubt both men were sensing the tension between me and Maddox. I was half-tempted to take him up on the offer but the reality was, Maddox and I needed to clear the air, especially if Newt and I were staying for a little while.

"No, it's okay," I said.

I left the barn and walked up the trail toward Gentry's pen, which was on the side of the property where the rest of the larger, more dangerous animals were kept. As I walked, Jerry the zebra started walking along the fence line that bordered the path. I couldn't help but laugh as I remembered Maddox's fake horror at the thought of the striped menace biting him. Despite the animal being so far out of its natural habitat, I couldn't help but think it looked at home as it plodded comfortably through the thick snow.

"You behave yourself tomorrow," I said as I eyed him. "I heard what you did to Nolan when he started," I added as I shook my finger at him. I stopped when Jerry hung his head over the fence and began shaking it like he was agreeing with me. It did not bode well for me come tomorrow.

"I think you can take him."

I jumped a good foot at the sound of Maddox's voice. This time he wasn't behind me, but just a few feet ahead of me on the path where it split.

"Son of a mother!" I shouted. "God, will you please stop doing that?" I groused as I tried to calm my racing heart.

Maddox seemed amused as he said, "Sorry."

I didn't quite believe him.

"I thought you were working on the mountain lion fence," I said.

"Finished," was all he said in response. He looked yummy in his navy parka. Unlike Dallas, who regularly wore a jumpsuit of some kind to keep his clothes clean, Maddox wore just jeans and heavy work boots. His parka was buttoned, but I'd seen that he was wearing a thick hunter-green knit sweater earlier in the day.

Right before he'd hugged me.

"What are you doing?" he asked.

"Bringing you," –I looked down at the sandwiches at my feet– "lunch." At least I'd managed to hang onto the Thermos.

Maddox stepped forward and it was all I could do not to move. He bent down in front of me to pick up the sandwiches. The plastic baggies had kept them protected from the snow, so he merely brushed the little bit of ice off them. "Thank you," he said.

Man, the guy was going for a record with the polite thing. I almost wanted to look to see if Newt was around to account for his behavior. The reminder of my brother and the events of the morning had me handing the Thermos to him. "I want you to stay away from me and my brother while we're here. Newt especially," I blurted.

If he was surprised by my comments, he didn't show it. "Why don't we talk inside?" he said as he motioned to the building behind him. I knew it was the place Dallas kept orphaned babies in the spring. As far as I knew, it was empty at the moment.

Not that being in a room with a bunch of baby animals would have made any difference, but somehow the idea of being alone in a building with him made me nervous. But Maddox didn't give me a chance to respond. Instead, he turned and went into the building, leaving the door open for me.

I forced myself to follow because I wasn't afraid of him.

I wasn't.

When I entered, the lights were on and Maddox had placed the sandwiches and Thermos on a small table in the middle of the room. I watched him strip off his gloves so he could wash his hands. The building wasn't warm, so I automatically put my arms around myself. If Newt and I were going to stay a little longer than planned, I'd need to invest in a heavier coat and some thicker sweaters. My plan had been to do so once we got to New York, but I'd also planned to have a lot more money to spend on stuff like that. As it was, I wouldn't get paid for this job for at least a week. Dallas had offered to pay me an advance, but I'd refused and, fortunately, he hadn't argued with me.

But it was definitely going to suck having to work in the icy conditions without the right clothes. As it was, Dallas had let me borrow one of his older coats, but it was too big on me and would make cleaning awkward. At least I had enough clothes for Newt that I could bundle him in layers. And I had enough cash that maybe I could go to the thrift shop and find him some snow pants and actual winter boots, especially if we were going to be spending more time outside.

I was silent as Maddox took his time getting cleaned up. He shrugged his coat off and pushed up his sleeves before reaching for one of the sandwiches. My belly dropped out at the sight of the dark hairs on his muscled forearm.

"So you were saying you want me to stay away from Newt... and you?" Maddox asked. He took three bites and the sandwich was gone.

"Yeah, that's right," I said. I felt a shiver go through me, but part of it was the cold.

Maddox reached for the second sandwich but hesitated, then he was moving toward me. I automatically stepped back before I could stop myself. But he just walked past me and closed the door, which I'd inadvertently left open. When he returned to the table, he stayed on my side of it. There were only a few feet separating us. A row of cages was at my back, preventing my escape.

Maddox reached for the Thermos and took a sip of the coffee, then handed it to me.

The actual Thermos, not the cup that came with it. And the way he'd turned the container, if I took it just like it was and drank, my lips would touch the same part of the opening that his had.

Had he done it that way on purpose?

Jesus, Isaac, get a grip. The man isn't attracted to you.

I sighed and took the Thermos. I should have thanked him but didn't. I'd made the damn coffee, after all. I didn't often drink coffee because I just wasn't a big fan, but it was hot so I didn't care. I handed it back to him and watched as he took another drink. There was no doubt that his lips covered the spot where mine had been.

Despite the cold, my dick responded accordingly.

I needed to go. I was about to do that when Maddox's fingers were suddenly on my arm. I opened my mouth to protest, but snapped it shut again when all he did was grab his parka lying across the table and drape it around my shoulders.

"Is it true?" Maddox asked as he stepped back, giving me a little breathing room.

"Is what true?"

"Did I make you cry… again?"

"No," I scoffed, even as I got all hot inside. "What you saw at the motel—"

"Was it me you were talking about in your dream last night? Was it me you wanted to stay away from you?"

What?

"Or is Newt mixing me up with someone else?"

How the hell had we gotten on *this* topic?

"Look, I—"

"And if it was me, was it because I scared you? Because I don't want you to be scared of me, Isaac."

Jesus. What the hell was happening?

"I especially don't want to be the reason your brother is scared." I felt my stomach knot at that because it was the way he'd made the comment that had me on edge. He confirmed my thinking a second later when he stepped closer to me and whispered, "Are you both scared of *me?*"

I froze when his finger came up to trail my cheek gently. "Tell me who *he* is, Isaac, and I swear, he'll never touch you or your brother again."

CHAPTER NINE

MADDOX

It lasted about three seconds.
   That moment where I could see him desperate to answer me truthfully, to ask for help, to accept it, to trust in it.

But his eyes shuttered just as quickly, and his lips drew into a tight frown. "Don't use my brother to try and make up for the shit you did to yours," he said quietly, deliberately. As much as I would have liked to deny it, the barb hit its mark and I found myself stepping back. He took my parka off and tossed it on the table. His eyes were brittle as he said, "Stay away from Newt."

With that, he turned on his heel and left the building.

I took a few minutes to sip at the coffee he'd brought me, then closed the Thermos and tucked the remaining sandwich into my pocket. I got my parka back on and went to the office to leave the Thermos there, since I wasn't sure I'd be welcomed into the house. I went about the rest of my tasks on my list of things to do. Dallas found me just as darkness was starting to fall. I was in the process of cleaning up my tools and putting them back in the small cabinet in the building that was attached to Gentry's enclosure. I could hear music coming from outside. It was obviously Nolan playing, but I wondered if Newt would be up next, and would Isaac be watching again like he had been this morning?

God, I really was obsessed.

I shouldn't have promised Newt anything. Even if Isaac were willing to put any kind of trust in me, I didn't deserve it and I couldn't necessarily keep them safe from whatever they were running from. For all I knew, Isaac had done something wrong. Hell, he'd stolen that violin, so it stood to reason he could have stolen something else from someone. Or it could just be a vindictive ex. Maybe I could check out this Trey guy who'd tricked Isaac into taking that fancy violin...

What the hell?

Since when had I decided Isaac's version of events when it came to the Stradivarius were true?

I was so lost in thought that it wasn't until the inside lights were turned off and back on that I realized Dallas was trying to get my attention. How had I not even heard the door opening?

"Hey," I said.

He held up his hand in a simple wave, then approached me. He typed something out on his phone.

Didn't knock... didn't want to startle you.

I glanced at the door and understood what he was telling me. He'd used the lights to get my attention so he wouldn't inadvertently trigger an episode.

"Thanks. It usually takes several rhythmic bangs and they have to be pretty loud," I said. "But lights and any other kind of sound are probably a better way to go."

He nodded.

"How are you feeling?" I asked.

Good.

I tilted my head at him knowingly.

Tired, he admitted with a slight smile. *Nolan's mad at me.*

"He should be," I said. "You just had major surgery, Dallas. It's okay to take it easy and let others shoulder the burden."

Another nod. *Sawyer called. He finished up with his consultation and will be back tomorrow. He's agreed to work here until he gets his veterinary practice opened up in a few months or next summer. His only responsibility is on-call stuff.*

"That's good," I said. "He's a good guy."

What's going on with you and Isaac?

If that wasn't the sixty-four-thousand-dollar question, I didn't know what was.

I closed the toolbox and collected my gloves. "Have a good night, Dallas. Do yourself and your man a favor and sleep in tomorrow. Sawyer and I can handle things."

I reached out to touch his arm, then remembered I wasn't allowed to do that anymore. I had my back turned when I heard Dallas snap his fingers a few times. I turned and waited for him to hand me his phone.

Do you need a ride home?

I shook my head.

It's fifteen miles to the house, Maddox.

I wanted to tell him that I wished it was more than that, but he wouldn't get it, so I settled for, "I'll see you tomorrow," then turned and left. The Twinkle, Twinkle lullaby was playing as soon as I stepped outside, but I kept my eyes averted as I turned in the opposite direction. I could feel eyes on me, but knew they weren't my brother's or his boyfriend's.

I kept my pace quick as I cut through the back of the property and headed for the road. Thankfully, the sounds of the lullaby quickly faded away, but unfortunately, the memory of Isaac's haunted eyes in those three seconds that he'd wanted to take me up on my offer to help stayed with me for the entire walk home.

And long after.

My next encounter with Isaac didn't happen until Thanksgiving, which was a few days after his warning to stay away from him and his brother. It was another situation where he was forced to deal with me, much like when Newt had insisted on the hug-and-make-up moment. Isaac had done an admirable job of ignoring me at the sanctuary and I hadn't seen much of Newt either, a sure sign Isaac was keeping close tabs on his little brother. But Thanksgiving was a different story because Dallas had invited me to join him and Nolan at Nolan's mother's house. I'd suspected Dallas had probably invited Isaac and Newt to attend, but I hadn't asked. It'd been a form of plausible deniability on my part. I wasn't sure what Dallas had told Isaac, if anything, about me attending the dinner, since surely the young man would have declined if he'd known I was going to be there. But based on the look upon Isaac's face when I walked in the door after Nolan's mother opened it to me and welcomed me with open arms, I had to guess the young man had just assumed I'd avoid the event.

Under normal circumstances, I would have.

But nothing about my relationship with Isaac was normal, so why would this be any different?

Unfortunately, fate had thrown a wrench into my plans in the form of Sawyer Brower. He too had been invited, and as I watched him and Isaac sitting across the table from me chatting comfortably about nothing, I found myself experiencing an emotion that I was wholly unfamiliar with.

Jealousy.

The green-eyed monster.

And it was ripping into me with a vengeance.

"Would anyone like to say the blessing?" Nolan's mother asked, then pointedly looked at her son. I'd gotten the impression the relationship between mother and son was a complicated one. Nolan's father had only recently passed, so this was the family's first holiday without the man. But there was something more than just grief at work here. The tension and uncertainty between Nolan and his mother was palpable.

Nolan glanced at Dallas, who gave him an encouraging nod. Nolan was sitting at the head of the table while his mother sat at the other end. Sawyer, Isaac, and Newt were across from me and Dallas. Nolan reached for my brother's hand as he cleared his throat.

"Um, a lot of things have changed for us this year, but we have a lot to be grateful for too." Nolan glanced at Dallas. "We've had the chance to forgive the past and look to the future." Dallas pulled Nolan's hand up to his mouth and kissed the back of it. The move seemed to relax Nolan even more. His eyes shifted to his mother. "We've lost a part of ourselves, but we've found something new, too."

Nolan's mother smiled and nodded, and I saw her dab at her eyes.

"And we've welcomed new friends into our lives," Nolan added as he nodded at Isaac, Sawyer, and Newt. When Nolan's gaze shifted to me, I felt myself involuntarily tense up. Things had been going well between Dallas and me this past week, but it wasn't like we'd turned some big corner. Not enough that it deserved any kind of mention, anyway.

"We've also been given a second chance to make amends and to know the true meaning of family." My heart began pounding harder in my chest at his words. Was it his way of telling me I still had a chance at something with my brother? Dallas and I had avoided the topic of the past like the plague, but surely he and Nolan had discussed what my presence was doing to Dallas. Maybe his words meant things weren't beyond repair?

The young man looked around the table again. His eyes settled on his mother, then he released Dallas's hand and clasped his own together in prayer. Nolan's mother let out a soft cry and then she did the same. Everyone else followed suit. Like many of the residents in Pelican Bay, I knew Nolan's family put a lot of stock in faith and religion. I'd been to church enough times when I'd been home from West Point to remember that the Graingers had been devoted members of God's flock, though I'd never seen Nolan with them. So I had to assume that Nolan's gesture was an important one.

I closed my eyes and bowed my head as Nolan recited a simple prayer. Although my father had been a well-known reverend with a megachurch and huge following via his televised sermons, Dallas and I hadn't really bought into the man's teachings, especially after we'd realized that what the man taught and what he lived were two very different things. But there'd been a few times on the battlefield where

I'd sent a prayer heavenward, so I had no issue with thanking the man above for everything He'd seen fit to give me and the people around me.

When the prayer was done, everyone softly said their amens and then Nolan went to work on carving the turkey as conversation broke out again. Nolan's mother began passing bowls of food around, but I found myself preoccupied with watching Isaac, and it was all I could do to remember to actually spoon food onto my plate before passing it on.

The way he spoke with Sawyer was so easy and natural. And Sawyer was a good-looking guy. He was also really laid-back. I couldn't see him ever pushing Isaac too hard.

Or making him cry.

I felt a hand on my lower arm and saw that at some point Dallas had closed his fingers around my wrist.

I realized why when I saw my fisted hands.

And the multiple platters of food sitting by my plate waiting to be passed on.

"Sorry," I murmured, then went to work filling my plate, though I didn't really have an appetite. My eyes continued to move to Isaac of their own volition. Today was the first time I'd seen him a little more dressed up, though it wasn't a traditional formal outfit.

Which I was glad for, because Isaac was anything but traditional.

His jeans were as tight as ever, but they were bright white instead of black. He had a bright pink button-down shirt on that had little jewels sewn into the collar. The buttons were large and sparkly. He had his normal blue eyeliner on, but it looked like he'd added some kind of shadow to his lids and his lashes looked thicker than normal. They almost looked like they had a bit of a blue tinge to them, similar to his hair. He'd put some product in his hair to keep it from falling into his face and I couldn't decide if I liked it or not. On the one hand, I could see more of his gorgeous face. On the other hand, my fingers itched to run through the long strands that perpetually seemed to hang just above his eyes. I didn't see any kind of foundation makeup, but it looked like he was wearing a little bit of blush.

That, or something was naturally causing his cheeks to pinken.

God, if it was because of Sawyer, I was just going to lose it.

For the life of me, I just couldn't stop looking at Isaac's lips. They were shiny-looking as usual, but I suspected he'd used some kind of gloss with just a hint of color, because they were a pretty shade of pink. I'd kissed women who were wearing lipstick before, but my gut was telling me that the gloss wouldn't detract from the softness of Isaac's lips. There'd be no tacky texture or chemical or artificial taste.

It would just be Isaac.

God, what the hell was wrong with me?

But I knew the answer to that. I couldn't keep denying it anymore.

I was wildly attracted to Isaac.

More so than I'd ever been to any other person.

And it wasn't my mind playing tricks on me. Despite there being a hint of femininity in his features, I wasn't seeing him as anything other than a beautiful man who, for some inexplicable reason, stirred my blood.

I barely listened to the conversation going on around me. Dinner seemed to last forever, but I knew from the time it had taken us to fill our plates to the time Nolan's mother went to the kitchen to get the dessert, it hadn't been more than half an hour.

But it might as well have been a lifetime.

Because I'd had to watch Isaac make conversation with everyone but me. In fact, he'd gone out of his way to ignore me.

So much for trying to force him into acknowledging my presence.

He'd meant what he'd said. He wanted me to stay away from him and his brother. I needed to accept that. It was a good thing.

Right?

"Mrs. Grainger, thank you so much for having me," I suddenly blurted when there was a lull in the conversation as everyone began digging into their pie. The food I'd eaten was already feeling like lead in my stomach, so I pushed back my chair and added, "It was all delicious, but I couldn't possibly eat another bite."

"Oh, of course, dear, would you like me to wrap it up for you?" she asked as she motioned to the pumpkin pie on my plate.

"Thank you, that would be nice," I said, though in truth, I had no interest in the dessert. I had all the dessert I needed at home.

In the form of a large bottle of whiskey.

Mrs. Grainger stood and quickly took my plate to the kitchen.

"Happy Thanksgiving," I said to everyone, then I was hurrying to the front door where the coat rack was. I wasn't surprised when Dallas appeared at my side.

There was one single word typed onto the screen on his phone.

Stay.

On any other day, I would have been thrilled by the request. Today, it just hurt.

Because I couldn't give him that. It was just too damn hard. But I couldn't explain that to him.

"I should get going," I murmured. "It's a long walk."

I'll drive you.

I automatically shook my head.

You let Alex drive you to the meeting the night of the town council meeting.

Yeah, and it'd been a horrific ten minutes, especially since I'd had to work extra hard to make sure the deputy who I also considered a friend hadn't recognized how fucked-up in the head I was. It wasn't like I'd wanted to answer a lot of questions about why sitting in any kind of vehicle made me want to throw up.

As badly as I wanted to explain things to Dallas, I also really just needed to get the hell out of there. My skin felt like it had a million fire ants crawling beneath it and it was all I could do not to storm back into that dining room and drag Isaac out of his chair and ask him what the fuck the good-looking veterinarian could do for him that I couldn't.

Because I already knew the answer to that.

Everything.

"Please, Dallas," I said. My back was to him and my hand was on the doorknob, so I couldn't see his expression.

I didn't want to.

The only evidence I had that he was letting me go was when he reached past me and gently pushed my hand out of the way so he could open the door himself. I hurried through it, not looking back as I tugged the collar of my parka higher. It was cold out and there was a little bit of light snow falling, but nothing too bad. The chilly air felt good against my heated skin, so I didn't search out my gloves right away or button up my coat.

I would in a few minutes.

As soon as I no longer felt the need to crawl out of my own skin.

I'd just reached the curb where Dallas's truck was parked when I heard someone call out, "Maddox."

I stilled because I knew who it was.

I didn't turn around, so when Isaac reached me, he had to step in front of me.

"You shouldn't be out here," I automatically said when I saw he wasn't wearing a coat.

The light from the streetlamp above us illuminated his frown. Snowflakes began to collect in his hair. The stark white was bright against the dark strands.

"You forgot this," Isaac said as he handed me a little bag. "Mrs. Grainger said to add whipped cream to make it even better," he added. "You also forgot this."

He thrust a folded envelope at me. I tucked the bag with the pie beneath my arm and took the envelope, then looked into it.

It had money in it.

"What is—"

"I told you I don't want your charity," Isaac bit out. "I don't need it." He started to turn away, then spun around. "And frankly, I think it's pretty cowardly to make your brother do your dirty work for you."

I knew then what he was talking about. The money was the salary Dallas had offered to pay me for working at the sanctuary. The salary I'd told him to give to Isaac instead.

"I told you I didn't need help!" he continued, his skin flushing as his anger grew. "And even if I did, you'd be the last person I asked."

With every word he spoke, I felt my agitation growing. All I heard in my head was Sawyer's name repeated on a loop. He'd take Sawyer's charity, he'd ask Sawyer for help, he'd be okay with Sawyer being around his brother, Sawyer would make him laugh, he'd let Sawyer touch him...

He wasn't saying any of that, of course, but it was all I heard, and I knew if I didn't do something and do it quickly, I'd lose it completely. I wanted to tell him to go back inside, back to goddamned Sawyer, but I couldn't even rein in my frustration enough to speak, so I simply turned my back on him and began walking.

"Oh yeah, that's right," he called. "Walk away. That's what you're good at, right?"

I told myself to keep walking. I practically demanded it of myself. But the part of me that had yet to be able to successfully let go of the strange pull Isaac had on me failed once again and I found myself turning around instead.

Isaac's back was to me as he started walking back up the walkway toward the house, but it was too late.

He'd pushed just a little too hard.

And I was too far gone to do anything but push back.

CHAPTER TEN

ISAAC

I hated the pinpricks of tears at the corners of my eyes.

I mean, what had I expected? For him to apologize? To tell me he didn't see me as a charity case? To offer some explanation for humiliating me yet again? Even the memory of Dallas handing me the envelope full of twice as much cash as there should have been for a week's worth of pay caused my cheeks to burn all over again.

Although Dallas hadn't been willing to give up his brother, it hadn't taken a genius to figure out where the money had come from. I'd been pissed at Dallas but hadn't been willing to pick a fight with him because I understood the loyalty he felt to Maddox, despite all the pair had been through. It was that way with me and Newt. My brother would always come first, no matter what.

So when Dallas had refused to rat out his brother right after he'd given me the money, I'd let the issue go, intent on dealing with Maddox myself. I hadn't expected to see him at Thanksgiving, though, so my plan had been to confront him at the sanctuary the following day. But after spending the past hour enduring endless, undeserved glares from a pissed-off-looking Maddox, it had just been too much. He'd ruined what should have been a fun night of harmless flirting with Sawyer.

I liked the vet a lot, but he and I both knew there was nothing there. He was sweet and kind and great with Newt, and totally gorgeous, but that spark just was completely absent. We'd fallen easily into being friends and I suspected he was just as okay with that fact as me.

But Maddox had fucking ruined it all as usual.

Even when he was doing exactly what I'd told him and leaving me alone, he was still ruining things. The fact that I was ready to burst into tears all over again was proof of that. I just really needed to pack up Newt and get the hell out of Pelican Bay. It'd been less than a week and we were becoming way too comfortable. Dallas had even talked about me and Newt moving into the apartment above the garage if we wanted to make staying in Pelican Bay a more permanent thing.

Not because either man didn't want us in the house with them, but because they seemed to be bending over backward to try to make us feel as welcome as possible.

I'd thought maybe they'd just become overly attached to Newt, but I was beginning to wonder if maybe, just maybe, they liked having me around too.

But no, it'd all been another one of Maddox's elaborate schemes.

Because he still didn't see me as someone who could take care of myself and my brother.

Well, he could go fuck himself.

I turned around to tell him just that, not about to mince my words since Newt wasn't within hearing range, when I suddenly slammed into a hard body. I let out a little gasp, but when I tried to pull back, thick fingers curled around my upper arm.

Tight.

Enough so that I couldn't get away.

I could see Maddox's expression in the lamplight.

He looked more pissed than I'd ever seen him.

Shit, I'd really gone and done it this time. I opened my mouth to tell him to let me go, but before I could do more than let out a squeak of sound, he yanked me forward.

And then his mouth crashed down on mine.

I was so surprised that I didn't react at first. Maddox was kissing me. Why was Maddox kissing me?

I expected him to shove me away as soon as he came to his senses and remembered who I was... and wasn't. But instead, he drew me forward and wrapped one arm around my waist as his other hand rooted in my hair. His mouth moved effortlessly over mine and he didn't even hesitate to slide his tongue against mine.

I couldn't help the moan that escaped my throat at how good it felt. Fire simmered in my blood and my dick reacted painfully as Maddox forced my head back so he could completely plunder my mouth in any way he wanted.

And that was exactly what he did.

I was completely at his mercy.

As he bent me back over his arm just a bit, I reached out to grab his waist to support myself... to have something to hang onto in case he let me go.

But I needn't have worried about that.

From the way he was holding onto me and owning my mouth, hell, my whole body, I wasn't going anywhere anytime soon.

It occurred to me that I should be stopping him, but he just tasted too damn good. Despite the cold air around us and the snow landing softly against my face, I felt warm all over.

And safe.

So very safe.

I was panting by the time Maddox pulled back just a little. He kissed me gently, just once, then softly brushed the tips of our noses together. At some point I'd wrapped my arms around his waist beneath his parka. He was just so big and built...

"Isaac," Maddox whispered, then his mouth was covering mine again. His teeth gently closed over the piercing in my lip. When he gave the metal hoop the softest of tugs, I felt it in my cock. Then I was the one latching onto his lips and plunging my tongue into his mouth.

Kissing wasn't something I did often, and never with clients. Trey had been the one exception. But I couldn't remember kissing anyone and having it affect me like this.

Like my body wasn't mine anymore.

Like I wanted to crawl inside of someone else and bury myself so deep that I never had to feel alone again.

Warning bells were trying to sound off in my head that Maddox was straight and this was all some big mistake, but my hands and mouth weren't listening to my brain anymore.

They hadn't been from the moment his mouth had sealed over mine.

Maddox's hands somehow ended up covering my ass, but just as he began to grip me like he was going to lift me up, I heard Newt calling my name from the direction of the house. Amazingly, the snow had started to fall more heavily, but I hadn't even noticed. I was covered in thick flakes.

Maddox carefully pushed me back to put some space between us as Newt called for me again.

"You should go," was all he said. And just like that, he was the one who turned and walked away.

Without another word.

Not even to say it was a mistake or that it was amazing or that it shouldn't happen again.

Nothing.

And worse, he'd somehow managed to put the envelope back in my hand. The envelope with all the money still in it.

My body turned icy cold as I watched Maddox get swallowed up by the snowfall. The bag with Mrs. Grainger's pumpkin pie was on the ground at my feet. I felt sick as I leaned over to pick it up.

"Isaac?"

This time it was Sawyer's voice calling me.

"Coming," I called as I turned to head back toward the house. I was cold and wet and covered in snow, but it was nothing compared to how frigid I felt on the inside.

And empty.

So very empty.

Again.

"Hey, I'm talking to you!"

Ignore them. Just ignore them.

I repeated the words on a loop as I forced myself not to speed up my pace as I made my way back to my car. It was the day after Thanksgiving and I'd taken advantage of Dallas and Nolan's offer to babysit so I could run to the thrift store in Pelican Bay to pick up a few things. I'd managed to finally find snow pants for Newt, along with an array of winter gear that would keep him warm when he was outside building the snow fort he and Dallas had been designing on paper for the better part of a week. I'd managed to find a coat for me too, though it'd been a little pricier than I would have liked. But it was good quality and fit me well, so I knew I'd get a lot of use out of it, even in Chicago or New York or wherever we ended up. As it stood, though, I didn't have a ton of cash left.

Unfortunately, in addition to the clothes, I'd picked up a couple of things I hadn't intended.

And they were currently following me down the sidewalk toward the alley next to the thrift shop where I'd left my car.

I'd dealt with bullies all my life, so it shouldn't have surprised me that I'd run into them here in Pelican Bay. But these guys were proving to be pretty persistent. They'd already followed me throughout the thrift shop. Fortunately, I'd been on the tail end of my shopping, so I'd only had to put up with them for a few minutes. I'd figured they'd let me go once I left the store, but clearly the bullies in Pelican Bay had been hankering for fresh meat and I was their prey.

I wasn't particularly scared because I knew most bullies backed off if you ignored them or stood up to them, but admittedly, I was too preoccupied to adequately deal with this shit today.

Maddox kissed me.

That particular phrase had been repeating on a loop from the moment I'd stepped back inside the Grainger house and Sawyer had hurried to get me a towel so I could dry off. I'd lied and told everyone I'd had to run to catch up to Maddox to give him the pie so that's why

I'd been covered in snow. It hadn't been until Newt had pointed out I still had the bag with the pie in it that I'd had to lie a second time and say I hadn't been able to find him. I suspected Newt had been the only one to buy my story.

It was bad enough I couldn't stop reminding myself that Maddox had kissed me, but I couldn't stop remembering *every single detail* of that kiss. The way he'd smelled, tasted, felt. The way he'd made me feel... at least before he'd turned his back on me. Well, in truth, I was also remembering the humiliation after he'd walked away too.

I'd read way more into that kiss than I should have.

The man had just been frustrated and pissed and he'd wanted to send me a message. I'd tossed that cruel barb at him about walking away and using his brother and he'd wanted to punish me for it.

God, what a mess.

It was just another reason to leave Pelican Bay.

It would be even harder now to avoid the man at the sanctuary. I'd done an okay job of it the past few days, but it'd taken a lot of effort.

"Those holes in your ears make you hard of hearing, freak?"

I sighed at the pathetic barb. God, bullies weren't even unique anymore. I stopped suddenly and swung around, surprising my would-be tormenters who nearly slammed into me at the move. Clearly, they'd been hoping to confront me in the privacy of the alley while I was trying to make my escape.

"Okay, what's the plan here?" I asked tiredly as I scanned the men in front of me. There were four of them. Three were just a few feet from me, but a fourth who looked a little younger than the rest was standing back a bit, looking particularly uncomfortable. I dismissed him as nothing more than a follower and studied the other three. The one directly in front of me was definitely the leader. His pinched expression and triumphant smirk told me as much, not to mention the other two kept looking to him as if waiting to see what he'd do. The leader was older than me, maybe early thirties. In addition to needing some serious fashion advice, he also looked like he needed to lay off whatever artificial substance he used to escape the world.

Based on the smell of pot wafting off him, my guess was that he preferred drugs to alcohol to escape whatever shitty life he led. He was tall but scrawny and had greasy long hair and yellow teeth. His friends looked a little more average, though I suspected with how wide their eyes were and how they couldn't stand still for even a second, they were indulging in the same shit, just not as heavily. The fourth guy, the quiet one, just looked like he wanted to be anywhere but there.

"Is it just the names thing or are you going to threaten me with a beatdown or actually give me a beatdown?" I sniped. "Because I've got stuff to do and frankly, I don't think your little town here wants the blood of some random fag lining their pretty little sidewalks because some redneck wannabe couldn't figure out a better way to hide his homosexual tendencies."

The leader's face fell in surprise, then quickly grew red. He reached out to grab me by the collar of my shirt and slammed me up against the wall of the building next to his. The move caused my cheek and temple to scrape the brick and while it hurt, it fortunately didn't disorient me. The man's fist came back and I steeled myself for the blow, hoping it didn't knock me on my ass, because that would make it so much harder to come up with a good comeback. But before he could let the punch fly, the quiet man from his group grabbed his arm.

"Jimmy, let's just go!" the man said, his voice thick with fear. "Mom's waiting."

"Shut the fuck up," the guy, Jimmy, snapped and shoved the other man hard. He hit the ground.

Neither of the other men made a move to help him up, but one blurted out, "Jimmy, your bail—"

"Shut up!" Jimmy bit out. His free hand was around my throat and while he wasn't cutting off my airway, his hold was forceful enough that I'd probably end up with bruises. Jimmy's dark eyes landed on me as he pulled back his arm, but I spoke before he could take the swing.

"You're Jimmy Cornell, aren't you?" I said. "You're the asshole who attacked Gentry," I added. "Takes a big man to prey on helpless animals who can't fight back. Or queers half your size."

Jimmy's face got even redder, but I didn't care. I had a lifetime of dealing with the Jimmy Cornells of the world under my belt. Besides the manhandling he was doing by holding me against the wall like he was, I doubted he'd do more, and even if he did throw a few punches, it wasn't like I was a stranger to that shit. But if I backed down now, this guy would be coming after me every time he saw me.

"You little piece of—"

"So you're out on bail, huh?" I said. "Guess that means if you get into any kind of trouble, your bail gets revoked. Straight to jail. Do not pass go." I kept my voice light and casual, even though I was scared. I knew standing up to bullies was the only way to stop them, but it wasn't like I was excited about getting my face bashed in. And so far, not one of the few people out and about on the quiet street had done anything but look the other way as they'd hurried to the opposite sidewalk.

"Just remember this when you're letting your fists fly, Jimmy. My first stop after you're finished *will* be the police station because I'm not some defenseless animal who can't stand up for itself and point the finger at you," I lied, because no way in hell was I going to go to the cops. But he didn't know that. I dared to get in his face. "And I will be pointing every one of my fingers" –I held up my hands to show off my sparkly nails– "at you."

Jimmy scowled and I saw that his temper was going to get the best of him. But the man who'd tried to intervene grabbed his arm and jerked him back. I watched in horror as Jimmy punched him instead. "Don't ever put your fucking hands on me again, little brother!" he snarled. Jimmy shot me a glance, but since he had a new and seemingly less threatening outlet for his anger, he didn't come at me. Instead he grabbed the younger man's arm and jerked him forward. Jimmy's eyes held him until the younger man looked away like when a submissive animal cowered to a more dominant one. The move seemed to satisfy Jimmy because he thrust the man–his own brother, apparently–away and snapped, "Let's go," to the rest of his little crew.

I waited until they were out of sight before I relaxed enough to take a deep breath. My heart was racing in my chest and I could feel a little bit of warmth on my cheek. When I touched the spot, my fingers came away with a little bit of blood on them, so I used the hem of my shirt to dab at both my cheek and temple until I got most of the blood off. Then I reached down to pick up my bags and hurried to my car.

My fingers were shaking as I got my car started, and I was still on edge by the time I got back to the sanctuary. I parked in front of the office and found Nolan and Dallas looking at something on the computer. I didn't see Newt among the kittens that were in the cordoned-off area in the corner.

"Hey," Nolan said. "Newt asked if he could go down to the cat building to get that wand cat toy. He really wanted to go by himself. Sawyer is down there vaccinating the cats, so we told him that Newt is on his way down and to look out for him. I hope that's okay."

"It's fine," I said with a nod. Newt had been begging me for more independence over the past few days, so I'd been letting him run little errands for me when I was working in the livestock barn. I'd checked the design of every single animal enclosure, including the ones for the animals who weren't considered dangerous, and every habitat had security features on them that would keep a child of Newt's size from getting into them. The only animals he could come into direct contact with were the livestock, dogs, and cats, and he'd been around those enough now for me to see none of them were dangerous. Even Jerry the Ornery Zebra had been uncharacteristically careful with Newt.

Me, not so much.

No, I hadn't ended up in the water trough on my first day working in that enclosure like Nolan had his first time out, but Jerry had somehow managed to leave a pile of zebra poop right in my path when I wasn't looking, and I'd stepped into it while wearing my canvas sneakers. The striped hooligan was the reason I'd splurged and also bought myself some decent winter boots at the thrift store today.

Dallas made a grunting sound, then pointed to my face.

"Oh my god, what happened?" Nolan asked as he got up from the chair he'd been sitting in.

"Oh, nothing, I just fell on the sidewalk," I lied. That fucker, Jimmy, had caused them so much grief already, I didn't want to give them another thing to have to worry about. I was pretty sure I'd managed to get the asshole off my back, so I wasn't overly concerned that he would continue to be a threat.

I would, however, watch my back when I was in town.

Well, I'd watch my back *more*.

Before Nolan or Dallas could question me further, I quickly backed out the door and said, "I'm going to go check on Newt. I'm sure he's going to want to try on the snow pants I got him."

I hurried from the office and rounded the corner. That was when I saw Loki come racing toward me.

Just Loki.

The big animal stopped in front of me and began whining, then he circled me several times.

"Dallas?" I called. I yelled his name louder when Loki became more restless. But when the large animal suddenly grabbed my arm between his teeth, I panicked.

"Dallas!"

Fear went through me at the wolf hybrid's behavior, but the animal quickly released me, then gently grabbed my arm again and tugged.

And a whole new kind of fear went through me.

Newt.

Panic ripped through me as I began running. I heard Nolan call out to me, but I didn't stop to respond to him.

"Dallas!" I heard someone shout. "Sawyer!"

It was Maddox's voice.

And he sounded scared.

Oh God, Newt.

I tore around the corner of the livestock fencing and ran down the path leading to the cat building. The snow made it feel like I was going so slow I may as well have been walking backward.

"Newt!" I screamed as Loki flew past me and raced down the trail.

"Here!" Maddox called. "He's here!"

I almost fell as I turned onto the smaller path that led to the building, and my heart nearly stopped in my chest at the sight that was waiting for me.

CHAPTER ELEVEN

MADDOX

It'd been a shitty morning, but that was only fitting since it'd been a shitty night the evening before.

Well, except the kissing Isaac part.

That had been unbelievable.

Like life-altering kind of unbelievable. He had the sweetest mouth, and the way he'd clung to me as I'd plundered it and made it mine…

I shook my head as my dick responded to the memory. Sadly, I knew the cold wouldn't do much to calm my raging libido, since it hadn't the night before when I'd walked home. The only thing that had managed to make me forget Isaac's delectable mouth and the red-hot jealousy I was *still* feeling about him and Sawyer this morning had been the alcohol I'd consumed.

And it had taken quite a bit of it.

Enough that I was nursing the mother of all hangovers this morning. It was the first day in the better part of a few weeks that I'd actually wished I didn't have an obligation to the sanctuary. Normally, I welcomed both the walk to and from the center and the work that kept my mind occupied throughout the day, but today was different.

Today, Isaac was in my head more than ever and he wasn't going anywhere.

Besides Isaac, the fact that I'd kissed a guy and loved it was pretty much leaving me questioning a lot of things. Was I gay and I'd just been in denial this whole time, or was I straight and something about Isaac just called to me? Maybe I was bisexual because I had, in fact, been attracted to women in the past, and maybe I'd also been attracted to guys and just not recognized it for what it was?

But how was that even possible? I was thirty-two years old, for God's sake. Shouldn't I have known all this shit about myself?

As I made my way from the aviary where I'd been doing some repairs, I let my thoughts drift to Jett and the time he'd kissed me. I couldn't say I'd particularly enjoyed it, but maybe that was because Jett was my best friend. I hadn't hated it, either. If anything, I'd just been caught off guard by the kiss.

I'd briefly debated calling Jett to talk to him about the whole thing but had decided against it. I still didn't know what that kiss had meant to him so many years ago. If he'd been crushing on me, he'd never acted on it. That one night had been the only time I'd even had a hint that he saw me as anything besides a friend. He'd come out to me almost as soon as we'd met and I'd never gotten the sense he was disappointed I was straight.

Fuck, I hated labels.

My parents had been fond of labels.

I sighed and realized there was only person I really wanted to talk to about the whole thing, but he and I weren't on sure enough footing for that yet. If I was going to talk to Dallas about anything, it probably needed to be to figure out exactly where we were at in terms of our relationship. I hadn't thought he'd give me a second chance, but Nolan's words the day before at Thanksgiving dinner had given me an odd sense of hope.

Hell, what I needed was just to focus on work. My next task was to start ripping down one of the dilapidated sheds on the property to make way for the new habitats Dallas wanted to build. Dallas had indicated we could wait until spring, but I wanted him to be able to break ground as soon as the snow was gone. And the location wouldn't be easy to get any excavating equipment to, so the building would need to be taken down by hand and the debris trucked out at some point.

As I rounded the corner to follow the trail that led to the office, I heard a muffled thump and a whining sound. I was just walking toward the narrow path that cut through to the cat building when I saw a streak of white flash by me. Loki changed direction when he saw me and began whining in earnest as he darted back toward the cat building, then came back to me. I dropped my tools and began running, because I had no doubt what was bothering the animal.

My heart was in my throat when I saw the familiar bright-blue parka covered in cartoon cars and the red knit cap. But the cap was currently lying in the snow next to Newt's little thrashing body.

"Newt!" I screamed as I ran to him and fell to my knees next to him. His eyes were open and his face was contorted into an expression of confusion and fear. His mouth was wide open and there was some spit forming at the side of his mouth. His arms and legs were jerking in the snow.

Jesus, he was having a seizure.

I automatically began searching for my phone but remembered I'd left it in the office to charge.

I ripped off my gloves and put my hands on Newt's face.

"Newt, buddy, I'm here," I said. I wasn't sure if he could hear me or not, but I desperately wanted him to know he wasn't alone. His expression didn't change–it was like he was seeing right through me.

"Dallas! Sawyer!" I yelled. I knew Isaac had left to go to town earlier because I'd crossed paths with him in the office as he'd been saying his goodbyes to Newt, Dallas, and Nolan. He hadn't spoken to me, but I'd overheard Newt begging him not to forget the snow pants.

I had no clue what to do for Newt, though my gut was telling me not to restrain him. I checked the area around him to make sure there was nothing his body would come into contact with, like a tree limb or large rock sticking out of the snow. The evening's previous snowfall had left a soft layer of snow on top of the iced-over layer, so my hope was he hadn't hurt himself when he'd fallen. I didn't see any kind of bleeding or marks on his head, but there could very well be an injury on the back of his head.

I fought the urge to gather the thrashing little boy in my arms and instead continued to talk to him so he would know he wasn't alone. I was about to yell for Dallas and Sawyer again when I heard Isaac calling Newt's name. It was then that I noticed Loki had taken off.

God, I fucking loved that wolf.

"Here! He's here!" I shouted.

Less than ten seconds later, Loki, then Isaac came barreling around the corner.

"Newt," Isaac cried out, and then he was falling to his knees on the other side of Newt's body. Loki began licking Newt's face and whining frantically.

"I think he's having a seizure," I said. "Where's your phone?"

Surprisingly, Isaac was calmer than I would have expected him to be when he said, "He is." He put his hands on Newt's upper body and said to me, "Help me get him on his side. We need to keep his airway clear and ride it out."

I did as he said. As I held Newt in position, Isaac got down next to his face and checked his mouth, then began quietly talking to him.

"I'm here, Newt. It's okay, buddy. It'll be over soon, okay? I'm not going anywhere. Just listen to the sound of my voice."

He kept talking to Newt even as Sawyer suddenly appeared. Within seconds, he was kneeling next to us. "What happened?" he asked.

"He's epileptic," Isaac responded.

Sawyer nodded and then began running his fingers gently over the back of Newt's head. Dallas and Nolan appeared, and Nolan quickly pulled Loki back as the animal continued to try and lick Newt's face.

"I'm not finding any head wounds," Sawyer said. "This snow is soft enough that it would have cushioned his fall."

"Do we need to call someone?" Nolan asked. We were all on our knees in the snow. Dallas yanked his coat off and draped it over Newt's still-jerking body.

"No, it'll be over soon," Isaac said. His voice was still calm, but I could hear a line of fear in it. Even if he'd witnessed an episode like this before, it had to have been scary as hell each time.

I knew I was scared shitless.

And felt so fucking helpless. Newt's little body felt so frail beneath my hands, but his limbs just kept jerking. He was making grunting sounds too.

It was a good minute before his moves began to slow. It was only when his body began to tick rather than jerk that Isaac lifted Newt onto his lap and cuddled him against his chest. I grabbed Dallas's coat and tucked it against Newt's body as best I could. Then I stripped my own parka off and draped it over Isaac's shoulders.

"Newt," Isaac said softly just after Newt's eyes rolled shut. I saw Newt's fisted hands relax and then lift so they were pressed close to his chest. He let out a soft little cry and tucked his head under Isaac's chin.

"It's okay, buddy," Isaac said. "It's over."

"Is he in pain?" Nolan asked.

Isaac shook his head. "No, he's just confused. He doesn't remember the actual episode, but when he comes out of it, he doesn't know where he is or what's happened. He just needs a minute."

"Here," I said as I reached for Isaac's elbow. "Let's get you up."

Sawyer supported Isaac's other arm while we helped Isaac climb to his feet.

"Isaac?" Newt whispered, his voice thick and hoarse with tears.

"I'm here, Newt," Isaac said as he gave Newt a gentle squeeze. "Everything's okay. You're safe."

Newt nodded but didn't say anything else.

"Let's get him inside," Nolan said. "Can you carry him?"

Isaac nodded. We all ended up making a little cocoon around Isaac as he walked. I kept my arm around him to make sure if he stumbled, he wouldn't fall. Nolan and Dallas were leading the way to the house, Loki was practically glued to Isaac's other side, and Sawyer was right behind us.

"I need to get him warm," Isaac said as we reached the house. He looked at Nolan. "Can you get a bath ready, but make sure the water isn't too hot?"

"Of course," Nolan said as he hurried to do Isaac's bidding.

"I'm going to go run and get my medical bag," Sawyer said. "I just want to take a listen to his lungs."

"Is there something to be worried about?" I asked.

"No," Sawyer quickly said. "Just a precaution."

"Thanks," Isaac nodded. To Dallas he said, "There's a thermometer and some children's aspirin in my bag in our room. Would you get that for me? Also his pajamas? He's going to need to rest once I get him warmed up."

Dallas nodded and hurried upstairs. Isaac and I followed.

"Do you want me to carry him up the stairs?" I asked.

"No, I'm okay," Isaac said. He sounded much more tired than he had a moment earlier, likely because his adrenaline was starting to crash. "Just, um, can you keep your arm around me?" he asked. "So I don't fall."

I didn't bother to tell him that had been my plan all along. Isaac felt so slight against my body that I found myself tucking him up against my side in the hopes of offering him even more support. When we got to the bathroom, Nolan had the bathtub already filled. It wasn't a big space, so he stepped out of the way. Dallas appeared and handed me the items Isaac had asked for.

"Do you need anything else?" Nolan asked. "How about we heat up some soup?"

"He won't eat for a bit," Isaac said.

"Okay, how about some hot chocolate?"

Nolan clearly was rattled because his voice was shaking, and I guessed that Isaac responded with, "Sure, that would be great" more to give Nolan something to do than anything else.

After Nolan and Dallas left the bathroom, Isaac said to me, "We're okay. You can go too."

I heard one thing but saw another. And even if I hadn't, I wasn't going anywhere. As calm as Isaac was, I could see his hands were shaking and there was a tremor running through his body. This might not have been the first time he'd had to deal with this kind of episode, but fuck if he was going to deal with it alone.

"Tell me what you need me to do," was all I said.

Fortunately, he didn't argue with me. He hesitated, then nodded. "Can you hold him while I get him undressed?"

I carefully took Newt from Isaac. The little boy didn't even seem to notice the transfer because he was practically asleep. My eyes fell on a couple of abrasions on Isaac's cheek and temple, but I didn't ask him about it.

Now wasn't the time.

I held Newt as Isaac quickly worked his clothes off him. It was a little awkward maneuvering him around, but Newt slept through it. Sawyer appeared.

"Can I take a listen?" Sawyer asked Isaac.

Isaac nodded and stepped back, leaving me to hold Newt while Sawyer listened to his lungs. I held my own breath for the handful of seconds it took for Sawyer to say, "Everything sounds clear."

"Thanks," Isaac said.

"From what I've read, you just need to monitor him for fever or more seizures, right?"

Isaac nodded. "He's usually fine after a couple of hours of sleep. But I'll take him to the doctor if he's showing any abnormal signs."

Sawyer nodded and patted Isaac on the upper arm. "I'll be downstairs if you need anything, okay?"

"Thanks," Isaac murmured.

Sawyer left, and Isaac and I carefully got Newt settled in the tub. The little boy stirred awake as he was surrounded by the warm water. I kept my arm around him to keep him from slipping beneath it.

"How you doing, buddy?" Isaac asked as he got the thermometer.

"Sleepy," Newt whispered.

"I know. You can sleep in a few minutes, okay? Just need to take your temperature."

Newt nodded and accepted the thermometer. I couldn't help but sigh in relief when the temperature read normal.

"Did I get the shakes?" Newt murmured as he tried to curl into my arm. Isaac was using his cupped palm to scoop some water onto Newt's head to try and clear some of the lingering chunks of snow from it.

"Yeah, Newt, you did," Isaac said.

"Do I gotta wear the hat?" he asked.

Isaac hesitated and said, "We'll talk about it later, okay?"

"Don't wanna," Newt said as he began to cry. "People will laugh at me."

Isaac quickly lifted Newt and pulled him out of the tub, not caring that the little boy was getting him wet. I snagged a towel and wrapped it around Newt's body. Isaac tucked the ends between his and Newt's body, then settled Newt on his lap as the little boy cried. He kissed the top of his head and said, "No one will laugh at you, Newt. Promise."

My heart broke for the little boy as he shook his head and cried. I suspected what Newt might be talking about. A kid I'd gone to grade school with had suffered from severe epilepsy. He'd had to wear some kind of soft-padded helmet to protect his head if he fell. The kids had teased the boy mercilessly.

Newt was inconsolable as he sobbed, and I could see that every second that passed was breaking Isaac down further and further. Although he was being strong for his brother, I could see it was taking every ounce of strength he had not to lose it himself.

"Hey Newt, do you remember when you helped save Loki that night? When you told all the people how nice he really was?" I asked.

Newt nodded.

"Do you remember afterwards when your brother had to help me leave the room?"

"'Cause you were scared?" Newt asked.

I nodded. "That's right." I felt Isaac's gaze on me, but I didn't allow myself to look at him. "I got scared when the man was banging the gavel and all those people kept bumping into me."

"You don't gotta be scared of that," Newt said.

"I know I don't need to, but I am just the same."

"Why?"

"Because it reminds me of some scary stuff that happened. But you want to know what's scarier?"

"What?"

I began drying his hair but made sure not to cover his face with the towel while I was doing it so he could still see me.

"I'm afraid people will laugh at me when they find out I'm scared of those things."

"It's not funny," Newt said softly.

I let my eyes hold his as I said, "No, it's not. Just like it's not funny that you have to wear a hat sometimes to keep you safe."

He nodded but didn't say anything.

"So I'll make you a deal," I said. "I promise that if anyone laughs at you because you're wearing your special hat, I'll let them know it isn't funny if you promise to do the same for me if someone laughs because I'm scared of loud noises and being around too many people."

He only thought about it for about two seconds before he said, "'Kay."

"Okay," I declared, then I spit into my hand and held it out to him. His tired eyes went wide. "What, you've never spit on it before?" I asked.

His eyes remained wide as he shook his head. He looked both horrified and fascinated at the same time.

"A spit handshake is like a promise you can't ever break. Ever," I declared. "You only spit on it when you really, really mean it."

Newt glanced at Isaac who said, "You gotta really mean it, Newt." He ran his hand over Newt's damp hair.

The little boy seemed to think long and hard on it, then he spit into his hand and shook mine. I nearly laughed at the big gob of spit that met my palm.

"It's done," I said solemnly as I gave him a firm nod of my head.

Newt nodded. "Done," he repeated as he laid his head on Isaac's chest. His eyes began to slide shut, so I quickly dried off the rest of him, then helped Isaac to his feet while he was still holding Newt. When I went to open the door, Loki pushed into the bathroom.

"Loki," Newt murmured as he let his arm hang so Loki could lick his fingers. The wolf hybrid followed us to the bedroom Newt and Isaac were sharing. I'd remembered to snag Newt's pajamas from the bathroom, so Isaac stood Newt on the bed and told him to stay standing as he quickly got the PJs worked onto his little body. Then he was settling Newt into the bed. The moment he covered Newt with the blanket, Loki jumped up onto the other side of the bed and lay down next to Newt. The child buried his fingers into Loki's fur, then his eyes drifted shut and I knew he was out by the time Isaac leaned down to kiss his forehead.

When he straightened, Isaac just stared down at Newt for the longest time. I instinctively put my arm around Isaac's waist and drew him back against me. The fact that he leaned into me pretty much right away was proof of how far gone he was.

"He's okay," I reminded Isaac when I felt his body begin to shake.

Isaac nodded and held there for a moment. Then a harsh, agonized cry bubbled up from his throat. He slapped his hand over his mouth to try and stop the sound, but it escaped anyway. It wasn't loud enough to wake Newt, but I knew that wasn't why Isaac had tried to hide it.

"It's okay, Isaac," I said as I nuzzled the back of his neck. He'd gone stiff in my hold as soon as the strangled sound had erupted from his throat, but when I wrapped my other arm around his upper chest, another muffled sob broke loose. I dropped my mouth next to his ear and whispered, "I've got you, baby. Just let go."

I wasn't sure if it was the endearment or my hold or him just being too exhausted to do otherwise, but whatever it was, he broke in the most heartbreaking of ways. He let out another painful-sounding sob, then turned in my arms and pushed against my chest. I held him tight as he cried against my chest. I placed my hand against the back of his head and just held him like that as he clung to me. His fingers were curled into the fabric of my shirt along my waist, but the longer I held him, the more he began to relax as his cries started to ease. His arms drifted to my back and then it was just him hanging onto me as the fight seemed to leave him completely.

"Why don't you go lie down in Dallas and Nolan's bed for a bit?" I suggested.

"Can't leave him," Isaac whispered.

"We'll all take turns sitting with him," I said. "I'm sure Dallas and Nolan are freaking out downstairs with not being able to do anything."

Isaac hesitated, then nodded against me. I took him by the hand and led him from the room, leaving the door open so we'd hear Newt if he cried out or if Loki needed to get out of the room to find someone if Newt had another seizure.

I knew Dallas and Nolan wouldn't mind if Isaac used their bed to lie down for a bit, so I didn't ask them first. I led him into the room and pulled back the covers, then had him stand by the bed. He was so exhausted, he barely seemed aware of me or anything else.

"What happened here?" I asked as I skimmed my fingers over his temple, then his cheek. He seemed confused at first, but when I touched one of the marks, he winced and said, "Nothing. I fell."

I was inclined to believe him until I reached for the hem of his shirt and helped him get it off his body.

That was when I saw some light bruising around his throat.

"Isaac, what happened?" I asked, barely keeping the rage out of my voice.

To my surprise, Isaac dropped his forehead to my chest. "So tired, Maddox," he said softly. "Please, I'm just so tired."

I managed to stifle my need for answers and brought my hand up to caress the back of his neck. "Okay, I'm sorry."

He sighed, then straightened and started to sit down. "Wait, let me get these off," I said as I motioned to his jeans. "They're really wet."

He didn't argue with me, so I reached for the snap and then the zipper. I'd managed to get the pants open and was just sliding them down when Isaac suddenly cried out, "No, wait!" His hand shot out to capture my wrist, but he was too late.

I froze at the sight of the bright white, lacy material covering the part of his upper groin I could see. It tapered to a narrower strip of fabric that was more sheer and rode high on his hip. Isaac frantically tried to pull his jeans back up, but it didn't matter. I already knew what I'd seen, even if I couldn't make sense of it.

He was wearing women's underwear.

Even if I could have somehow mentally tried to convince myself they were a feminine version of men's underwear, his reaction to my discovery was enough to tell me I was right and that there was nothing else the scrap of material could be other than panties.

"Oh God," Isaac cried, then he ripped my hand from his jeans and yanked them up. He took off out of the room before I could stop him, even though I was too shell-shocked to even consider doing so.

CHAPTER TWELVE

ISAAC

"So is this how it's going to be?" I snapped the second I stepped into the electrical room in the small animal building and my eyes searched out Maddox. He was leaning over some kind of piece of equipment that I knew had something to do with the automatic waterers that each habitat included. "I'm not a freak, you know!" I practically yelled.

Maddox straightened and eyed me but didn't say anything.

Which only served to piss me off even more.

It'd been two days since he'd discovered my secret.

Two whole days.

And he hadn't said even one single word to me about it. He hadn't said even one single word to me *at all*.

He'd talked to Newt a few times when he'd stopped by the house to check on him the day following the seizure, and he'd said hello in passing to Sawyer and made conversation with Nolan and Dallas.

But me...

He'd ignored me like I... like I didn't even exist anymore.

"It's totally normal!" I spit out. "A lot of guys do it. Straight ones and gay ones," I insisted. Some of my fire began to die off the more Maddox stared at me. But the humiliation made it impossible for me to keep my mouth shut. "And it's not like you had any right to find out like you did... or at all!" My throat closed up when he suddenly began walking toward me. To my horror, I started backing up at the same time, but I couldn't stop talking.

"You're just embarrassed," I insisted. "You kissed a guy and you liked it and you can't deny it and now you find out he... he..."

Jesus, what the hell was happening to me? I'd come down here full of righteous indignation and with a plan to rip him a new one, but one look at his hard eyes and tight jaw and I was a blubbering mess.

Where was the man who'd spoken so sweetly to Newt? Where was the guy who'd held me in his arms and called me baby and taken care of me? And why the hell had I let that happen? Why had I let myself believe he'd be different? And why in the name of all that was good and holy hadn't I remembered I was wearing the underwear until it was too damn late? I never, ever wore them when there was even the smallest chance my secret could be discovered, choosing instead to wear them in private and only for short stints at a time–long enough to get what I needed out of them. But I'd needed the security and confidence the pretty underwear never failed to bring me after the devastating kiss Maddox had laid on me the night before, so I'd worn them despite the risk.

"You're the one with the problem," I yelled, even as my voice broke a bit. "You're so narrow-minded and uptight and controlling—"

I stopped talking when my back hit the wall behind me. Maddox kept coming at me. He had some kind of tool in his hand. I knew he wouldn't hurt me, but the shame and humiliation were like a raw nerve flayed open wide somewhere deep inside me and my instinct to keep attacking would not be quelled, even if my brain was screaming at me to shut the hell up.

"I didn't ask for your help that day and I don't need it! Newt and I are fine, we're... we're..."

Jesus, why couldn't I even get the word out?

Maddox's chest brushed mine just as I managed to whisper "fine."

"Are you finished?" he asked, his voice obscenely calm.

I wanted to hit him.

He'd reduced me to a quivering mess and he was acting like I was just a kid throwing a temper tantrum. He had no clue what he'd done to me.

And it had all started in that fucking motel room when he'd asked me to put on my lip gloss.

I didn't answer him. Instead, I tried to duck out from between him and the wall, but his arm shot out to stop me. His palm slapped against the wall next to my head. I closed my eyes.

"Open them," Maddox ordered, his voice hard and unyielding. I was helpless to do anything but obey, and I kind of hated him for that.

I made myself look into his eyes, even though all I wanted to do was look at the floor.

No one, not one person, knew about me what he did. I'd had one thing left in my life that had well and truly been mine, and he'd taken that from me.

And now it was like I was mourning its loss.

"Are you finished?" Maddox repeated.

I was at the point that I wanted to beg him to let me go, to give me back the scrap of dignity I'd stupidly thrown away by confronting him. But before I could say anything, his mouth was on mine. I gasped in surprise and he quickly took complete possession of my mouth. I was breathless by the time he pulled back.

"Are you wearing them now?" Maddox asked, his mouth practically brushing mine as he spoke.

"Wha... what?" I croaked.

"Are you wearing the same ones or ones like them?" he asked. His eyes actually dropped to my groin. Heat sizzled beneath my skin as my dick responded to the question. He kissed me again until I felt too dazed from the sheer pleasure of it all to even consider my words.

"No... I... no, I don't... what?" I whispered, completely confused.

This time I was kissing him because kissing him was so much better than trying to form actual sentences. I felt his hand slide down to my ass and then he was pulling me forward against him, his big hand splayed over my backside.

"I don't think you're a freak," he said softly against my mouth. "I think you're the most beautiful thing I've ever seen." He nibbled at my lip piercing before settling his mouth on mine once more.

By the time he let me come up for air, I was dizzy from the pleasure of it all. At some point I'd moved my hands up to his shoulders. I threaded my fingers through his short hair. There wasn't enough of it to tug on to force his head back down, but it wasn't really necessary. The slightest bit of pressure against his scalp had him leaning down to kiss me again.

It could have been minutes, hours, or days when he finally released my mouth.

But not me.

His hand wasn't on my ass anymore, but it was resting on the small of my back. His other hand was still against the wall and he was resting his forehead against mine.

"Are you gay?" I asked.

"No idea," he responded.

I let out a dry laugh and said, "It's not a trick question."

"Does it matter?" he asked with a sigh.

"Um, yeah, it kind of does."

"Why?"

"Because..."

Yeah, that was all I had. *Because*.

"Tell you what," Maddox murmured against my mouth before brushing a kiss over my lips. "You tell me what I am, okay?" Before I could respond, he cut me off with another kiss, then said, "You're not the first guy I've kissed. And I've kissed plenty of women too."

My interest in the conversation went south quickly at that point, because I definitely did not like hearing about the other people he'd kissed. He must have sensed my imminent protest, because he kissed me again. He kept at it until I was basically jelly in his arms. Only then did he continue.

"But you're the only person I've never wanted to stop kissing. You're the only one who keeps me awake at night as I imagine what it would be like to be inside you. *You*. Not Isaac the *man* or Isaac with the makeup or Isaac, the guy who wears women's underwear. Just you."

This time when he kissed me, I let out a little whimper because I was still reeling from his words. He ripped his mouth free of mine and ground out, "I want to punch Sawyer every time he looks at you. I want to hunt down whoever put those bruises on your throat and the marks on your face. I want to never see the fear I saw in your eyes the day the sheriff showed up here and you thought he was here for you and Newt. I never want to see another tear roll down your cheek for as long as I live, and I want to kill any man who thinks it's okay to use you and throw you away like you're nothing. And I want to know how the fuck it's possible to feel so much in so little time. So tell me, Isaac, what does that make me? Gay? Straight? Bi?"

I could barely breathe as he held my gaze for a moment, then released me. I felt the loss almost immediately.

"Isaac, you in here?" I heard Nolan call before I could respond to Maddox or beg him to take me back into his arms.

"Yeah," I somehow managed to get out. "Is Newt okay?" I asked.

"He's fine," Nolan said. When he came around the corner, his eyes shifted between me and Maddox and I could tell he knew something was up. "Everything okay here?" he asked.

I swallowed hard and nodded. "Just clearing the air," I murmured. "We're good."

I risked a glance at Maddox and saw him watching me. He looked agitated and I wondered if it was because of what I'd said about clearing the air.

"Yeah, we're good," Maddox muttered, then he went back to the electrical room.

I forced myself to look at Nolan. He and Dallas had been incredible in helping me watch out for Newt these past two days. Even though Newt was fully recovered from his seizure, I'd still made him stay in the house and rest. But most of that had been because I was terrified of what would happen if he had another seizure while outside. We'd gotten incredibly lucky that he'd been found so quickly and that he hadn't hurt himself when the seizure had hit. It'd been a long time since the last seizure and deep down I'd thought that meant he'd been cured of them, so I was nursing the disappointment that came along with knowing he wasn't. And I was projecting that onto him.

Not to mention I'd been a complete mess because of everything that had happened with Maddox.

Of course, none of that had changed.

Well, not in a helpful way, anyway.

I was more confused than ever about what was happening between us.

"What's up?" I said to Nolan.

"Oh, I'm having problems with that spreadsheet. It won't open and I know it's because I'm doing something wrong."

"Okay, yeah, I'll take a look," I said. "No problem." I told myself not to look back toward the electrical room as Nolan and I walked toward the exit, but I did anyway.

Just as I'd expected, the doorway was empty. And despite telling myself I was glad about that, I still couldn't ignore the pang of disappointment that went through me.

And stayed with me for the rest of the day.

CHAPTER THIRTEEN

MADDOX

It was nearly three days before I saw Isaac again, and when I did, it wasn't by choice. I'd spent the better part of those days ripping down the old shed, which had kept me on the back part of the property where there was little around. Dallas had started helping me on the second day and while we hadn't talked much–which wouldn't have been easy to do so anyway, since Dallas was still following doctor's orders not to try using his voice yet–we'd still managed to find a certain rhythm that had felt like its own form of communication. The fact that he'd even taken the time to work with me when he could have been doing other things around the sanctuary had been the one bright spot in my existence.

The rest was all just a dark, jumbled mess of shit.

Between Isaac and Jett, I was a roiling mass of uncertainty that no amount of walking would alleviate. With Jett, it was the same situation–he was refusing to talk to me beyond a few words telling me he was fine when he was clearly anything but. My fear for his mental health was starting to ratchet up. On the one hand, I knew it was normal for him to mourn the loss of his old life, but on the other, I'd nearly lost him once to his own demons and I was terrified that there'd be a day where his obligation to his grandmother wouldn't be enough and he'd finish what he'd started. But I also wasn't sure that going down there was the answer. Maybe seeing me would push him over that same edge. He'd told me many times he didn't blame me for what had happened, but I knew that couldn't be one hundred percent true.

I'd been in charge that day.

I'd made the decision that had led to him losing his legs and nine other men losing their lives.

It would be too much to expect that he'd ever forgive me for that.

I'd never forgive myself for that.

But as bad as things were with Jett, Isaac was the one who consumed most of my thoughts.

I'd clearly scared him by telling him so much about what he made me feel. I didn't even know the man who'd said all that shit because I wasn't that guy. I didn't talk about my feelings. I didn't do relationships and emotions. If I felt the need to give in to my body's desires, I took care of it and then moved on.

But none of those rules seemed to apply to Isaac.

I'd already gotten past the fact that he was a guy. Maybe it was so easy because of the more intense emotions he stirred in me that went way past desire. Or maybe because I'd always been someone who dealt with a situation head-on and then moved forward. I didn't ruminate or wonder or waffle back and forth. I saw something, I made a decision about it, and I moved on to the next thing.

So being attracted to a guy was kind of easy in that sense. My dick responded whenever I was around Isaac and I accepted what that meant.

But the emotional shit...

That was a whole other ballgame.

I may have stuck to my routine of saying what I thought when I'd spit out all that stuff about how he made me feel, but now what the hell was I supposed to do? Straight, gay, or bi... didn't matter. I needed the damn handbook that told you how to deal with the stuff that came in addition to attraction and desire.

I glanced at my brother where he was tossing debris into the back of his truck. I still had half the building to tear down, but Dallas was making good progress with cleaning up the scattered lumber. It'd been a couple of weeks since his surgery and he'd only recently gone with Nolan to Minneapolis to follow up with his surgeon and to have the stitches removed. He had another appointment in two weeks where the surgeon would actually do the testing to see if Dallas's voice would fully return and that it was safe to start using it more regularly. If things went well, he'd be working with a speech therapist on a regular basis. Fortunately, he'd found one in Pelican Bay he'd be able to work with, so he wouldn't need to travel for those appointments.

Pain suddenly lanced through my hand as I reached for a piece of wood to throw on the pile.

"Son of a biscuit!" I snapped as the sharp edge of a piece of broken metal I hadn't seen ripped through my glove and into my palm.

Blood began pouring from the wound as I pulled my glove off. Dallas was by my side instantly. He pulled a bandana from his pocket and quickly wrapped it around my hand. Blood immediately seeped through the material.

"Stupid," I muttered more to myself than anything else.

Dallas quickly typed something into his phone and handed it to me as he grabbed me by the arm and led me toward his truck.

You need stitches. Come on. Nice swear word, BTW.

I smiled to myself at the last part. All of us adults had started to temper our language in deference to Newt. And while I hadn't been around the little boy as much, I'd heard the stories of the various punishments Newt and Isaac had been inflicting. Nolan had, in fact, missed out on a coveted pedicure and Sawyer had yet to actually get his nails done because the man cursed worse than a sailor.

My humor lasted about as long as it took me to realize Dallas was leading me to his truck. The second he opened the door for me, I broke out into a cold sweat and it became hard to breathe. I was backing away before I could even stop myself.

"It's fine," I said. "I just need a bandage."

Coward that I was, I didn't give Dallas a chance to respond using his phone. I just turned around and hurried up the trail that would lead to the office where the first aid kit was. Not surprisingly, Dallas's truck was sitting outside the office by the time I got there and four sets of eyes settled on me the second I walked in the door.

True to form, my eyes zeroed in on Isaac first. He was wearing what had to be the most boring clothes I'd ever seen on him. A simple cable-knit sweater that looked a little big on him, his dark skinny jeans, and boring navy-blue moon boots. I couldn't help but wonder what he was wearing beneath the jeans. At least the sweater was bright pink and he was wearing his normal eyeliner and gloss.

"You're going," Isaac said, his arms crossed.

I glared at Dallas, who'd clearly ratted me out.

"Where's Sawyer?" I asked. "I'm sure he can take care of it."

"He had an emergency call," Nolan interjected. "You need to go to urgent care."

I opened my mouth to protest, but Isaac shook his head. "You're going and I'm driving you and that's all there is to it. Any questions?" he asked. His pretty lips were pulled into a tight line and I just wanted to kiss the frown away.

"Fine," I said. My whole body immediately reacted and it felt like all the air had been sucked out of the room. Isaac was there, his soft hands framing my face.

"Look at me," he said firmly.

I did and while it didn't automatically calm me down, just being able to focus on his voice, his touch, helped keep me from tearing out of that room and walking away.

"It's going to be okay," Isaac said. "We're going to take it slow and easy, okay?"

I managed a nod.

"I'm going too, Mad," Newt announced as he stepped over the barrier that kept the kittens in the corner with him. He handed the kitten he had in his hand to Nolan and said, "Snotrod is lonely. Can you hold him till I get back?"

"Absolutely," Nolan said. "I won't let him out of my sight."

It was then that I realized the kitten area in that corner of the office was empty. Which meant Nolan and Dallas must have managed to find homes for all the kittens except the spindly-looking one in Nolan's hands.

"You sure you want to come, buddy?" Isaac asked as he took the keys Dallas handed him. I figured that meant we were taking Dallas's truck, which would at least be a little better than being stuck in Isaac's tiny tin can of a car.

Newt nodded. He was wearing a simple black soft-padded helmet. "We spit on it," he announced. Then suddenly he spit in his hand and held it out to me. I didn't have the heart to explain a spit shake only needed to be done once. I somehow managed to find enough saliva to spit in my uninjured hand and shook Newt's.

"Okay, we really need to talk about you guys switching to pinkie swears or something," Isaac said as he snagged a couple of tissues and handed them to each of us. He took my arm and said, "Let's go."

Humiliation went through me as we neared the pickup truck and I stopped walking. It was like my body was shutting down.

"Maddox," Isaac said gently as he closed his fingers around the ones on my uninjured hand. "Just focus on me and Newt, okay? No matter what else, just listen to the sounds of our voices."

I managed a nod.

To Newt, Isaac said, "Newt, we're gonna play the I Spy game. Can you explain how it works to Maddox?"

I only half-listened as Newt began explaining the rules. Shame curled through me as Isaac had to do everything for me, including get my seatbelt on and close the passenger door.

"I spy with my little eye something... white," Newt announced.

Isaac was just climbing into the driver's seat when Newt spoke, and I tried to listen to him start spouting off guesses, but my heart felt like it was going to pound out of my chest and it was getting harder and harder to breathe. I didn't even feel a bit of pain in my injured hand. It was a sure sign I was on the verge of completely losing it.

"Maddox, baby," Isaac said softly. The endearment was enough of a surprise that I looked at him. He closed the fingers of his right hand around mine. "Just focus on me, okay?" He leaned across the seat and touched the back of my neck, then whispered into my ear, "You can do this," then kissed my cheek.

He quickly got the car started and in gear, then his fingers once again wrapped around mine. I tried not to hurt him as I held onto him, but admittedly, it was hard to temper my reaction as the car began moving. The snow in front of me disappeared and was replaced with sand and rock and dirt and a deserted road that had dozens and dozens of tire tracks on it.

The steering wheel felt comforting beneath my fingers. As a senior officer, I rarely drove, so it was a nice change of pace. And we'd just finished our last mission, so I was willing to break protocol this one time.

After all, we were going home.

But as I turned onto the road, something in my belly tightened. My guys were joking and laughing in the Humvee, even as they kept their eyes on our surroundings, and I had no doubt the guys in the vehicle behind us were doing the same. I tried to ignore the lead weight in my gut, but as it grew worse, I reached for the radio.

I listened as my commanding officer reassured me the road had just been swept for IEDs. I wanted to argue, but the need to respect senior leadership was ingrained deep within me, so I ended the call and put my foot on the gas.

And then my body was flying through the air and everything was dark.

I couldn't stop the pounding.

Thunk...

Thunk...

Thunk...

"...pink."

The word caught my attention. There was nothing pink out here. We were in hell. There was no such thing as color in hell. The only bright color in this godforsaken place was blood.

And it was everywhere.

"...an elephant?"

Elephant? Huh?

"Maddox, do you think it's an elephant?"

The roaring in my ears was so loud, I almost didn't hear my name being said. "What?" I managed to croak. Why was Jett asking me about elephants?

"Do you think Newt spies a pink elephant?"

Newt.

Reality slowly returned as I realized it was Isaac asking me the question. No, Isaac couldn't be in the desert. It wasn't safe for him or Newt. I was about to yell at both of them to run when I felt a soft caress along the back of my neck.

I knew that touch.

I *craved* it.

Isaac.

He was here.

And here wasn't that terrible, too-quiet road outside Mosul.

The blackness disappeared and all I saw before me was white.

Snow.

Lots and lots of snow.

Because I was home.

"Maddox," Isaac whispered, his voice sounding strangled.

I didn't like when he sounded like that. It meant he was upset and I didn't like when he was upset. I turned to look at him. He looked like he was on the verge of tears. "Breathe, baby," he whispered as his fingers continued to toy with the back of my neck.

I didn't want him to look so scared anymore, so I did what he said and pulled in a deep breath. My lungs screamed in relief and the pain in my chest eased just a little. So I did it again.

And again.

I kept sucking in huge lungsful of air in until the pain and noise in my head receded and my chest no longer felt like it had an anchor sitting on it. My body was shaking and I couldn't relax my hands, but I was able to focus on Isaac and Newt.

"Maddox," Isaac said carefully. "Do you think Newt spies a pink elephant?"

The game.

Right.

I glanced over my shoulder at Newt, who was watching me with worried eyes.

"No," I managed to somehow say. "I think he sees pink clouds."

There was a beat of silence and then Newt let out a long, "Nooooo."

"Is it elephants?" Isaac asked, even as he kept glancing at me.

"Nooooo."

"Okay, I guess we need another hint," Isaac insisted.

"I spy something with my little eye that's soft."

I continued to slow my breathing as Isaac made another silly guess. When it was my turn, I reached out to run my fingers over the hem of Isaac's sweater. "Is it Isaac's sweater?" I asked as I held Isaac's gaze. He was forced to keep looking back at the road in between exchanging glances with me, but there were a whole lot of things he said to me with those looks.

Most of all, that he was relieved.

As I managed to calm down, the pain in my hand returned, but I happily welcomed it.

"Yes!" Newt said. "You win. It's your turn."

We played the game for the entire drive to town. Every guess was silly and the game grew more boisterous as we argued and joked about the hints and the answers. By the time we reached the doctor's office, I was feeling a little steadier. Though admittedly, I was more than happy to get out of that truck.

When we entered the clinic, Newt went quiet and tucked himself against Isaac's side and I quickly realized why. His helmet had gained the attention of several people, including a couple of children who were in the kid's area of the lobby. I reached down for Newt's hand and tucked it in my uninjured one. I crouched down to his level and said, "Do you trust me, Newt?"

Newt hesitated, then nodded. I looked up at Isaac who didn't even hesitate to nod. I felt my heart swell at that. I wanted to kiss him then and there but managed to refrain. I led Newt over to where the kids were playing. I kept my bloody hand out of view so I wouldn't scare the kids and said, "Hey guys, this is my friend, Newt. You mind if he hangs out with you while I get my hand fixed up?"

The little boy who was maybe a year older than Newt shrank back a bit, but the girl who appeared to be closer to eight or nine eyed Newt's helmet. Newt automatically pressed against me and I put my arm around him.

"Why's he wearing that?" the girl asked.

"Hmmm, well, you know how your mom probably makes you wear a seatbelt or sit in a car seat when you're in the car?" I asked.

"Uh-huh, it's to keep us safe," the girl said as she motioned between her and the boy, so I figured they were likely siblings.

"Well, Newt here needs this hat to keep his head safe just in case he falls. Even though he can walk and run and play just like you guys, sometimes he just needs a little bit of extra protection."

The girl studied me and Newt for a moment, then looked at her brother. "It's like your bed," she said to him. Then she looked at me and said, "Justin's gotta have a fence on his bed to keep him from falling out when he sleeps."

I smiled at that because I knew she was talking about the safety rails that parents sometimes used on younger children's beds to keep them from rolling out of it and onto the floor while they were sleeping.

"Exactly," I said. "It's like that."

The girl hesitated, then handed Newt a small plastic doll that was part of the tabletop train set the kids were playing with. "You wanna be the driver?" she asked.

Newt nodded shyly. The girl's brother still seemed hesitant so I said to the kids, "Do you guys wanna know a secret about Newt?"

My statement caught the interest of both kids and they eagerly nodded. I lowered my voice and said, "His best friend—" I looked around me dramatically like I was making sure no one could overhear us— "is a wolf. A white wolf."

Both kids went wide-eyed. "Really?" the little boy asked.

Newt eagerly nodded. "Yeah, and his name is Loki and he sleeps in my bed with me each night."

I stepped back as the kids pressed forward to pepper Newt with questions. When I turned around, I saw Isaac watching me with what looked like watery eyes. I went to him and, not caring who was watching, closed my uninjured hand around his. He looked down at our joined hands in surprise but didn't say anything. He just followed me to the reception desk so I could check in, and I couldn't help but think that despite the pain in my hand and the little bit of tension I was still feeling after the car ride, things had never felt more right in my world than they did at that very moment.

CHAPTER FOURTEEN

ISAAC

The trip back to the sanctuary wasn't quite as bad as the drive to town, and it took less time to bring Maddox out of whatever trance he seemed to automatically fall into the second he got into the vehicle. Newt had been so enamored with his new friends that he'd talked all the way back to the sanctuary about little Emily and Justin Knapp. The kids' mother had even asked me if Newt wanted to come over for a play date sometime and had handed me her cell phone number.

I'd been too preoccupied with Maddox at the time to really give it much thought or even respond, but as I stared at the computer screen, I couldn't stop thinking about it.

And everything else that had happened in that short span of time.

Maddox had held my hand.

In public.

And not because he'd been in the midst of a panic attack.

He'd been Newt's savior and then he'd held my hand and I didn't know what any of it meant.

Except there was one thing I *did* know.

Newt and I needed to leave Pelican Bay.

Like yesterday.

Not only was this thing with Maddox fucking with my head big-time, Newt and I had gotten in way too deep with Dallas and Nolan. Somehow in the span of two weeks, they'd become like uncles to my brother. We spent every evening having dinner as a family and then we'd either watch a movie or play a game. I usually woke up after Newt, only to find him helping Nolan make breakfast before we all got to work caring for the animals. Loki had taken up residence in the bed I'd been sharing with Newt, so Dallas and Nolan had cleared out a guest bedroom and brought a spare mattress in from the apartment above the garage for me. Everyone, including Sawyer, was mindful of always keeping an eye on Newt in case he had another seizure, but they didn't baby or coddle him so that he'd feel self-conscious about his disorder or the fact that I was making him wear the dreaded helmet.

And now Newt had some new little friends.

Friends he already couldn't stop talking about, on top of everything else.

Friends who knew his real name, a parent who knew mine... not to mention that I stuck out like a sore thumb in Pelican Bay. It was just a matter of time before someone got curious and started asking questions. And if the cops started looking into me and Newt...

A chill went through me at the prospect of Gary finding us.

No, I just couldn't risk it.

Nothing was worth Newt's safety.

Nothing.

I glanced at Newt who was quietly coloring as the kitten, Snotrod, lay on his lower back and Loki was resting his head on my brother's butt. I pulled out my phone and snapped a picture and set it as my new wallpaper.

God, how was I going to give this up? How was I supposed to make Newt give it up?

I heard the office door open and immediately felt warmth flow through me as Maddox walked in. His eyes landed on mine and I felt it everywhere.

Yeah, Newt and I definitely needed to go.

I only had the cash from my second paycheck, minus the part I'd had to take out that Dallas was still including–Maddox's salary. It would be enough to get us to Chicago and maybe secure a motel room for a few nights, but that was it.

Which meant I'd have to find a few tricks…

Bile rose in my throat at even the thought. How the hell was I supposed to let any man touch me after Maddox? It just felt so wrong on every level.

God, he'd completely ruined me for other men, because I doubted I could even bear the idea of someone who wasn't a client touching me the way Maddox had.

"Hey," Maddox said.

Butterflies danced in my belly with the simple greeting. Hell, he could probably read me scores from the sports page and I'd still pop a boner.

"Hey," I said.

Smooth, Isaac. Real smooth.

"Hey, Newt," Maddox said.

"Hey, Mad," Newt returned, though he didn't look up from his coloring book.

Maddox approached the desk. Even with the piece of furniture separating us, I felt like I could feel him all around me.

It was the strangest thing. It was like there was this current between us that had a wire running to both my dick and my heart. Usually it didn't matter what he said or did, both body parts responded accordingly.

"How's your hand?" I asked.

He glanced at his bandaged hand and said, "It's good." There was an awkward silence between us before he leaned over the desk and said, "Listen, I wanted to talk to you about what I said in the small animal building the other day—"

My heart constricted painfully in my chest. "It's okay, I know you didn't mean it."

I expected him to flash me a smile of relief, but instead, his eyes hardened just the tiniest bit, then he was leaning across the desk until he was practically in my face. "I meant every freaking word I said, Isaac," he whispered. Then to my surprise, he brushed his mouth over mine. I was about to grab him and lay the mother of all kisses on him when he pulled back just a little because, *come on*, between that kiss, his words, and the fact that he'd deliberately chosen not to swear... a guy could only resist for so long.

But the sound of the office door opening had me keeping my hands to myself.

Maddox straightened as Loki got up from his spot and went to check out our guest. It wasn't until Maddox moved out of the way that I recognized the man.

It was Jimmy Cornell's brother.

I automatically stood up and began looking for Jimmy, but there was no one else with him. The man's eyes landed on mine, but he didn't seem particularly surprised to see me. I didn't miss the fact that he had fresh bruises on his face.

"Hi," he said to me.

Maddox looked between me and the man as I came around the desk. "Hello," I returned. I liked it when Maddox automatically moved closer to me.

"My name's Ford," the man said. "Ford—"

"Cornell," Maddox finished for him. "You're Jimmy Cornell's brother," he said. His voice had gone cold and Ford automatically stepped back a bit.

"I am," he murmured.

"You two know each other?" Maddox said to me.

"It's nothing," I said with a shake of my head. If it'd been Jimmy standing in front of us, I wouldn't have hesitated to tell Maddox about the incident in town, but my gut was telling me Ford wasn't like his brother.

Maddox eyed me, then Ford. To me he said, "Did he do that to your face?" as his fingers came up to skim the faded marks on my temple and cheek. "Your throat?" he said more softly. His voice was positively scary now. He was already stepping toward Ford when I grabbed his arm.

"He didn't," I said quickly. "It wasn't him. He tried to stop it."

Maddox hesitated, then eased up a bit. "It was Jimmy?"

I swallowed and nodded. "But I took care of it. Jimmy and his friends were hassling me after I left the thrift store." My eyes flicked to Ford briefly. "But I knew Jimmy is nothing but a bully… his attack on Gentry proved that. So I pretty much told him and his friends they could go fu… fudge themselves." I looked awkwardly at Newt and saw he'd gotten up and was holding Snotrod close to his chest while he listened in on our conversation. "Jimmy was going to take a s-w-i-n-g at me, but Ford stopped him."

Newt had moved to my side while I'd been talking, but fortunately he hadn't gotten the gist of the conversation. I had no interest in him knowing I'd nearly gotten attacked.

"Mad," Newt said softly.

"Yeah, buddy," Maddox said, his eyes on Ford.

"Someone hurt him," Newt whispered as he looked at the other man, his eyes on the bruises on Ford's face. Ford's skin went bright with color, a sure sign he was embarrassed. "You should spit on it," Newt added.

At that, Ford actually went wide-eyed and I couldn't help but smile as I put my arm around Newt's shoulders. "He means *spit shake* on it."

"Yeah," Newt said. "Mad can promise to keep you safe and you can promise him something and then you spit on it and it's forever."

Ford actually smiled briefly. "Good to know," he said softly to my brother. To me he said, "I'm sorry about," –his eyes fell on Newt and then came back to me– "that thing that happened in town. I wish there was something else I could have done."

I sent him a nod because I believed him.

"What are you doing here?" Maddox asked. He still sounded suspicious and I couldn't really blame him.

"Um, I came to see you, actually," Ford said as he focused on Maddox. "This is, uh, for you. I… I got it done sooner than expected so I thought I'd hand-deliver it." Ford stepped forward enough to hand Maddox the large paper shopping bag he'd been holding.

Maddox glanced in the bag and then pulled out what appeared to be some kind of receipt. He looked at Ford in surprise. "You're Chaotic Creations?"

Ford nodded. "Yeah."

I had no clue what either man was talking about. Maddox must have seen my confusion because he said, "I was looking for someone to design a special art project for me. I wasn't expecting to find someone local, though."

"That site you used," Ford cut in. "It's like that Fiverr site but for artists. I get notified for certain kinds of jobs. Yours stood out not only because of what you wanted, but because you were from here. I, um, recognized your name so I bid on it."

"Why?" Maddox asked, clearly suspicious.

Ford shifted nervously back and forth on his feet. "I just, I... I know what my brother did to your brother, and I knew I couldn't just come out here and tell him how sorry I was but I wanted to do *something* and then I saw your name on the design job and I just... I don't know," Ford said awkwardly. Then he was rooting around in his pocket and pulling out some money. "I, um, can't give it all back to you because I needed to use some of it to buy the" –his eyes shifted to me, then Newt, then back to Maddox– "the, um, *it* and the art supplies because I didn't have enough money to pay for that myself, but the rest of it is here, I swear."

Ford thrust the money at Maddox.

I couldn't help but feel sorry for how rattled Ford was. I wasn't the least bit surprised when Maddox didn't take the money. He studied Ford for the longest time and the younger man began to shift even more uncomfortably. I guessed Ford to be in his mid-twenties at the most. He was a really good-looking guy, the bruises notwithstanding. Unlike his brother, he was fit with short black hair that was neatly styled and a carefully trimmed beard that was just a little bit long to be considered scruff. His eyes were a really bright blue and his body looked muscular beneath his snug jeans and beige long-sleeved shirt. He was on the shorter side and his clothes, while clean, had a threadbare look to them.

Maddox suddenly handed the bag back to Ford, whose face fell as he had no choice but to take it. My stomach dropped out, but I held my tongue.

"It's not for me," Maddox said. Then he motioned to Newt. "It's for Newt, here."

I felt my brother shift next to me. "You got me a present?" he asked excitedly and then he was hurrying toward Ford. He suddenly remembered the kitten in his hands and did an about-face. But instead of handing Snotrod to me, he handed him to Maddox, then threw his arms around Maddox's lower body as he hugged him. Before Maddox could even respond, Newt was rushing to Ford who knelt down and set the bag on the floor.

I felt like I was going to cry as I watched Newt's excitement as Ford pulled out a large box and carefully opened it enough so Newt wouldn't have to struggle with it. I couldn't remember the last time anyone besides me had thought to give my brother a gift.

Ford held the box as Newt carefully opened it. I moved enough so I could see his reaction to whatever was in the box.

"Lightning!" Newt yelled as he clapped his hands together. Ford eased the item from the box and when I realized what it was, I did start to cry.

It was a soft-padded helmet, but it was painted to match the colors of Lightning, the race car from the *Cars* movies. Even the car's number was painted onto it.

Newt let out a cry of delight as Ford turned the helmet so Newt could see all of it. "Here, look," Ford said as he showed Newt the front of the helmet. "It's like what all the race car drivers wear. It's even got a microphone so you can talk to your pit crew."

I knew the microphone wasn't real, but Ford had definitely managed to make it look that way. It even folded out of the way for when Newt would be doing something like eating or drinking.

"Isaac, look!" Newt exclaimed, then he grabbed the helmet and brought it to me and began showing me all the features. I wiped at my eyes as I met Maddox's gaze over Newt's head.

"It's amazing," I said to Newt, though admittedly, it was hard to breathe with all the emotions that were clogging my throat. Newt ran back to Ford.

"Can I wear it now?" he asked.

"Of course," Ford said with a smile. He seemed genuinely pleased that my brother loved the helmet as much as he did. He carefully began working the straps of Newt's existing helmet loose. As he helped Newt put the new one on, I went to Maddox and just walked into him. I didn't even wait for him to open his arms.

But he did anyway. He kept the kitten cuddled against one side of his broad chest and gave me the other as his free arm went around me.

"Thank you," I whispered so only he could hear.

I felt his lips skim the top of my head.

"You're welcome, baby."

He held me until Newt came to show us both how the helmet looked on him. But it wasn't until Maddox knelt down and began talking to my brother about how he was a real race car driver now that I made my decision and hoped like hell it wouldn't come back to bite me in the ass.

Because there was just no way in hell Newt and I were going anywhere.

We'd have to leave at some point, but today wasn't that day and I hoped like hell that day, whenever it was, was way off in the future.

Really way off.

CHAPTER FIFTEEN

MADDOX

"Okay, buddy, it's way past your bedtime, I think," I said softly as I stared at the small form curled against my chest. The kitten seemed to respond to my voice because it stretched a little and dug its nails into my shirt, all without opening its eyes. I ran one of my fingers over its little body. The kitten was smaller than all its littermates who'd already been adopted out, but Dallas had assured me the baby was strong. In addition to its size and general scrawny look, the kitten had been born with one of its back legs deformed and tucked up against its body. But it didn't seem to slow the kitten down because he'd been following me all around the lower level of the house as I'd tried to figure out where to put the small box I'd found for his litter and the plastic containers acting as his temporary food and water dishes. I'd settled on putting the stuff in one of the lower-level bathrooms for the time being, since it wasn't too far from the living room where I spent my evenings.

Snotrod had eaten quite a bit, then lumbered after me and crawled up my pant leg after I'd sat down in the armchair by the fire. He'd been asleep for hours now, and I'd found myself spending most of that time running my fingers up and down his back. The little rumbling sounds he made were oddly comforting, and I felt on the verge of falling asleep myself.

I still had no clue how I'd ended up agreeing to adopt the kitten.

Yes, you do.

I sighed because my inner voice was right.

Newt had talked me into it without even really talking me into it. After he'd gotten done hugging me and repeatedly thanking me for the "best present he'd ever gotten" I'd tried to hand him Snotrod back, but he'd told me I should take the kitten home with me so I wouldn't be scared when he and Isaac weren't around. He'd also said something about Snotrod not having a mommy and daddy but that I could take care of the orphan like Isaac took care of Newt. That was when he'd gone to his brother to hug him, and I hadn't had the heart to turn down the suggestion.

In theory, I had no room in my life for a cat, but looking around the spacious, darkened living room, I realized I had more than enough room, both literally and figuratively. I was starting to think I had enough room for a lot of things that I'd never planned on before.

To say I'd been surprised to discover it was Ford Cornell who'd accepted my custom art request was a shock, to say the least. I had mixed feelings about the man, since he didn't exactly come from a great family. Between his brother and the former sheriff, Curtis Tulley, who was Mrs. Cornell's cousin, I had to wonder if Ford didn't have some ulterior motive for what he'd done. But I couldn't discount what Isaac had said–that Ford had tried to intervene when Jimmy had gone after him. The fact that Ford was sporting those bruises also had me wondering if he was less tormentor like his brother and more victim.

Ford had still been in the office when Dallas and Nolan had come in from feeding the animals their evening meal, and things had gotten pretty tense pretty fast when I'd told them who Ford was. But Newt, who'd been clueless about the situation, had been so excited to show off his helmet that it'd given Dallas and Nolan a few moments to process Ford's presence and the bruises on his face. I knew next to nothing about Ford Cornell, other than he was a good five years younger than Jimmy and had ended up getting into some pretty serious trouble shortly after high school. My plan was to ask Alex if he knew anything about what exactly it was that Ford had done and if he thought the young man was a bad seed like his brother.

After Newt had finished telling Nolan and Dallas about his present and shown them the microphone that Ford had added on his own and which I thought had been a pretty clever idea, Ford had sputtered an awkward apology and promised he'd never bother any of us again before he'd hightailed it out of the office. Nolan had actually tried to stop him, but Ford had been out the door too fast to even try to get any more information out of him.

I hadn't had time to talk to Dallas about any of it, but I definitely wanted to see how he was feeling about the whole thing when I saw him the following day, since I'd been the one who'd brought a member of the Cornell family back into his life, inadvertent as it was. I also wanted to talk to Alex about Jimmy's attack on Isaac, though I knew I'd need to talk to Isaac first, because I still had no idea what he and Newt were running from and as much as I liked Alex, I couldn't risk exposing Isaac in any way.

Not until he told me the truth.

But the truth was a long ways off. At this point, I couldn't even get Isaac to spend more than a few minutes in my company unless I was in the midst of a raging panic attack.

I should have been more embarrassed by the fact that Isaac had seen me yet again at my weakest, but in truth, it didn't bother me. I'd accepted that even though I saw myself as weak for not being able to just get over my fears, Isaac didn't see me that way.

He wouldn't.

He just wasn't that kind of person.

I sighed as Snotrod stretched again before getting up and snuggling right up against my neck. "Okay, Snot, I'm calling it," I said. "Bedtime."

It wasn't particularly late, but it'd been a long day and for once, I wasn't interested in losing myself in half a bottle of alcohol.

I was in the process of getting to my feet when the doorbell rang.

With Snotrod tucked against my chest, I went to answer it, assuming it was Alex stopping by to say hi. But when I saw who it was on the other side of the door, my breath caught in my throat.

"I come bearing gifts," Isaac said loudly.

A little too loudly.

He held up what looked like a litter box, a bag of cat food, a plastic bag that had something in it I couldn't see, and a plush cat bed with a mouse embroidered on the cushion.

"Newt and I went to the pet store after you left. You really should have let us drive you," he said.

Since I'd figured I'd pushed the limits of my mental health with the one car ride already that day, I'd ended up declining the offer to be driven home, choosing instead to just tuck Snotrod into my coat and hold him against my chest for the walk home. The kitten had slept the entire time.

"And don't worry, I didn't pay for any of this myself. I used the money you kept telling Dallas to give me, so you paid for it. Not that I would have minded paying for it after what you did for Newt, which was awesome by the way. He wanted to sleep with the helmet on. I finally told Dallas and Nolan just to let him. They're babysitting. Did I say that already? Because they are. Just until I get back. Dallas let me borrow his truck again and told me how to get here. I mean, I know it could have waited until tomorrow but I wanted Snotrod to be comfortable—"

"Isaac," I cut in, since I knew he was so nervous he'd ramble on all night if I let him.

"Yeah?"

"Do you want to come in?"

Isaac looked past me as if expecting the house to be some kind of doomsday lair. He finally nodded. "Yeah, okay, thanks."

Butterflies danced in my belly as he moved past me. He smelled really good and he'd swapped out the pink sweater for a teal and black top and was wearing purple skinny jeans instead of his typical black ones. There wasn't enough light in the hallway to see his makeup, but

I could see the tempting sheen on his lips, which told me he was wearing the gloss. I just didn't know if it was the regular clear gloss or the one with the tint.

I really didn't care.

Isaac stood nervously just inside the door. "Should I take my boots off?" he asked. "I should take them off," he amended before I could respond. "Not because I'm staying but because I don't want to mess up your floors."

His show of nerves was both disheartening and exciting at the same time. On the one hand, he'd had this same level of verbal diarrhea when he'd been upset with me that day in the small animal building. On the other hand, I had to believe he'd made the trip out here to do more than just deliver cat supplies.

"Where do you want this stuff?" he asked as he lifted the items in his hands. He'd toed off his boots. I smiled at the sight of his rainbow-colored socks.

"I've got him set up in here," I said as I motioned to the bathroom at the end of the hall. Isaac nodded and hurried past me. He talked incessantly about each item as he set them up in the sizeable bathroom, but I was so busy ogling his slim frame as he moved and his delectable ass every time he bent over, I barely heard anything he said.

Was he wearing the feminine underwear?

Did I want him to be?

The answer to that was an unequivocal yes.

But I'd be just as happy if he were wearing boring boxer briefs, white granny panties, or going commando. I doubted I'd have a problem with anything this man was wearing because he was just so very beautiful.

And he was all that without even trying.

"Dallas said Snotrod will probably want to sleep with you, but you should still put out this bed for him just in case. It's not new–it's from the sanctuary. It's the one he and his brothers and sisters slept on, so it'll smell like them," Isaac explained as he approached me. I was standing in the doorway of the bathroom, so there was no way for him to get out. When he realized that, his nerves kicked up even more and he suddenly thrust the bed at me and took Snot from my hands and cuddled him to his chest.

"Where are you going to put it?" he asked as he motioned to the bed. He pressed a kiss to the top of Snot's head and all I could think was, *damn lucky little cat*.

I didn't respond, choosing instead to turn and head to the living room, knowing Isaac would follow. I put the cat bed between my sleeping bag and the fireplace. There was a grate around the fireplace, so I didn't have to worry about Snot inadvertently wandering too close to the flames. I turned and saw Isaac looking around the dimly lit room. It was a massive space that was overdone with rich blue, white, and gold colors. My parents had had both lavish and garish taste.

Isaac moved closer to me as he explored, and when he reached me he just nodded. "It's nice," he finally said.

"No, it isn't," I responded.

I couldn't stop looking at him. With the added light from the fireplace, I could see that he was wearing a different color eyeshadow altogether this time. It was some kind of blend between brown and pink. His lashes looked impossibly long and thick and he had just a little bit of eyeliner on. His lips looked plump and wet but not overly pink, which meant he was wearing his regular gloss, not the tinted stuff.

Isaac's fingers were almost frantically petting Snotrod, but his touch was gentle and the kitten had once again fallen asleep.

"What you did for Newt was incredible," Isaac whispered. "I can't thank you enough. He doesn't get a lot of presents."

"What about you?"

"Oh, um, I try to give him presents whenever I can. Especially on his birthday and—"

"No," I interjected. "I mean, when was the last time anyone got you something?"

He seemed surprised by the question. "Well, Newt always makes me something. He's such a great kid."

"He's got a great brother," I said. I hadn't missed the fact that whenever the conversation steered toward him, Isaac always tried to turn it away again. I wondered what drove the behavior.

The air grew thick between us as electricity danced around our bodies. The longer the silence, the more agitated Isaac became. He finally said, "I should go."

But he didn't move.

And that was when I knew why he'd really come here.

My heart skittered through my chest in excitement. Admittedly, I was also nervous about what was to come. But I could tell that even though Isaac was clearly the more experienced one, whatever was happening between us was new for him, because he seemed frozen in place.

Which meant if I wanted this to happen, I needed to make the first move.

I reached for Snot and carefully eased him out of Isaac's hands. I was glad when Isaac didn't move as I put the sleeping kitten in his little bed. By the time I got back to Isaac, he'd wrapped his arms around himself like he was cold. But with the roaring fireplace, I knew it was a self-soothing gesture.

"Why did you really come here, Isaac?" I asked as I ran the tips of my fingers up and down one of his arms. He was still wearing his coat, so I couldn't actually feel his body, but he still shivered beneath my touch just the same.

God, what would it be like when we were skin on skin?

Isaac shook his head but didn't respond right away. When I bent to kiss him, he suddenly blurted, "I'm wearing them!"

I pulled back so I could watch him as he spoke because I was finding that what Isaac said and what he meant when he was upset were two very different things.

"I told myself not to because it would just freak you out and I don't want that because I really want this, but you already know about them and I'm not going to pretend that you don't, so if that's what you want..." His words dropped off and he looked at the floor. The insecurity was painful to watch, but I needed to let him get whatever shit was driving this out or it would stay between us.

And I really, really didn't want anything between us tonight.

"I could… I could just…" Isaac hesitated, then stepped forward. His hand slowly reached out to touch the waistband of my jeans. He pulled them away from my body just the tiniest bit, then looked up at me with uncertain eyes and whispered, "I could just make it good for you."

Even though my body reacted almost violently to the sensation of him running his long, slim fingers down the front of my jeans, I felt sick inside as I understood what he was trying to tell me.

He was willing to get on his knees for me.

Like he had with that piece of shit Tomlinson.

Like he had with all the other men who'd seen him as a body to use in exchange for a few bucks.

Well, fuck that shit. I sent a silent apology to Newt for the swear word, then stepped closer to Isaac and used my fingers to tip his chin farther up so there was no way he could *not* look at me.

"Show me," I whispered.

Isaac let out a little whimper and started to drop to his knees, but I clasped him around the back of the neck to keep him from moving. I dropped my mouth to his ear and used my free hand to skim his hip before releasing just the button on his pants. "Show me," I repeated.

Isaac gasped as he finally got my meaning. He stayed stiff in my hold for a couple of beats, then seemed to melt into my touch as a huge breath whooshed out of his lungs. Then he was nodding.

I stepped back to put some space between us. Isaac's shaky fingers immediately went to his pants.

"No," I said firmly. When he looked at me, I took a few more steps back until I felt the chair just behind me. "Slowly," I ordered as I lowered myself into it.

Isaac was frozen in place for several long moments. I didn't breathe until he carefully shrugged off his coat. It fell to his feet, but all he did was kick it away. I noticed the shirt he was wearing had an oversized opening at the throat, so it exposed one of his shoulders. My mouth watered at the sight of his pale, creamy skin.

Isaac's hand ran down the middle of his shirt as if to smooth it out. He fingered the hem and I could see he was still having doubts. But I remained silent as I held his gaze.

I saw the exact moment something shifted, and I wanted to thank God for whatever had finally made him realize that between the two of us, he was the one with all the power. Instead of just removing his shirt, Isaac's palm flattened on the lower part of it and he slid his hand up, dragging the hem of the shirt up in the process and exposing the flatness of his belly.

Isaac used his free hand to hold the hem up enough so he could run his fingers over his stomach. Despite how graceful his moves were, my gut was telling me they weren't practiced.

He wasn't acting cool enough for that. There was still that little bit of a tremor in his fingers and a speck of doubt sprinkled in with the desire I saw in his eyes.

My cock pressed painfully against my zipper every time Isaac touched himself. When he finally snagged the end of the shirt and dragged it up and off his body, I was leaning forward in my chair so I could see him even better.

He was beautifully built.

Yes, he was slim and small, but toned too. His skin was smooth and flawless. There was a single tattoo on his left forearm, but I couldn't tell what it was of. I made a mental note to explore it later.

Isaac let his hands roam over his own body and I couldn't help but wonder if he was imagining that they were my hands. As badly as I wanted to get up and go to him, I was completely entranced by this new version of Isaac. Somewhere along the way, he'd gotten lost in the act of undressing. He was still very much with me, but the doubt and insecurity were gone. He wasn't being overly confident like it was all some big act. It was more like he was exploring his body in a new way... like he'd been freed to do so.

I was mesmerized as Isaac took his time removing his socks. Then his fingers were at his zipper. He tensed up just a little and I wasn't surprised, considering what he was about to reveal to me. His moves slowed as he got his zipper down and then put his hands at the waistband. But when he stilled and dropped his eyes, I knew I was on the verge of losing him.

"Isaac," I whispered.

I wasn't sure if it was my tone or what, but he lifted his eyes and I saw how pained they were. And I knew this was more than just him showing me something so many would consider taboo.

It was him showing me *him*.

"Show me, baby," I said so softly I wasn't even sure he heard me.

When he kept his eyes on me as he lowered his pants, I did the same. I actually didn't even move my eyes until he silently gave me permission by trailing his fingers slowly from his chin, along the column of his throat and down his body. My eyes connected with the underwear only when his own fingers did.

And the sight took my breath away.

He was gorgeous.

There was just no other way to describe him.

Yes, I could see the outline of his semi-erect cock through the lacy fabric, but that wasn't where my eyes stayed. No, they moved when his fingers did.

Over the spot where the narrow strip of material rode high on his hip near his waist, then lower over the slightly scalloped edge of the fabric along his groin and across the bulge of his dick that was pressing against the material. Isaac didn't move as I drank in the sight of him, but he seemed satisfied when I lifted what had to be wide eyes to his. My throat was too dry to make it possible for me to speak. I'd seen plenty of women in sexy lingerie, but none of them held a candle to Isaac and I didn't care why that was.

But it wasn't just the beauty of the fabric against his skin, it was what it did for him. The longer he stood before me, that confidence he'd been feeling before he'd lowered his pants returned, and that was when I knew that the underwear had been the root of that confidence.

My theory was confirmed after Isaac removed his pants

completely and then stepped closer to me until he was almost within touching distance.

Almost but not quite.

Isaac began running his hands all over his lower body and the fabric, like they were all one and the same. My dick was practically being strangled by my jeans, but I couldn't have moved even if I'd wanted to.

I was completely under his spell.

And then he turned around.

I whimpered.

Actually whimpered.

The line of his back on its own was a sight to behold, but to see how the dip of his waist flared just the tiniest bit into the curve of his hip stole my breath. And the underwear... Jesus Christ, the fabric rode high up his crease so that most of both beautiful cheeks were exposed. His skin was soft and smooth and tight.

"Fuck, Isaac," I breathed. I lifted my eyes to see him looking over his shoulder at me. His eyes were bright with some emotion I couldn't put my finger on.

Not satisfaction.

Not relief.

Not even pleasure.

Rightness.

The word somehow wasn't enough, but it fit the moment. I could see that whatever was happening between us, it felt right to him. That him sharing this part of himself with me was right.

For him.

For me too, but he wasn't doing this just to please me. He was doing it for himself as well.

I had my proof that I was right when he slowly turned around, closed what little distance remained between us, slid down onto my lap so he was straddling me and then whispered, "Thank you."

There was a host of emotion in those two little words and I felt every single one of them.

And it shook me to my core.

Isaac's arms went around my neck and then my arms were around his waist. He kissed me gently at first, then more deeply. I tried to restrict myself to just kissing him, but my hands refused to listen and began roaming all over his body and eventually ended up on his ass. I leaned back in the chair so I could watch what I was doing.

It was my turn to touch and feel and play.

And that's exactly what I told him.

CHAPTER SIXTEEN

ISAAC

My turn.

When Maddox had said those words, I'd thought he was talking about him getting undressed, but he quickly disabused me of the notion when I reached between us for the hem of his shirt. He grabbed my fingers and carefully eased my hand behind my back. Then he took my other hand and did the same.

"Leave them there," he growled.

I managed a nod because speech was pretty much impossible.

That's what happened when you were living out your fantasy.

When I'd made the decision to bring Maddox the cat supplies, I'd tried to fool myself into believing that was the real reason I was making the trek out to his house in the middle of the night. I'd even continued to sell myself on that particular story as I'd put on the sexy underwear and carefully applied my makeup. I'd spouted the lie so very easily to Dallas and Nolan when I'd asked them to keep an eye on an already sleeping Newt. Even when they'd mentioned they'd watch him for as long as needed, I hadn't allowed myself to believe any of what was currently happening was a possibility.

But the fact that I was sitting nearly naked on Maddox's lap, in women's panties no less, was proof that it was.

And the bulge I could feel pressing against my own hardening cock was the final evidence I'd been waiting for.

I'd thought I'd needed a label for what Maddox was, but gay, straight, or bi, I just didn't care anymore.

What he was, was mine.

At least for the moment.

And if I got my way, he'd be mine for as long as I could manage to keep me and Newt in Pelican Bay.

I expected Maddox to go for my ass, since one of his hands was resting right at the small of my back, just beneath my own hands. But when he reached up to close his big hand around both my wrists to make sure I couldn't move my arms, I nearly came right then and there. I could feel the pre-cum dripping from the head of my dick and dampening the delicate fabric of my underwear.

Maddox held me in that position for a moment as his eyes raked over my entire body, then his free hand, the injured one, settled on my throat and then ran all the way down the length of my chest. I automatically tipped my head back when he did the move again. The pads of his fingers felt rough against my skin and the bandage he was wearing added another level of sensation. Somewhere in the back of my mind, I knew I should remind him to be careful with his hand, but words were still something that were escaping me at the moment.

"Watch me," Maddox ordered when his hand came to rest on my belly. I obediently lowered my eyes to his. So many of the men I'd been with had enjoyed ordering me around and I'd always complied because that came with the job, but with Maddox, not only could I not deny him, I didn't want to. My body was his and not because he'd paid for it.

But because I wanted him to have it.

He'd earned every piece of me by *accepting* every piece of me. Sharing my secret with him had been one of the hardest moments in my life because it was the last thing I had left... my last line of defense against a world that was just sometimes too damn hard. He could have ridiculed me or made me take the underwear off in another room or just let me suck him off like I'd initially planned, but he'd understood what it had meant for me to give him this part of me.

Maddox waited until I dropped my eyes to his hand. He was still holding my own behind me so I had no control, though I knew if I told him to let me go, he would.

Maddox's finger trailed along the waistband of the underwear a few times, alternating between putting more pressure on the silky material, then my skin. He did the same to my hip, then finally moved his fingers lower to where the fabric met my groin. I couldn't help but moan when those rough pads dipped beneath the material and brushed over my skin. My cock was pretty much right there, but he didn't touch it and I was both disappointed and a little nervous about what that meant. He'd said he'd kissed a guy before, but I wasn't sure if he'd done more than that. And suddenly, the dreaded thought that I'd been trying to avoid ever since he'd kissed me the first time was back in my head.

I tried to force it away, but Maddox must have noticed something in my expression because his hand slipped from beneath the underwear and lifted to tip my chin up so I was forced to look him in the eye.

"What?" he asked. "Tell me what you're thinking."

I shook my head because it was too humiliating and because I was afraid of how he'd respond.

"Is it because I didn't touch you here?" he asked as he dropped his hand and brushed the backs of his fingers along my shaft. I cried out at how good it felt to have the silky material pressing against my sensitive flesh beneath the pressure of his hand. He was still holding my hands, so I couldn't even really move toward his hand to get him to do it again.

"Talk to me, Isaac," he demanded, then he did the move again.

I was panting when I blurted, "I'm not... I'm not a woman."

"I'm well aware of that," Maddox said, his voice completely serious. He straightened so our chests were touching. His lips gently brushed mine.

"No, I mean…"

What *did* I mean?

I shook my head because it was all just so pathetic, and I was mad at myself for ruining the moment. But Maddox didn't seem particularly fazed because he began nibbling along the edge of my jaw.

"You don't want to be a woman," Maddox murmured. "And you don't want me to pretend you are one."

Shame curled through me. "There's nothing wrong with people who want that," I whispered.

"No, there isn't. Even if you were transgender, Isaac, we'd still be having some kind of conversation about how we could be together."

"We would?" I asked in surprise.

He sighed and looked me straight in the eyes. "I don't want to make love to just your body, Isaac. I want to make love to *you*." His fingers stroked over my hair as his eyes seemed to search my face. "Tell me why you wear them," he said as he motioned with his eyes to the underwear.

I shook my head because I couldn't tell him *that*.

"Is it because they make you feel confident?"

I swallowed hard and nodded. "And beautiful," I admitted.

"You are beautiful in them, Isaac. What else?"

"Soft," I whispered. "I feel soft when I wear them."

"And you think that's wrong somehow?"

God, how had we ended up on this topic? I was sitting practically naked on the lap of the most gorgeous man I'd ever known and instead of him fucking me ten ways to Sunday, he was trying to dissect the jumble that was my brain.

"Why is it wrong?" Maddox pressed.

"Because I can't be soft," I admitted. "I… I have to be strong."

"So being soft means being weak?"

"No," I said softly.

Maddox was quiet for a moment and then said, "Being soft means being vulnerable."

I didn't answer him, but I didn't have to.

He knew he'd gotten it right.

Maddox's fingers began running up and down my side. The touch had my libido returning.

"Let's make a deal, okay?"

I nodded because what else could I do? Despite how embarrassed I was, I wanted him more than ever. I wanted to *be* with him more than ever.

In any way I could.

"When it's just you and me, you can be all the things you can't be when you're taking care of Newt or looking over your shoulder for whatever it is you're running from or when you're fighting battles you're not ready to let me fight with you. Sexy underwear or granny panties, doesn't matter."

I couldn't help but smile at the last part of his comment. "I'd turn you on in granny panties?" I asked.

Maddox smiled and kissed me. His mouth hovered against mine as he whispered, "Baby, you turn me on just by breathing." He kissed me again and kept kissing me until I was once again pliant in his hold. Not once during our talk had he released my hands and I found myself completely okay with that. I'd never liked when tricks got off on controlling me, especially using any kind of restraints, but this was so very different.

First off, it was Maddox who was doing it.

Second, *I* was the one getting off on it. Probably more than he was. Like the underwear, I felt free and open and powerful, even though I had no control. And that warmth was there in spades. Whenever I put the underwear on just for a few minutes, or even thought about it, I got a taste of that warmth that came with finally being allowed to be the real me, the complete me, even if it was just for such a short amount of time.

Unfortunately, that feeling never lasted.

With Maddox, I just knew that every time we came together like this, that warmth would be there.

It was like I could finally breathe.

I sighed as Maddox's mouth moved down my neck and over my chest. His sinful tongue toyed with my nipples as his hand once again began exploring the fabric of my underwear. He didn't touch my cock, but I got the idea the move was deliberate.

As he slid his free hand to my ass, Maddox's teeth closed gently over a muscle in my neck. He soothed the spot with a tongue, then kept repeating the move as his fingers trailed along the edge of the panties. While one finger rode along the material, the other was touching my skin and the contrast was making me crazy. Maddox's fingers disappeared between my crease and caressed me there for a moment before sliding down my ass and in between my legs. I automatically lifted off him enough so he could move his hand closer to my balls.

Which he didn't.

"Maddox," I said breathlessly as I dropped my head to his shoulder. "Please."

"Please what, baby? Touch you?"

I nodded against him. His mouth was next to my ear as he said, "Here?" and then he was caressing one of the globes of my ass. I managed something that was between a nod and a shake.

"Here?" he asked again, this time touching my other cheek.

I didn't respond this time, mostly because I was too breathless to do anything but wait to see where he would touch me next.

I opened my mouth against his shoulder and moaned when his finger disappeared into my crack and began rubbing my opening through the panties. I began grinding my dick against his and then I searched out the corded muscles of his neck as he toyed with me.

"So good, Maddox. *So* good," I breathed.

Without the use of my hands, I couldn't grab him the way I wanted. He turned his head and kissed me even as he continued to rub my entrance. When his finger pushed past the silk and touched my hole I jumped and moaned into his mouth. "Oh, God," I cried when he began rubbing me harder and harder. I kept trying to push back on him, but every time I did, he moved his finger away.

I was completely at his mercy.

And I loved it.

I tugged my hands and said, "Maddox, please, I have to touch you." The man was still fully dressed and I wanted to be skin on skin. To my surprise, Maddox released my hands. I instantly went for his shirt. As I dragged it off him, my eyes caught on the dog tags he was wearing and I made a mental note to explore them later. Maddox lifted his arms only long enough to get the shirt free, then his palms were on me again, smoothing over my body as if he was trying to memorize every line, every curve. His mouth was there too.

Kissing.

Teasing.

Tasting.

I grabbed Maddox by the ears to force his head up so I could kiss him.

Really kiss him.

He groaned as I fed on his mouth, but when his hand moved beneath the waistband of my underwear and slid over my ass, I let out a string of curses that would have made Newt go wide-eyed for sure.

And just like that, everything was moving too slow. I tore at Maddox's belt and practically ripped it out of the loops and flung it aside. He continued to rub my ass with both hands, the underwear pushed down to the backs of my upper thighs, but still covering my cock in the front. I was harder than I'd ever been and I could only imagine the wet spot I'd see on the panties if I looked down.

But I wasn't interested in my own cock.

I clung to Maddox's mouth as I frantically tried to get his jeans open. Maddox pulled his mouth from mine and nuzzled my ear. "Breathe, baby. I'm not going anywhere."

His lips moved so tenderly against my skin that it helped calm me and my fingers began to work in my favor as I opened his pants. I couldn't see what I was doing because I'd tipped my head back so Maddox could lick the column of my throat. But I could absolutely feel what I was doing. Maddox's underwear definitely wasn't loose enough to be boxers, but that didn't stop me from reaching my hand into them and fishing out his cock. I swallowed hard when I felt his girth. It was both intimidating and enthralling. For all the men I'd been with, there'd been few I'd actually found pleasure with. Even Trey, who I'd started to think of in my head as my boyfriend, hadn't been a satisfying lover.

Probably because he'd never been willing to cut out the games and the kink long enough to consider my needs.

I forced thoughts of Trey out of my head. I knew in my heart Maddox would never treat me like Trey had. Trey had been good with saying the right things, but his actions had never matched his words.

Maddox was the whole package. He meant what he said and he said what he meant. And he backed it up with his body. Even now as I stroked him, he was focused on my pleasure. He'd stopped rubbing my hole, but he was palming my ass as he kissed me.

"Wanna taste you," I breathed against his lips.

Maddox nodded but said, "Show me how to touch you first."

I was about to tell him he was touching me just fine when he moved one of his hands to my front and pulled my underwear down, freeing my pained cock in the process. His hand was hot and rough as he encircled my shaft. I put my hand down to cover his and said, "Tighter."

He tightened his grip.

"Do to me what you do to yourself," I murmured. "I guarantee I'll like it."

Maddox's intense eyes held mine as he firmly began to stroke me–so he could read me.

So he could know he was bringing me pleasure.

Oh God, I could fall for this man so easily.

I was scared I was already halfway there.

I forced myself not to focus on any of that and instead began pumping Maddox's dick to match the pace he'd set on mine. He was a quick study because it didn't take him long to figure out the things I liked that drove me higher. Like that I loved it when he flicked his thumb over the ridge just below the head of my dick. I was learning too. Maddox was extremely sensitive at the base of his shaft and he moaned every time I twisted my wrist just a little on the upstroke.

Within minutes, we'd moved so our bodies were flush and our hands were brushing each other's as we pleasured one another.

"Fuck, need you," Maddox bit out, then he kissed me hard and deep. I let out a little squeak when he suddenly grabbed my ass and held me to him as he climbed to his feet. I wrapped my legs around him and they were still that way when he lowered me to the sleeping bag he'd laid out by the fire.

"Is this okay?" he asked when he was lying full on top of me. I didn't know if he was asking about the position or the sleeping bag or what, but my answer was the same either way.

"It's perfect."

Somehow between us, we managed to get Maddox's pants and underwear off. I'd been forced to unwrap my legs for that to happen, but I was kind of glad I had because once my hands found his ass, I never wanted to move them. He was so much bigger than me but there wasn't an extra ounce of flesh on him. Even his ass was incredibly tight. The difference in our height meant our cocks weren't quite rubbing against one another as he ground his body against mine, but I was definitely okay with that because I got to feel the perfection of his muscled abs sliding over my weeping dick. My underwear was still wrapped around my lower body, but Maddox quickly took care of that with a sweep of his hand.

Finally, *finally*, we were skin to skin. The cool metal of his dog tags felt good sliding against my body as he kissed me all over my face, neck, and chest.

"Tell me how to get you ready," Maddox said.

I shook my head. "Nuh-uh, you promised me a taste first, remember?"

To my surprise, Maddox grinned.

And it was so damn adorable.

"So I did," he said. For someone who was about to have a man's mouth on his junk, the guy didn't seem the least bit worried. But I wasn't about to point that out to him.

"How do you want me?" he asked.

I had so many answers to that question, but there was one thing I really wanted when his cock was stuffed down my throat.

To see his eyes.

Not so I could know if he was disgusted, because I knew he wouldn't be. No, I wanted to see his pleasure and know I was the reason for it. So with that in mind, I put my hand on his chest and gave him a tiny push. "On your back, soldier."

CHAPTER SEVENTEEN

MADDOX

I expected his mouth to be like those of the women who'd given me blow jobs in the past, but it wasn't.

It was so very different.

In the best way.

He knew exactly how to tease, when to apply suction, when to ease up, which parts of my cock were just a little more sensitive than the others... it was like I was a finely tuned instrument and he knew exactly how to play me. But when he sucked me to the back of his throat, I lost all semblance of control and thrust my hips up. I immediately felt bad when Isaac gagged, but when I tried to drop my hips, his arms slid beneath my ass and he was sucking even more of me down. He swallowed around me and I shouted in response to the pleasurable sensation that raced up and down my spine and landed in my balls. I reached down to run my fingers through his hair and held onto him as I fucked his mouth. I used my elbow to lever myself up so I could watch him.

My heart flip-flopped crazily in my chest when his pretty blue eyes connected with mine. His gorgeous lips were stretched so wide it had to be uncomfortable, but his eyes were bright with so much pleasure that I didn't try to pull out again. In fact, I slowed my strokes down so I could both watch and feel him working me. When I was on the verge of blowing, I forced him to release me and dragged him up my body. His weight felt so good on me and I couldn't stop marveling over how soft and smooth his skin was. I suspected he waxed and while it should have seemed like a strange thing for a man, I loved it.

Even if I did wonder if part of the reason he did it was because of his occupation.

The reminder of what he'd been forced to do–and after having seen him at the center working and seemingly enjoying a regular job, I really did believe the prostitution had been something he hadn't really had a choice in–didn't belong between us, so I pushed it from my mind and just held him as we kissed. He slid his body up mine enough so that my cock was notched against his ass. I began bumping my hips up against his crease.

"I can't wait," Isaac ground out, then he was climbing off me. I was mesmerized by his body, hard cock included, as he rushed to grab his wallet from his discarded pants. He returned with a condom and packet of lube in hand and climbed on top of me. He kissed me and repeated, "I can't wait."

I was in the same boat, so I rubbed my hands up and down his supple thighs. "Then don't," I said. "Take what you need, Isaac. Anything, it's yours."

"God, Maddox, you gotta stop saying stuff like that," he whispered hoarsely as he leaned down to kiss me gently. I didn't really understand the statement but didn't have time to dwell on it because he straightened and moved back enough so he could slide the condom down my length. Then he was tearing at the packet of lube. A little of it was smeared all over my sheathed cock, but the rest he put on two fingers. I felt my mouth go dry as he reached behind himself.

I'd never had anal sex with a woman, so I didn't really know what to expect, but I knew at least some preparation with fingers was required. On the one hand, I was wound way too tight to learn exactly what it was Isaac needed when it came to being made ready, but on the other hand, I didn't want to miss out on anything, either. So I sat up and wrapped an arm around Isaac's waist to support him, then reached down to his ass with my other hand. Since my right hand was the injured one, I was using my left to explore what Isaac was doing to himself, so it was a little more awkward. Isaac was panting as he held my gaze. My fingers bumped up against his where they were sliding in and out of his body.

Two fingers.

Two slicked-up fingers.

More blood rushed to my cock at the knowledge that Isaac was fucking himself. I waited until he slid his fingers out and then gathered what lube remained on the slim digits and began pressing one finger into him. Isaac's hands landed on my shoulders as he threw his head back. His body didn't fight my entry too much, so I was knuckle-deep in no time. He was so tight and hot I could have come then and there. I could feel the slickness of the lube inside of him as I explored his inner muscles.

"Another," Isaac gasped right before he kissed me. I instinctively knew the second finger wouldn't be accepted as easily, so I took my time working it into his body. Isaac was the one who began rocking his hips so he could fuck my fingers. I could feel his cock between us. He was leaking enough fluid from the tip that it was smearing across my own lubed cock.

"Need all of you," Isaac said, then he was pushing me back down, forcing me to remove my fingers. He shifted forward and grabbed my cock. I let out a violent curse when the head of my dick was quickly swallowed into the tightest, hottest grip I'd ever known. I grabbed Isaac by the hips to help steady him as he carefully eased his body farther and farther down onto me. It seemed to take forever before his body completely swallowed my length, but he didn't give himself time to adjust. His face was contorted into a mix of pleasure and pain as he lifted up and slowly slid back down again. It was all I could do not to pound up into him. Instead, I focused on how lost in his own body he was as he rode me. His hands skimmed over his neck and chest and down to his belly. I was reminded of when he'd been removing his clothes. He was in that same state where he seemed completely free. There was no coyness or faked moans and groans like some of the women I'd been with had been prone to do. No, every sound, every move was about pulling every ounce of pleasure out of his body that he could.

And in turn, he was doing the same to me.

As he began to alternate between rocking against me and bouncing on my dick, my orgasm began to wind its way along all my nerve endings. The sounds Isaac made just drove me higher. Grunts, whimpers, mewling sounds–they all combined to create a picture of a man who'd never been more at home in his skin as he was in that very moment.

"Maddox," Isaac cried as he opened his eyes and looked down at me. His pupils were blown and I knew he was close.

Really close.

I wanted to watch him go, but I wanted to follow right after him too.

I quickly sat up and wrapped my arm around his waist and flipped him so he was lying beneath me. I managed to keep my cock buried deep inside of him. Isaac's arms wound around my neck as I pushed into him.

Hard.

Deep.

Really deep.

He cried out and wrapped his legs around me. I could feel his weeping dick between our bodies, but I didn't know if he needed me to jerk him off. From the way he was hanging onto me and jamming his hips up to meet my brutal thrusts as I pounded into his lithe body, my guess was that he didn't need the extra contact. He took the choice away from me when he suddenly dropped his legs and grabbed my ass with his hands and dug his blunt fingernails into my skin.

"Harder, Maddox! Harder!"

I braced my arms next to his head and proceeded to pummel him with one thrust after another. Our bodies writhed against one another in a rhythm that I never would have thought we could sustain. But it went on and on as our orgasms seemed to build and build. I knew enough that there was a spot inside of him that was guaranteed to send him over if I could just find it. So I began canting my hips and twisting them as I slammed into him. I knew I'd hit the mother lode when he screamed and bit down on my shoulder.

So I nailed him there again.

And again.

My name tore from his lips as he came. Hot liquid hit my belly and chest and mixed with the sweat that was coating both our bodies in a fine sheen. My dog tags were dragging back and forth over Isaac's chest as I kept fucking into him. It almost looked like he was wearing them.

The idea of him wearing something that important to me did funny things to me that I couldn't explain. It was like I claimed ownership over him in that moment merely because of that one image.

And that was when my body gave up the fight. Isaac's inner muscles were still flexing around my cock as he continued to ride out the orgasm. So between that and the idea of him wearing my dog tags, I was a goner. I dropped my mouth to his neck as I came. His hands had slid up my wet back at some point and he clung to me as I came deep inside of him. I kept pushing into him as I emptied into the condom, but he didn't protest the rough thrusts. If anything, he held onto me tighter with every single one. It wasn't until I completely collapsed on top of him that his fingers began toying with the back of my neck as I kept my face buried against the spot where his shoulder met his collarbone. Aftershocks tore through my body for what seemed like ages, but he never once tried to get me to pull out of him. I knew I was too heavy for him, but when I tried to lift some of my weight off him he whispered in my ear, "No, stay."

So I did.

It was a long time before I pulled out of him. I reluctantly got up to get rid of the condom and grab a washcloth for both of us. He was still sprawled out on top of my sleeping bag when I returned to the living room. I cleaned him and myself up and tossed the washcloth aside, then got us both into the sleeping bag. He snuggled up against my chest. There were a lot of things I wanted to say, but there was one thing in particular that had been haunting me from the night I'd met him and Newt.

"Isaac?" I said softly.

"Yeah?"

"What's your middle name?"

"What?" Isaac asked in surprise. His fingers were playing with my dog tags while I was running mine up and down his spine.

"The night we met, you and Newt were talking about how people couldn't hurt you with their words if they didn't know your middle names... because if they didn't care about you enough to know your middle names, it didn't count when they tried to hurt you."

Isaac was quiet for a moment and I fully expected him not to tell me. It was a big ask. But I didn't know how else to make it clear that what we'd just done hadn't just been about sex. That he meant more to me than that. I was afraid if I told him how I really felt, he'd run for sure. I could feel it there, just beneath the surface–the inherent fear of trusting someone else besides himself and his brother, of caring about someone else, of letting them care for him. But maybe if I could tell him without telling him...

He didn't speak for a long time and I figured that was his way of telling me we weren't there yet, but when he whispered, "Aaron," I felt the tension in my chest ease.

"Aaron," I repeated. It occurred to me then that I didn't know his last name, but I wasn't going to push on that one.

Not yet.

"Can I ask Newt to tell me his?" I said softly.

He nodded against my chest.

We were both quiet for a really long time and I actually thought he'd fallen asleep when he all of a sudden whispered, "Don't hurt him, Maddox. Please."

He'd said him, but I knew what he'd really meant to say.

Us.

Don't hurt *us.*

"I won't, baby. Not ever."

Isaac didn't respond other than to close his fingers around my dog tags and curl into my chest. But that in itself was response enough.

CHAPTER EIGHTEEN

ISAAC

"Will you tell me what happened that day?" I asked as I fingered Maddox's dog tags. After two weeks of spending nearly every night in Maddox's arms, the little stamped pieces of metal were becoming more of a familiar comfort rather than an object of fascination. I'd already memorized his blood type and religion along with the ten-digit number that Maddox had said was some kind of Department of Defense identifier. I'd asked him about his religion one night after making love and that was when he'd told me about his parents. I'd been surprised to learn his father had been a one-time televangelist and his mother had been a B movie actress. He'd spoken fondly of his early years with his parents, but something had clearly changed in the later years and while he hadn't said it out loud, I had a feeling that the alcohol that had played a role in the accident that had ultimately killed his parents and maimed his brother had also been the reason for his childhood turning into something negative rather than positive.

Despite the fact that Maddox and I were at a point where we seemed to know one another's bodies better than we knew our own, we'd been careful about the subjects we'd discussed.

Well, *I'd* been careful.

Maddox had been more open.

He'd tried several times to broach the topic of my past, but I'd adamantly remained silent on the matter, so he hadn't pushed. But I knew it was just a matter of time. For my part, I was trying to pretend Newt and I would be leaving any day now, but here we were, two weeks later, and I still couldn't find my way out of Maddox's arms... or bed.

But nights at his house were all we had, because I refused to engage with him at the sanctuary while we were working.

Not because I was embarrassed or worried about people finding out about us, but because I thought that by pretending that Maddox and I only had a physical relationship, it would make it that much easier just to pack up the car and leave.

So far, I hadn't even managed to pack our bags, let alone the car. If anything, Newt and I were settling more comfortably into Dallas and Nolan's house. To make matters worse, Maddox had recently started accepting the invitations Dallas had extended for him to join us for dinner. Which meant he was spending more and more time not only in my company, but Newt's as well.

And Newt was loving every moment of it.

Maddox had become his new hero and since all of the kittens and most of the cats had been adopted, Newt was following Maddox around the sanctuary during the day and helping him out with different projects, which Maddox didn't seem to mind even a little bit. Newt had confided in me only a few nights ago that he'd told Maddox his middle name, then he'd asked me if Maddox was going to be his dad or his brother.

So clearly, Maddox and I weren't fooling anyone in terms of our relationship.

But try as I might, I couldn't stay away from him.

And so little of it actually had to do with the sex.

It was phenomenal sex, of course, but it was the moments afterwards that I craved.

Like now.

"It was a roadside bomb outside Mosul. We'd just finished our last mission and I was driving," Maddox began. "The guys were celebrating, but still watchful, you know?" he said.

I nodded.

Maddox's fingers were alternating between stroking over my hip and petting Snotrod, who was tucked up between us. The little kitten was thriving under Maddox's care and he actually brought him with him every day when he came to the sanctuary. The baby usually spent the day either in my lap as I worked on the computer or with Nolan as he was dealing with the center's endless paperwork. For whatever reason, the kitten seemed to love the time it spent tucked inside of Maddox's parka as he walked to and from his house. Dallas had driven Maddox home a couple of times when the weather had gotten particularly dicey, but he still struggled with being in a car.

"I knew in my gut something was off, but I didn't listen to it. I chose to listen to my commanding officer instead. The bomb took out the Humvee behind us, killing everyone instantly. The Humvee I was in flipped. Those who weren't killed in the blast instantly fought the few insurgents who ambushed us. They managed to kill them all, but most of my guys were wounded in the process. I missed all of it because the blast knocked me out cold. When I came to, I was lying on one side of the vehicle. One of my men's bodies was on top of me—I think he'd been trying to drag me to safety. I managed to get to my knees. All I could hear was this pounding. Over and over. It was so loud, but that's all it was. Just pounding…"

Maddox's voice broke and I quickly covered his hand with mine where it was resting on Snot's back. I linked our fingers and began rubbing my thumb back and forth over his skin.

"I started checking the bodies to see if any of my guys were alive. I managed to call for help, but they were all dead. But the pounding wouldn't stop. I finally managed to crawl around to the other side of the overturned Humvee and that's when I saw him." Maddox's eyes sheened over with tears. "He was fucking pinned beneath the thing."

"Who?" I asked gently.

"Jett." Maddox shook his head. "He'd been using the butt of his machine gun to pound on the roof of the Humvee. I thought the pounding was in my head. Maybe if I hadn't ignored it for those couple of minutes..."

"You know a couple of minutes wouldn't have changed the outcome," I said. I didn't even know what that outcome was, but there was no doubt in my mind that from what he'd told me, he'd been completely helpless in that situation and if the other man had been pinned beneath a vehicle that had to easily weigh five thousand pounds, if not more, there was little he could have done, no matter the circumstances.

"Did you lose him?" I asked.

He shook his head. "We got him evac'd. But the doctors couldn't save his legs below the knee. When he woke up and found out, he just..." Maddox shook his head. "It was like he died in that moment, I guess."

"What happened to him?"

"I was discharged after about a week in the hospital. I went to see him and found out he'd... he'd tried to slit his wrists. He'd been transferred to a psych ward and restrained and heavily medicated because he was threatening to do it again. I lost it. I tore the place up until I myself had to be restrained and sedated. It was my fault—"

"It wasn't," I tried to interject, but Maddox just shook his head again.

"It was. I should have followed my gut. I should have—"

I kissed him to silence him. "It's not your fault, Maddox," I said softly.

He didn't respond, but he didn't try to push me away either. When he'd calmed down, I asked, "Where's Jett now?"

"Oklahoma. He lives with his grandmother. I haven't seen him since we got back to the states a few months ago. I call and text, but he doesn't want to talk to me. I'm... I'm worried he's going to try it again when his grandmother passes. He's all she has, so I think that's keeping him from hurting himself for now, but he's refusing to do physical therapy or get fitted for prosthetics and he's not getting any kind of counseling. As far as he's concerned, his life is over. I want to go check on him, but I'm afraid it'll just make things worse."

I didn't really know what to say, so I just held him and murmured, "I'm sorry, Maddox."

It was a good while later when I looked at my phone and saw it was well after two in the morning. Maddox had fallen asleep with his face tucked against my neck. Snotrod was curled up under his chin. I moved my hand up to ease the kitten off my shoulder and onto the sleeping bag as I began to get up, but Maddox's big arm tightened on my waist.

"Don't go," he said softly.

"I have to," I said.

This was the worst part of the night for me. That moment where I had to get up to leave and Maddox held onto me just a little tighter. But he'd never actually asked me not to go before.

"Dallas and Nolan know where you are," Maddox said as he levered up on his elbow after moving Snot to a position just above our heads but still on the sleeping bag.

"But Newt doesn't," I said.

"He's not the real reason, is he?" Maddox asked.

I turned my eyes away because the man was just too perceptive. He was absolutely right. I was using Newt as an excuse. Not once had my brother asked where I was going each night, which meant he hadn't woken up and looked for me.

"Stay, Isaac," Maddox murmured as he ran his fingers along my temple. "We can sleep in and go to work together."

"Unless you plan to carry me on your back the whole way there and back, that's not going to happen," I said with a laugh.

But Maddox didn't smile. Instead he remained fiercely serious as he said, "You could drive me."

This time my laugh was harsh. "You don't play fair, do you?" I would have given anything to be the one to keep helping him deal with his fear of cars. And the fact that he was willing to get in a car if it meant he could spend a little more time with me just broke my damn heart.

"Just stay, baby," he said as he kissed my shoulder. "We'll figure it all out, I promise."

I wanted to say yes, I really did. I could practically taste the word in my mouth. It would be so easy to utter that one little syllable and then curl into his chest. Maybe even make love again.

But I knew what I'd be saying yes to.

And I couldn't.

I just couldn't.

My gut was telling me that Maddox had gotten to the point that he could get past the fact that I'd broken the law in a big way–way bigger than even stealing that violin for Trey–which meant he'd do anything in his power to protect me.

And I couldn't risk that.

Or him.

He was finally reconnecting with his brother and building a new life for himself. No chance in hell was I going to put that in jeopardy.

It took every ounce of willpower I had to turn away from him and get to my feet. I quickly got dressed. I could feel Maddox's eyes on me the whole time, but he didn't try to stop me. I pulled on my plain pink cotton briefs and turned to face him. It was funny how I'd gone to hating not being able to wear my pretty underwear every day, or even just the nights when I came to see him. But I only had the one pair because I both hadn't wanted to risk anyone finding me with an array of women's underwear, and because I hadn't wanted to spend the money on the higher quality brands that made me feel the most confident in my own skin. As it was, I had to wash the one pair by hand in the sink and hide them so they wouldn't inadvertently be discovered. Maddox might not have an issue with me wearing them, but that didn't mean I wanted anyone else, including Newt, finding them.

But God, how I hated the feel of plain cotton on my skin now.

I began dragging my jeans on as Maddox watched me. He was clearly disappointed, but I was glad when he didn't say anything. It wasn't until I had my shirt back on that he got up and, completely naked, walked to me. My mouth went dry at the sight of his miles and miles of tanned skin and muscles. He wrapped an arm around me and kissed me passionately. I was just about to say fuck it and shuck all my clothes off again when he pulled back. His eyes held mine for a moment like he was trying to figure something out, then he softly kissed me and said, "Just so you know, Isaac, when it comes to you, I have absolutely no intention of playing fair."

CHAPTER NINETEEN

MADDOX

I was just in the process of confirming the door to Gentry's building was locked when my phone beeped. I recognized the tone I used for texts from Dallas, so I immediately pulled the phone from my pocket. Although Dallas's appointment with his surgeon had gone well and he'd gotten the go-ahead to start using his voice again, it was difficult to understand him, and it would likely take dozens of visits and a lot of work with his speech therapist before he got to a point that the majority of people would be able to understand what he was saying. Things like *yes* and *no* were easy enough to understand, but anything with more than a couple of syllables was still tough. I knew his raspy, barely there voice *also* embarrassed my brother, but he was still making an effort. I, for one, thought his voice was one of the best things I'd ever heard.

I looked down at the notification and saw enough that I didn't need to open the whole text.

Get up here. Isaac is leaving.

I barely held onto the phone as I sprinted up the path toward Dallas and Nolan's house. Nolan and Newt had already played their songs for Gentry while Dallas and Isaac had taken Snotrod with them up to the house to get started on dinner. I'd volunteered to do one last walk-through to make sure all the buildings and enclosures were secure before joining the family for dinner. I had no clue what possibly could have gone wrong between then and now because Isaac had seemed fine when he'd said his goodbyes to me. No, we hadn't been allowed to touch because he was still sticking to his ridiculous rule while we were anywhere but my house, but I knew Dallas and Nolan suspected Isaac and I were seeing each other. The fact that Dallas was texting me about Isaac was proof that he knew there was something between us.

I'd sensed Isaac's need to run. I'd *been* sensing it for a while. It seemed the closer he and I got, the more tense he grew when I pressed him for even the smallest of details about himself. In truth, I'd expected him to be long gone already, and every day I arrived at the sanctuary to find him working in the office or the barn and every night when I heard his tires crunching over the snow as he arrived at my house, I sent a little thank you heavenward that I hadn't already lost him.

I might know it was an inevitable thing, but I'd be damned if I was going to stand by and just let it happen without a fight.

I heard yelling long before I reached the house.

From what I could tell, it was Newt and Isaac going at each other.

"No, I don't wanna leave!" Newt shouted as I reached the final path that led to the house. It was dark out but the floodlight attached to the house was on, so I had a clear view of things. Isaac was carrying a flailing Newt down the small sidewalk that led to the driveway where Isaac's car was already running. The back seat looked packed full of stuff, just like it had when he'd arrived.

"Isaac, no!" Newt screamed.

"Newt, we have to go!" Isaac responded, his voice thick with tears.

"Mad!" Newt yelled when he saw me, then he was kicking and squirming in Isaac's arms until Isaac was forced to put him down. The little boy came barreling at me and I scooped him up when he reached me. His face was wet. "Tell him we can't go!" Newt cried in my ear.

Isaac was frozen in place and I could see he was silently crying himself.

"It's okay, Newt, just calm down," I said as I rubbed my hand over his back. I made my way to Isaac, who was pale as a ghost.

"Isaac, talk to me," I said as I stopped a few feet from him. I wanted to reach out and touch him, but he looked like he could completely shatter at any moment. He was caught right on that line that said he was about to have a complete meltdown, but I didn't know what that would look like. He could do something foolish like get in the car and drive away and possibly end up in a wreck, or he could sink to his knees right there in the snow and go completely silent.

I just didn't know.

And I didn't want to find out.

His wet eyes met mine and I could tell he'd been crying for at least a little while because his eye makeup was starting to streak just a bit. "They want to buy him Christmas presents," he whispered.

"Who? Nolan and Dallas?" I asked as I spied both men standing near the bottom of the steps leading into the house. Nolan was holding onto Loki to keep the wolf hybrid from following Isaac. Dallas had his arm around Nolan.

"We're not your family," Isaac whispered. "We can't be."

"Yes, we can!" Newt cried. "Lightning and Mater and Sally and all the others became a family!" The little boy turned to look at Isaac but refused to release his hold on me. "You said I could tell them my middle name 'cause they care!" he accused. "I don't wanna leave!"

Every word Newt lobbed at his brother seemed to tear something open in Isaac and it was scaring me how quiet he'd gone.

"Newt, buddy, will you go into the house with Nolan and Dallas and Loki so I can talk to Isaac?"

"You gotta make him let us stay, Mad!" Newt said. He spit into his hand and held it out. "Please, Mad, we gotta spit on it."

My heart broke for the little boy and I wrapped my arms around him. "I promise I'll spit on it just as soon as I talk to Isaac, okay?" As badly as I wanted to tell Newt I'd make it so he could stay, I wouldn't do that to Isaac.

Newt let out a sob and nodded against my neck. When I put him down, he turned and ran past Isaac to Nolan and Dallas and Loki. The wide berth he gave Isaac seemed to be the final straw for Isaac because he sank to his ass in the snow and tucked his legs up against his body. His long arms wrapped around his legs and he began rocking back and forth. I was moving toward him when Newt suddenly came barreling back at Isaac and threw his arms around him from behind. The little boy began sobbing again and that seemed to snap Isaac out of his daze because he lifted an arm and curled it around Newt. Newt was in Isaac's lap by the time I reached them.

Isaac didn't say anything as he rocked Newt back and forth over and over. I put my arms around them both and was glad when Dallas came up behind the pair and draped his coat over Isaac's shoulders. I had to guess Isaac's coat was in his car. Fortunately, Newt had his parka on. As eager as I was to get both of them off the ground, I wanted them to have this moment. When Newt had calmed, I ran my fingers over his hair and said, "Newt, can you go inside with Dallas and Nolan? Isaac will be along in a little bit."

Newt nodded against Isaac's body. He held onto Isaac for another second and whispered, "I love you, Isaac."

"I love you too, buddy."

"Are you mad at me?" the little boy asked.

Isaac let out a choked sob and shook his head. "No, Newt, I'm not mad. I'm not leaving you, okay? Not ever. Do you hear me?"

Newt nodded and then got up and took Dallas's proffered hand. Dallas's eyes met mine and I saw him motion toward the garage. I knew what he was saying and nodded my thanks. I reached down to help Isaac to his feet. I wrapped my hand around his and led him toward the garage. The apartment Sawyer had been using while he'd taken care of the sanctuary during Dallas's recovery from surgery was above the garage. He'd only recently moved out, so I knew Isaac and I would have the privacy we needed.

I led him up the stairs to the apartment, which fortunately wasn't locked. The heat was turned off so I led Isaac to the little gas fireplace and got it going, then pulled a blanket off the back of the couch. I sat us both down in front of the fire and wrapped the blanket around us as I put Isaac between my legs so he was facing the fire and his back was to my front. For the longest time I just held him, because I knew he'd talk when he was ready. There was no doubt in my mind the incident with Newt had fundamentally changed something for Isaac. The fact that he was still so quiet meant he was trying to process things. It was a testament to how deeply troubled he was, not only by whatever had sparked the whole encounter, but Newt's and his own reaction to it.

"We shouldn't have stayed," he finally said. "Newt and I were doing fine till now."

I wasn't sure I agreed with that statement, but I didn't even get a chance to say anything because Isaac said, "He didn't really know what he was missing, you know?" He shivered against me, so I rubbed my hands up and down his arms.

"Family was just something he saw on TV. He didn't actually know what it was."

"You guys don't have a family?" I asked.

He shook his head. "It was us and our mom, mostly. She was young when she got pregnant with me—only eighteen. It was just her and her father and he'd had all these plans for her to go to college but when she got pregnant with me, he kicked her out."

"What about your father?" I asked.

"I don't know who he is. He was never in the picture."

"What did your mom do?"

"What most young single mothers do, I guess. Worked odd jobs and stuff. But when I was old enough to take care of myself, she went back to college. She was super smart. Like genius-level smart. She actually got accepted into MIT before she got pregnant with me. She reapplied when I was ten and was accepted. Full ride. When she graduated, she started teaching there."

"What did she teach?"

"Math. She loved numbers."

He said it with a certain wistfulness that had me asking, "Did you and she get along?"

He was quiet for a moment before nodding and saying, "I didn't know there was anything wrong with her, you know? She was just my mom. I thought it was normal when she'd wake me up in the middle of the night and start writing formulas out on the wall while trying to explain all these principles to me. She loved to play loud music and dance at all hours of the night, and sometimes she'd keep me home from school just so we could drive to the beach and go swimming or look for seashells or whatever. Every day was a new adventure. And it made sense to me that after all that, she'd need to sleep, sometimes for days on end."

"She was bipolar," I offered.

Isaac nodded. "It wasn't until I was maybe fourteen that I realized she was sick. She'd go on and off her meds all the time. She didn't even tell me she was pregnant until she was almost six months along. I don't think she even realized it herself."

"How old were you?"

"Seventeen."

"And Newt's father? Was he around?"

I felt Isaac stiffen. "Gary. He'd been living with us for almost two years at that point." Isaac hesitated for a moment and then said, "She had really bad luck with guys. She usually found them when she was manic, so she wasn't exactly picking winners, if you know what I mean."

"Did they hurt her?"

"Some did," Isaac admitted.

"And you?"

He shrugged. "A few. They'd knock me around here and there, but they usually weren't around long enough to do any real damage."

My heart dropped out at his words. He was just so nonchalant about it…

"What about Gary?"

"Gary was different. Smarter. More manipulative. My mom made good money at MIT and despite all her crazy behavior, she didn't spend a lot of it. So I guess he saw her as a cash cow."

"And you?" I asked. "How did Gary treat you?"

Isaac drew in a deep breath. "Gary was not my biggest fan. Not of the clothes or the makeup or the hair or pretty much anything I did.

But he treated my mother decently, even though he was using her. He made sure she stayed on her meds. He was just doing it because he wanted to make sure the money kept coming in, but me... he didn't mince words with me."

"He hurt you?"

Isaac nodded.

"Your mother didn't notice?" I asked as I tried to quell the growing rage inside of me.

"My mother was a genius, but she wasn't good at picking up on social cues. She couldn't really read other people and sometimes even when you told her something, she didn't necessarily understand it. Numbers were the only things that really made sense to her. But she did her best."

I didn't exactly agree with him, but I didn't want to argue the point since he was finally talking to me.

"Sometimes I think Gary got her pregnant on purpose," Isaac said. "As a way to bind her to him. It wasn't that he wanted Newt, though. He just wanted something that would guarantee his supply of beer was never-ending and there was always cash in his wallet. I heard him and my mom arguing about the pregnancy when my mom finally did learn she was pregnant–it wasn't until a doctor at an ER told her after she slipped and twisted her ankle. Like I said, she was really smart, but some of the most basic things about life stumped her."

Isaac shifted so he was facing sideways. He snuggled into my arms and rested his head on my chest. "I'd always planned to leave as soon as I graduated high school. I loved my mom, but I couldn't keep sharing a roof with Gary. Not if I wanted to be myself."

I took that to mean that to avoid Gary's fists, Isaac had been forced to forgo the things that made him so uniquely him. I couldn't even imagine what that had been like for him.

"Once Newt came along, I knew I wasn't going anywhere. Gary wasn't interested in taking care of him and my mom was too busy with work or dealing with the occasional manic-depressive episode."

"So you raised him," I said.

Isaac nodded. "It wasn't a hardship," he added. "I fell in love with him the first time I held him." There was a long pause and then Isaac said, "I did everything for him. Fed him, changed him, played with him, took care of him when he was sick, made sure he got regular checkups. All of it. After our mom died when Newt was two, I thought for sure Gary would take off and just leave me and Newt alone."

"He didn't?"

"No," Isaac said with a shake of his head. "I tried to take Newt and leave one day, but he told me *I* could go, but Newt wasn't going anywhere. I didn't understand why at first."

"But you found out?"

"Yeah, he wanted Newt because my mom left behind a life insurance policy naming Newt as the primary beneficiary. She and Gary were never married. Since my mom understood numbers, she calculated that Newt would need the majority of the money, since he was only two. I was over eighteen, so she saw that as me being able to earn my own income. Gary too. So Newt pretty much got all the money. I told you, my mom understood numbers."

My heart broke for him as I considered what that must have felt like. To know his mother had made plans for Newt to be financially taken care of, but not him.

"I'm sorry, Isaac."

He shook his head. "It wasn't about me," he said firmly. "Since Newt was underage, he needed a guardian. Gary was his father, so he got custody. But the money was in a trust, so he could only use a set amount every month and it was meant to care for Newt. There was even a trustee overseeing the account. It was a lot of money. Almost two million dollars. So the monthly amount was pretty sizeable."

"I'm assuming very little, if any, of the money went to caring for Newt?" I said.

"Enough just to satisfy the trustee. The trustee would occasionally make random visits to check on Newt's welfare."

"So Gary wouldn't let you just leave and take Newt with you," I guessed. Before Isaac even confirmed my statement with a nod, I knew what all this was leading up to. "You kidnapped him, didn't you?"

Isaac didn't respond at first. When he did, it was just with a simple nod.

"Why?"

When he didn't answer, I turned his face so he was forced to look at me. "Why did you take him, Isaac? I know it had to be for a good reason."

He tugged free of my hold and pressed his head back against my chest. Clearly, it was easier for him to talk to me without actually looking at me.

"Gary never hurt Newt like he did me, so I thought it was safe to leave him alone with Gary every once in a while at night. I was taking college courses to try to get a degree in computers. One night I got a call that Newt was in the ER. When I got there, he was being treated for a head injury. Gary told the doctor Newt had fallen down the stairs."

"You didn't believe him," I said.

"No, I didn't. The injury was on the side of Newt's head by his temple." Isaac pointed to his own head. "I got the same kind of injury when Gary slammed my head into a wall when I was sixteen. Before I could tell anyone, Gary threatened me... said if I said anything, he'd make it so I never saw Newt again. He had custody and I was just a twenty-year-old unemployed college student. I knew they'd believe him over me."

"What happened with Newt?"

"He was treated for a week in the hospital and made a complete recovery. Then the seizures started. The doctor said it could either be from the head injury or he could just be epileptic. There was no way to be sure. Gary didn't really care, as long as it didn't affect the money from the trust. About a month after he got out of the hospital, I finally got Newt to admit Gary had hurt him, and it hadn't been the first time. I took him that night."

"Where did you go?" I asked.

"All over. Any big city I thought we could get lost in. We'd only stay for a month or two at the most. Miami, Dallas, Los Angeles. Then came San Francisco."

"That's where you met Nolan's ex."

Isaac nodded. "When I took Newt, I tried to get a regular job, but the money just wasn't there. Newt's anti-seizure medicine was really expensive because I had to buy it illegally… I knew Gary or the cops would find us if I ever tried to get him a prescription for it. I just couldn't make ends meet. One of the guys I approached about selling me the medication told me I could make a lot of money escorting… said I had 'the right look.'"

Isaac dragged in a deep breath. "When I told him there was no way I could do that, he offered me the drugs for free if I let him fuck me. Those pills cost almost three hundred dollars for just a month's supply. So I did it. I hated it, but it was so damn easy. When we moved to the next city and our car suddenly died and I was running out of the medication, I thought about what he'd said. So I started looking at online ads, then I placed my own. I made more letting one guy fuck me than I'd made in a week washing dishes. There was no looking back after that."

"And Trey?" I asked.

"I met Trey through an ad. He was different, or so I thought. A lot of my tricks would sweet-talk me, but I learned pretty quickly it was all part of the act. But Trey was better at it. He'd bring me flowers and presents whenever we'd meet. He'd show an interest in my personal life, and it didn't take me long to fall for his bullshit that he wanted to take care of me. He was into some really kinky shit, which I hated, but he was so sweet afterwards that in my mind, he became two different people. Trey, the trick and Trey, my boyfriend. And I was willing to do a lot for Trey, my boyfriend."

"The violin," I said.

Another nod from Isaac. "I fell for his story that Nolan had stolen the Stradivarius from him hook, line and sinker. He painted Nolan out to be just the most horrible person and that Trey was the victim. And the amount of money he offered me to go to Nolan's apartment and take the violin was more than I'd make in a week turning tricks. Between the money and wanting to help my boyfriend out, I did it."

"And when you realized he'd lied to you, you set him up in order to clear Nolan of the crime."

"I shouldn't have fallen for his act," Isaac said. "I was smarter than that."

I doubted smarts had anything to do with it. I figured Isaac had been desperate for love and acceptance, not to mention he must have been unbearably lonely and scared. He would have been looking for anyone he thought he could trust with his secret who would help him get his life back and keep Newt safe.

"Do you know for a fact Gary is still looking for you?" I asked.

"I googled Newt's and my name. It says I kidnapped him and the cops are looking for us. I don't think it ever made the national news or anything, though. I tried to teach Newt that we needed to use fake names, but he usually forgot and then he'd do what he did when he got here—he'd point out what my real name was. I was sure the whole Isaac Newton thing would sink us, but most people don't seem to notice it. Luckily, unless you know our last name, it takes a while to get past the real Isaac Newton search engine results to the stories about me and Newt."

"Isaac Newton," I said with a smile as I realized I'd never even noticed it myself. "Like the scientist."

"Mom was a fan," Isaac murmured.

I let my fingers stroke over his hair and up and down the back of his neck. He was still tense and his skin remained a bit chilled, but the fact that he was leaning into me so heavily gave me hope that maybe he was past the worst of his near-breakdown.

"What's in New York?" I asked.

Isaac shook his head. "Nothing. Just another place to get lost in for a while."

"Don't get lost again, Isaac," I blurted. "Please, let me help you."

"I'm quicksand, Maddox. I'll just take you down with me."

I sighed and wrapped my arms around his upper body, then dropped my head on top of his. "I have money, Isaac. Lots of it. More than I could spend in a lifetime. I'll get you the best lawyers... a whole damn team of them, if that's what it takes."

"It's not just me I'd be risking if I exposed myself, Maddox. I can't let Newt go back to him."

"If the lawyers can't help us, we'll run. We'll go somewhere the law can't touch us."

Isaac turned so he was facing me. He sat cross-legged so he could be close to me.

"Running is so damn hard, Maddox. It's not something I would wish even on my worst enemy." When I went to open my mouth, Isaac gently covered it with his hand. "Are you really willing to risk giving up your home, your *brother*, to spend the rest of your life looking over your shoulder? Do you really want to worry that every second of every day you could do or say something, slip up somehow, and put not only me at risk, but Newt too?"

Did I *want* to do what he was saying? Of course not. Just like I didn't want him and Newt to have to do it. But *would* I do it?

Hell fucking yes, I would. But I could see in his eyes he wouldn't accept my words as truth. If I'd learned anything about Isaac in these past few weeks, it was that he was unfailingly stubborn.

Isaac's hand went from my mouth to the side of my neck as he clasped me there. His finger brushed over the shell of my ear.

"Stay through Christmas," I said. "Let Newt have that. Let yourself have that."

Isaac began shaking his head, but I leaned down to brush my mouth over his. "He's going to hurt whether you leave now or in a couple of weeks," I said. "At least give him some more good memories to hang onto."

I didn't mention the fact that I had my own ideas about how I'd be spending the next couple of weeks.

For every second I wasn't with Isaac, I'd be talking to every lawyer under the sun to see what could be done. The reality was that Isaac had broken the law. Kidnapping was a felony and if he'd never reported what Gary had done to him when he was growing up, proving the fucker had been abusing Newt would be tough. Even if

Newt remembered some or all of the details of Gary's abuse, he'd only been a toddler at the time, so his credibility would most certainly be called into question. And since Isaac had had him for the better part of a year, any prosecutor worth his salt would imply that Isaac had used that time to brainwash Newt against his biological father.

But that didn't mean I was throwing in the towel. And I'd meant what I'd said–if I couldn't get Isaac out of trouble, I'd follow him to the ends of the earth. It would hurt like hell to have to leave my brother just as we'd started to rebuild our relationship, but losing Isaac would kill me.

There was no doubt in my mind that I was in love with him. Head over heels, crazy stupid in love. But I knew if I told him that, he'd completely panic. My only hope was that the fact that he was trying to protect me by warning me off coming with him and Newt meant he felt the same, or close to it.

Isaac was quiet for a long time.

Too quiet.

I pulled back to see that his eyes were on my chest. He eased my dog tags out of my shirt and began running his thumb over the indentations that spelled out my name. He often did the same thing after we'd made love.

"Promise me you'll let me go when the time comes."

When I didn't respond, he gave the dog tags just the slightest tug. "Promise me, Maddox. Promise me or Newt and I are gone today."

I felt the air whoosh out of my lungs at that because I knew he wasn't going to budge on that particular threat. I could hear it in his voice.

"You don't play fair, Isaac," I said softly.

"I learned from the best," he said as he looked up at me. I was trapped in the hold of his blue eyes.

"I promise when you're ready to leave, I won't try to stop you."

But I'd sure as hell go with him. Even if I had to take enough drugs to knock out a horse, I *would* be in that car with him when it sputtered down Dallas's driveway for the last time.

I could tell he wasn't happy with my half-assed promise, but he didn't call me on it. Instead, he got up on his knees and wrapped his arms around my shoulders and buried his face in the crook of my neck. "No matter what, don't let Gary get Newt. Please, Maddox, if you care about me at all—"

"He's never touching you or Newt ever again, Isaac. That I *can* promise you," I vowed.

I held Isaac for a few minutes, then stood and helped him to his feet. We walked hand in hand toward the house, stopping only long enough to turn off Isaac's car, which was still running. When we entered the house, we found Newt sitting between Dallas and Nolan on the couch. At some point, one of them had taken Newt's helmet off him and the little boy had his head pressed against Dallas's side while his hand was holding Nolan's. Loki was lying next to Dallas, his head on his lap, his nose pressed against Newt's other hand and Snotrod curled against the wolf hybrid's side. There was a cartoon playing on the television, but none of them seemed to be watching it.

As soon as we walked into the house, Newt jumped off the couch and came tearing up to Isaac. Isaac dropped to his knees and wrapped his arms around Newt. I couldn't hear what he whispered into the crying boy's ear, but whatever it was, it had Newt nodding vigorously and wiping at his eyes. Isaac leaned back and helped Newt clean off his face. Dallas and Nolan had both gotten up in the meantime and took turns hugging Isaac.

Then they were hugging me.

"Okay, how about dinner?" Nolan announced. "It's Newt's favorite, liver and onions!"

Newt's expression was a mix of horror and shock as he stared at Nolan. "Gotcha!" Nolan said, and then Dallas was snatching Newt off his feet to carry him over his shoulder to the kitchen. The little boy led out a raucous laugh as he struggled in my brother's hold. Isaac went to join them, but I snagged his hand before he could get away from me and pulled him back. I brushed a soft kiss over his mouth and was glad when he didn't protest, despite the presence of others.

Neither of us said anything as we held each other's gazes, but we said enough without the need for words. He took my hand in his and said, "Help me set the table?"

I nodded.

It ended up being one of the best family dinners we'd had to date.

Now I just needed to figure out how to make sure it wouldn't be the last one.

CHAPTER TWENTY

ISAAC

I couldn't contain the warm feeling when I saw Maddox's front door open before I'd even pulled my car around in the circular driveway. It wasn't unusual for him to be waiting for me, since he'd been doing it every night since the first night we'd slept together. What was unusual was that I still hadn't gotten used to it or the warm, gooey feeling that would go through me when I'd see his big frame standing in the doorway.

God, I really was a goner at this point.

I had no doubt I was in love with Maddox. I wasn't sure exactly when it had happened, but I was tired of trying to pass it off as some other emotion. Even though our time together was winding down at a frighteningly fast rate, I wouldn't cheapen what I felt for him or pretend it would go away as soon as Newt and I left Pelican Bay.

I hadn't told Newt we were leaving after Christmas, both because I hadn't wanted a repeat of that terrible night when he'd fought me, and because I wasn't ready to admit it myself. It was the day before Christmas Eve, so we had a couple of days left at the most. I wanted Newt to have every ounce of fun he could before I had to tell him it was time for us to go. This time when I told him, I'd go about it a different way rather than panicking and just packing up our stuff like I'd done after Nolan and Dallas had asked me if it was okay for them to buy Newt some Christmas presents. There was no doubt in my mind that Newt would be devastated, but I'd taken on the role of parent a long time ago and that meant doing what was best for Newt, even if he hated me for it.

Pain lanced through me as I remembered the way he'd walked around me after Maddox had told him to wait in the house with Dallas and Nolan. Newt had looked at me like I was no better than Gary. In my mind I knew he didn't really see me that way, but it'd hurt just the same. I'd ended up staying at Dallas and Nolan's house that night because Newt had still been terrified that I was mad at him by the time his bedtime had come around. I'd slept in the bed with him with Loki on one side of him and me on the other, but when I'd woken up in the middle of the night, I'd been stunned to find Maddox asleep in the big armchair in the room. Snotrod had been curled up in the crook of his arm. It was the first time he and I had spent the night together, and while it hadn't exactly been the way I'd pictured it, waking up the next morning to his kisses had been heaven. Newt had already gone down to help make breakfast, so it had just been me and Maddox. He'd been lying in the bed with me, his big body curled around mine. He hadn't spoken other than to wish me a good morning, but it had just been so very perfect.

The only way it could have been better was if I knew we'd wake up like that every morning for the rest of our lives.

It was scary to know that someone else now knew my secret, but I also knew Maddox would take it to the grave with him. He hadn't pressed me in the past two weeks to try to find some alternative solution to Newt and me leaving, but I suspected that was because he was planning to come with us. He hadn't said as much, but I hadn't missed how he'd only promised not to stop me when I left.

I didn't know what to do with that.

On the one hand, the answer was obvious—Newt and I would need to leave after Maddox had left to go home for the evening so he couldn't stop us.

But on the other hand, a little part of me wanted to let him make that kind of sacrifice for me, even if it was wrong.

I was just so very tired of fighting this thing by myself.

And the idea of being away from Maddox for even more than a few hours…

I shook my head as I stared out my windshield.

I needed to stop thinking about it. It already consumed all my thoughts when I was by myself. I could barely sleep as it was. Food was something I had to force into my system and more often than not, I was looking over my shoulder.

Not for Gary.

But for Maddox.

Because I just couldn't bear to be away from him.

Yeah, I was so far gone it wasn't even the least bit funny.

I climbed out of the car and hurried up the walkway to the front door. Maddox didn't say anything as he held out his hand to me. As soon as he had me in the hallway, he shut the door and then he was pushing me against it, his mouth devouring mine. I shrugged my jacket off and went for the button on his jeans, but he was lifting me before I could even protest.

Not that I would have.

I wrapped my legs around him and kept kissing him as he walked to the living room. We both laughed when he kept bumping into things like the wall and some of the little side tables that littered the front hallway.

"God, I just can't get enough of this," I muttered against his mouth.

I'd finally stopped trying to hide my relationship with Maddox at the sanctuary, especially in front of Dallas and Nolan, since they'd clearly known for a while that he and I were seeing each other. I hadn't been so sure about whether or not Sawyer had known, but Maddox had taken care of that by grabbing me and kissing me while I'd been in the middle of talking to Sawyer in the office. The attractive vet had been asking if Newt and I wanted to come check out the hobby farm he'd only recently purchased. I hadn't considered the invitation a date of any kind, and I hadn't gotten the impression Sawyer had intended it as such, but Maddox had heard something he hadn't liked and had proceeded to kiss me silly in front of the man. I probably should have been pissed that he'd been like a wild animal marking its territory, but secretly I'd been really turned on. Who knew I went for the possessive, growly type? Sawyer, completely unfazed, had waited until Maddox had finished, then proceeded to invite him to come along with me and Newt to see the place. To my surprise, Maddox had accepted. It'd meant a tense car ride, but that was something else that had changed in the past couple of weeks.

Although Maddox was still walking to work every morning, he was letting Dallas drive him home each evening. I couldn't help but wonder if he was trying to challenge himself in the hopes he'd be able to cope with his fear better when it came time for me and Newt to leave. I had mixed feelings about that, because while I really wanted Maddox to start to heal from the trauma of it all, I didn't want to be encouraging something for the wrong reasons.

It was just another thing I was trying really hard not to think about so I wouldn't be forced to make any kind of decisions about anything.

Maddox carried me into the living room. I expected him to take me right to his sleeping bag, but he stopped and let me slide down his body until I was forced to stand on my own. I was about to protest when he pulled his mouth from mine and whispered, "Turn around, baby."

I gasped when I took in the room. The fireplace was going as usual, but instead of a sleeping bag in front of the blazing fire, there was now a mattress there. A Christmas tree decorated with what seemed like hundreds of tiny bright white lights stood in the corner. There were more lights strung up along the windows overlooking the back yard, and pillar candles were set up on just about every piece of furniture, making the room glow. Dozens of brightly wrapped presents were beneath the tree.

"What did you do?" I asked in disbelief.

Maddox took my hand and led me to the mattress. "Sit there," he said, as he pointed to the middle of it. I did as he said and watched as he went to the Christmas tree and grabbed half a dozen packages and carried them to the bed. He put them between us and said, "Merry Christmas, Isaac," then leaned in to kiss me. He maneuvered himself so he was sitting with his legs on either side of me with the packages between us.

"What is this?" I asked as he handed me one of the presents. My throat felt tight as humiliation swamped my system. "You got me presents?" I whispered. "Oh my God."

I began to cry. Although we hadn't talked about getting something for each other, I'd just assumed Christmas would be about Newt. "I didn't get you anything," I said in horror. I looked up at him. "I'm sorry, I've never—"

He cut me off with a toe-curling, mind-numbing kiss.

"Isaac, sweetheart," he said after he pulled his mouth free of mine. "You have no idea what you've given me. Even if I could find the words, it would take me until next Christmas to make you understand what it's meant to me that you…" He shook his head, then kissed me again. He picked up the package I'd ended up dropping on the bed and said, "Open it."

My fingers shook as I ripped into the present, and I couldn't stop sniffling as I tried to hold back my tears. Trey had gotten me gifts, but they'd always been generic things like flowers and candy and the occasional sex toy that had been more for him than me. He'd never given me anything that was *me*.

Beneath the wrapping paper was a plain white box. I carefully took the top off and felt my heart seize in my chest. There, nestled in the softest of tissue paper, were pale pink panties that looked like they were made of pure silk. There were a few small flowers carefully stitched along the waistband. They were exquisite.

I covered my mouth with my hand as I tried to stem my emotions.

"Are they okay?" Maddox asked, his voice thick with tension, and I realized it was because all I could do was stare at the box. I managed a nod.

"They're so beautiful." I carefully took them out of the box and turned them around. The silk felt like water between my fingers and I instinctively knew he'd spent a lot of money on them. In addition to the pink ones there were another half dozen of the same style but in an array of colors.

"Open the rest," Maddox said.

I did as he said and felt my heart swell painfully in my chest with every box I opened. There were lacy teal boy shorts that rode high in the back, a barely there string bikini in soft yellow, and a racy set of black panties that looked normal from the front but had thin strips running horizontally across the backside. I just knew those strips would hug my ass so deliciously.

The final box was a little bigger than the first few. In it was what looked like a normal set of white lace panties, similar to what I already owned, but when I turned them over, there was a large opening running right down the middle of the back side.

I nearly choked as I realized what it was for.

So the wearer could easily be fucked while still wearing the beautiful panties. My eyes lifted to Maddox. He was watching me hungrily and my dick instantly responded. "There's more," he said as he nodded at the box. I looked down and carefully pulled a layer of tissue paper away and saw a pair of silk stockings that were completely sheer except for a wide band of lace at the top that matched the lace of the panties.

"I wasn't sure if you liked wearing something like that," Maddox began nervously. "But it was part of the set so I figured why not and if you didn't like them you could just get rid of them—"

I lunged forward and threw my arms around him. He caught me as I kissed him. "I love them," I said. "Thank you."

"I got you other things too," Maddox quickly added. "Some clothes and some gift cards. Some makeup from the brands you already use, but I can return any of it you don't like and we can pick out something different. I figured you could open all that stuff at Dallas and Nolan's tomorrow but that you should open this stuff here."

His verbal diarrhea was so cute I wanted to cry.

"I can't believe you did this."

"Newt helped." Maddox blushed and quickly added, "Not with the underwear of course, but some of the other stuff. He definitely has better fashion sense than I do."

I laughed at that.

Maddox nuzzled my neck. "Try something on," he said as he motioned toward the packages between us.

Oh, I had every intention of trying them all on. And I was going to enjoy every second of it.

So was Maddox.

I kissed him and then leaned back and looked over my selection. I started with the first ones he'd given me. I slowly took my time getting undressed and then sliding the scrap of silk up my legs. Between the luxurious material and the way Maddox was hungrily watching me, I felt like the most powerful person in the world. I let my hands run indulgently over the material and reveled in the way Maddox watched my hands move.

Out of the corner of my eye, I could see my reflection in the large windows that overlooked the back yard, so between Maddox and the mirror-like windows, I could tell what a sensual picture I made.

I'd never *felt* more beautiful in all my life.

It was like that with each pair of underwear.

When I got to the final pair that came with the stockings, I took my time running the sheer material up my legs. I loved the contrast between the silk and the lace band that hugged my upper thighs where the stockings came to rest about halfway up. The combination of the sexy panties and the stockings made me feel like a million bucks. I moved closer to the window so I could see myself.

I couldn't stop touching the fabric.

I saw Maddox come up behind me in the reflection. He kept moving forward until I was practically pressed against the glass. I put my hands out to steady myself and let out a rough sigh when Maddox ran his fingers over the front of the panties, then the back. He paid particular attention to the opening that exposed my crease. The material was snug around my body, hugging my hard cock. But there was enough give that it wasn't uncomfortable. Maddox let his fingers slide over the stockings as he crowded me against the window with his big body. He nuzzled my neck and whispered, "So beautiful, Isaac. So fucking beautiful." Then he was kissing me. His hands roamed all over my chest, back, and sides and within minutes, I was writhing against him.

"Fuck me, Maddox," I practically demanded.

He growled in my ear and then pushed me forward so the cool glass was pressed against my bare chest. I heard the telltale sign of his zipper being drawn down, then foil tearing. Some lube was swiped over my hole a moment later and I smiled at the fact that Maddox had probably started carrying condoms and lube packets in his wallet. It'd likely only been a recent thing after I'd searched him out in the electrical room of one of the animal buildings at the sanctuary a few days earlier. I'd been particularly horny and Newt had been napping, so I'd taken advantage of the privacy to hunt my man down. Unfortunately, neither of us had had condoms, so we'd ended up blowing each other and then Maddox had taken us both in hand and gotten us off at the same time. For someone who'd never had his mouth on a man's junk, Maddox was a quick study. His lack of inhibition when it came to sex was so freeing for me.

I groaned when it was Maddox's cock I felt at my entrance a moment later, rather than his fingers. His thick cock breached me just as his hands closed over my hips. I let out a harsh cry of satisfaction as he split me open. He took his time filling me, but when I felt his jeans rub up against my ass, he grabbed my hair and forced my head back. "Look at us," he practically snarled. I looked up and gasped at our reflection. Him fully clothed and looking larger than life behind me. Me, my face alight with pleasure and my body splayed out for him, the gorgeous white panties and stockings framing my body so beautifully. My cock was hard enough that the tip was peeking out from the waistband of the panties, but then Maddox's hand was there, forcing my dick back down beneath the material. He palmed my cock as he began fucking in and out of me and I knew what his plan was.

He wanted me to come in the panties.

With one hand wrapped around my hip and the other working my cock, I knew I wouldn't last long. Maddox's shaft pulsed inside of me as he fucked me hard and fast. His clothes scraped over my exposed skin while the stockings and underwear added a level of softness that made my throat hurt.

I couldn't stem the tears as I realized the depth of what this man had given me by just letting me be me. And not even with just the damn underwear.

With everything.

"It's okay, Isaac," Maddox whispered as he leaned over my back and wrapped an arm around my chest. His strokes were still hard and deep, but they slowed just a little bit, dragging the pleasure out until my whole body felt like it was one raw, exposed nerve. "You're so perfect, my love. So beautiful."

I let out a harsh sob at his words and reached one arm behind me.

Because as he'd spoken those words, I'd seen his eyes in the window and I knew in my heart why he'd called me that particular endearment. I was afraid to believe it, but he wasn't even trying to hide it.

I wanted to say the words back, but they got stuck in my throat. I turned my head to kiss him and hoped he could *feel* the things I couldn't say. Nothing between us was resolved, but in that moment, they didn't exist.

It was just him and me.

And he loved me.

Me.

I clung to him with one arm and kept the hand of my other against the glass to support my body as he increased his thrusts. His fingers rubbed up and down my shaft. The material of the lace panties tempered the normally rough pads of his fingers but exposed me to a whole other kind of sensation.

Maddox began fucking me harder as he changed the angle of his hips. He nailed my prostate and I gasped at the white-hot pleasure that singed my every nerve ending. My whole body shook with the need to come. Between Maddox's hand on my cock and his dick shuttling in and out of me, I couldn't move. His free hand moved from my waist up to cover my hand on the glass. When he linked our fingers and bit down gently on my shoulder, I was a goner. The orgasm ripped through me, threatening to send me to my knees. I locked them so I could stay upright. Warmth surrounded my cock as cum filled the panties. Maddox fucked me through the orgasm for a few more seconds, then roared my name in my ear as he came. His fingers dug into mine on the window and I managed to look up to see him covering my body with his. Him fully dressed, me in nothing but the panties and the stockings. It was so incredibly beautiful.

I watched him long enough to see his face contort into a mask of pure pleasure as he came deep inside of me. In that moment, I wished more than anything that he could have been bare, so I could have felt his cum burning my insides. But I had to settle for the warmth of his juices through the latex barrier. His body jerked now and again as the aftershocks rippled through him and seeped into me. I was still trembling all over and trying to catch my breath when Maddox eased his hand from my cock. I looked down and gasped at the sight of a little bit of cum in his hand. When he pulled his hand back, white fluid began seeping from the fine openings of the lace and dripping onto the floor.

"Don't worry," Maddox said as he leaned over my shoulder to watch my cum pool on the floor at my feet. "We'll wash them. Oh, and I'm buying you one of these in every color they have available," he added with a kiss to my shoulder.

I laughed and then angled my head so I could kiss him. He eased out of me and then led me to the shower, where he proceeded to wash me from head to toe and then just held me under the spray of water for a while. Then he was getting us under the covers of what seemed to be a new duvet. The mattress itself felt like heaven compared to the sleeping bag, but I also kind of missed it.

"Um, don't get mad, but I bought you something else that I want you to make use of tonight."

"Not sure my ass can take another pounding like that right now, babe," I said with a smile. Maddox chuckled and kissed me lightly.

"Not that... at least not yet, anyway." He leaned across me to grab something off the floor. It was an envelope. He opened it for me. "Put out your hand."

I did and as soon as he tipped the envelope, a key fell into my palm. A car key.

My heart flip-flopped as I realized what it was for.

"It's nothing fancy," Maddox said. "It's just an SUV, but it's got all-wheel drive and good safety features. And a DVD player so Newt can watch movies in the car."

I opened my mouth to protest, but he kissed me hard. "It's bought and paid for, Isaac. It's in my name so you don't have to worry about any kind of paper trail. I'm paying the insurance too, and I bought the maintenance plan that will cover everything under the sun on the car for five years, even the oil changes. All you have to do is say yes."

"Maddox, I—"

"Just give me this," he whispered. "I'm terrified you're going to drive off in the middle of the night when I won't be around, just so you won't have to tell me I can't come with you."

My chest seized because that was exactly what I was planning to do.

"At least give me the knowledge that you're in a safe, reliable car when you do that. I'll store your car here and maybe someday you'll come back for it."

I felt like I was going to die. The way he was talking, it sounded like he was going to let me go, after all. But it was what I wanted, right?

"No, don't do that," Maddox whispered as he stroked my cheek with his thumb. "I'm still planning on being in the passenger seat of that car," he said. "In fact, I might withhold sex until you agree to let me come with you."

I let out a watery laugh at that because I knew he was trying to lighten the moment. I looked at the car key.

I couldn't.

I just couldn't.

But I closed my hand over it. "I'll just borrow it for the few days we're still here," I said.

Pain lanced through my body at the crestfallen look on Maddox's face. It clearly wasn't the answer he'd wanted. But he nodded silently, then took the key from me and put it on the floor. "I have one more thing I want to give you."

"Maddox, it's too much," I said.

But he ignored me and reached beneath the pillow I had my head on and pulled out a simple white box with a red bow on it. I was lying flat on my back with him on his side next to me so he could watch my expression as I opened his gift. I worked the top off and gasped when I saw what was inside.

"Maddox, no," I cried in disbelief, then I was sitting up. I glanced at his chest to confirm what I was seeing was real.

It was his dog tags.

In the box.

Not on his chest.

He was giving me his dog tags.

"Maddox, I can't," I breathed, even as I reached into the box to take the tags out. "They're so important to you," I said. "They're... they're who you are."

"Which is why I want you to have them," Maddox said as he took the tags and eased the chain over my neck. "I want to know that a part of me will always be with the man who's managed to steal my heart."

I gasped at his words. He put his fingers to my chin and said, "If you won't let me be with you, Isaac, then I want you to at least see me every time you look in the mirror, every time you feel the weight of these against your heart. That's me there. Cherishing you, protecting you... loving you."

I closed my eyes because it hurt too much to look at him. But it didn't matter. He was there in my mind's eye too.

He loved me.

Maddox loved me.

He wanted to be with me.

He wanted to take care of me and protect me and make it so I was never alone again.

He loves me.

I couldn't say the words back.

I just couldn't. But for once I was going to ignore my brain and follow my heart.

I wrapped my arms around him and whispered, "I love you so fucking much, Maddox. So much." I wasn't even sure he heard me because my voice was cracking so damn bad, but when he let out a little sigh and cradled the back of my head with his hand, I knew he had. I could feel the dog tags pressed between us, but the weight of them around my neck terrified me as one question kept repeating on a loop in my head.

How the hell am I supposed to walk away now?

CHAPTER TWENTY-ONE

MADDOX

"Lieutenant Kent!"

I stiffened at the familiar title and turned around to see who was calling out to me. Most of the people in town called me by my military title, though I'd asked them repeatedly just to call me by name.

It was Ford Cornell who was calling to me as he hurried to catch up to me on the sidewalk. I felt a shimmer of anger go through me when I saw that Ford was once again bruised, this time on his neck.

Much like Isaac had been bruised the day Jimmy had attacked him outside the thrift shop. I'd wanted to hunt Jimmy down and beat the shit out of him, but my fear of exposing Isaac in any kind of way to the authorities had kept me from doing it. As it was, Isaac was avoiding going into town whenever possible. The only thing he'd done that had anything to do with the residents of Pelican Bay besides interacting with those who were still occasionally coming out to the shelter, was to arrange some playdates for Newt with Justin and Emily Knapp. I'd been shocked when he'd reached out to the mother of the kids from the urgent care clinic waiting room a few days after Christmas, but he had. He'd ended up taking Newt over to the Knapp house and had stayed and chatted with Brenda Knapp as Newt had played with his new friends for a couple of hours. The Knapp children had come to the sanctuary the day before for a personalized tour and for Newt to show off Loki to them. Then they'd watched all the *Cars* movies in Dallas and Nolan's house and had even ended up making it a sleepover.

If that event hadn't been enough to have me thinking that something might have changed for Isaac in regard to leaving Pelican Bay, the fact that it was the day after New Year's was a pretty big indicator that he wasn't in the same rush to leave. He'd been so adamant about leaving right after Christmas, but when that day had come, the issue hadn't even come up.

I liked to think it was a combination of things that were making it hard for Isaac to pack up and leave.

My biggest hope was that my admission that I loved him was one of the things holding him here. I also hoped that the taste of family he'd gotten Christmas morning had played a part too. I'd ended up spending Christmas Eve at Nolan and Dallas's house, and for the first time ever, Isaac and I had gotten to sleep in the same bed the whole night through. We'd woken up in each other's arms when Newt had jumped on the bed and declared that Santa had come.

And Santa had come in a *big* way.

There'd been dozens and dozens of presents under the tree. And while most had been for Newt, there'd been plenty of others to go around. Even Dallas and I had exchanged gifts. But the best part had been when he'd hugged me that morning and in his raspy voice had said, "Merry Christmas, Maddox. Welcome home" in my ear.

Admittedly, I'd held him for a long time after he'd said those words.

And he'd let me.

When I'd finally let him go, we'd sat around and watched Newt rip into his presents. Isaac had opened the ones I'd gotten for him that I'd deemed "family-safe" and he'd loved every single one. He was also driving the SUV I'd bought him, though every time I saw him in it, he assured me he was just borrowing it. He'd started driving me home at night so we could have some alone time but then we usually ended up back at Dallas and Nolan's house to actually spend the night there. I'd been leaving Snotrod at Dallas and Nolan's because the kitten had become quite attached to Loki and usually ended up sleeping with the wolf hybrid and Newt every night.

Nolan's mother had joined us on Christmas Day for the opening of presents followed by a huge breakfast of pancakes, French toast, bacon and eggs, and just about every other breakfast food imaginable. Mrs. Grainger had also cooked a virtual feast for dinner, too.

It'd been a perfect day and I'd been so sure it was the last. But when the next day had come and gone and Isaac hadn't packed up Newt and left, I'd started to let myself hope a little bit. And that hope grew each day he stayed.

Since making his admission that in the eyes of the law he'd kidnapped his brother, I'd been quietly making calls to a couple of criminal and family lawyers to see what could be done. I was also in the process of hiring a private investigator to find out more about Gary. My hope was that there'd be something in his background to prove he was an abusive prick. Maybe that would help with the charges against Isaac.

At the same time that I was trying to see if I could get Isaac out of the mess he was in, I was also looking into how to get him and Newt out of the country if it came to that. There were quite a few nice places that had no extradition treaties with the US. So as long as Isaac didn't step foot outside the country, he'd be safe. It was a last resort, but I wanted to cover all my bases. And my plan was still to go with him and Newt if running ended up being the route we needed to go. I hated the thought of leaving Dallas, but I knew my brother would understand. He knew how deep my feelings for Isaac ran.

"Lieutenant," Ford said as he tried to catch his breath.

"It's just Maddox," I responded. The man's timing was good because I actually wanted to talk to him about a project that would be a surprise for Dallas for his birthday the following month. I ignored the pang in my chest as I realized I might not be around for that. My eyes lingered on the bruises and it took everything in me not to ask the man if his brother had done that to him.

"Maddox," Ford said with a nod. "I need to tell you something—"

Ford's voice dropped off the second a police car rolled around the corner. I wasn't surprised when it pulled over to the curb where we were standing because I could see Alex behind the wheel. I'd considered talking to Alex about Isaac but had decided against it, since doing so would only put Alex in the awkward position of having to choose between his duty as a law enforcement officer and his friendship with me. And the bottom line was that I wasn't willing to risk Isaac's safety with anyone except Nolan, Dallas, and Sawyer.

Alex got out and came around the car. "Maddox, hey," he said as he held out his hand. I didn't miss how Ford tensed up and took several steps back as the deputy approached us. The passenger door of the police cruiser opened up and an older man got out. He wasn't overly muscular, but he was tall and fit with hair that was silver mixed with a little bit of black that was just a little bit longer on top than the sides. I guessed him to be around forty years old or so. A slight five-o'clock shadow covered a chiseled jaw as his intense dark brown eyes swept the area before settling on me, then Ford. It looked like the man homed in on Ford's bruises and the younger man quickly dropped his eyes and shifted back and forth on his feet.

"Maddox, I wanted to introduce you to Camden Wells. He's the new sheriff."

"Sheriff Wells," I said with a nod as I held out my hand. His handshake was strong.

"It's Cam," the man responded. "I'm not big on formality," he said as his eyes shifted again to Ford.

"Ford," Ford managed to get out when Cam patiently waited for him to speak.

"He's Jimmy Cornell's brother," Alex said softly.

Cam's eyes narrowed a bit, but he didn't say anything. Instead, he stepped forward and extended his hand to Ford. "It's nice to meet you, Ford."

Ford looked like he wanted to be anywhere but there, and I was reminded that he'd had some kind of run-in with the law when he'd been a teenager. I hadn't remembered to ask Alex about the details.

Ford managed a stiff nod and quickly shook the sheriff's hand. But when he tried to step back, the sheriff held onto his hand just a little longer than necessary and I saw something flash between the two men that I couldn't quite put a name on. Ford once again dropped his eyes and after a moment, Cam finally turned back to me. "Alex is just giving me the lay of the land. I'd like to stop by and meet your brother and Mr. Grainger so I can introduce myself. You think that'd be okay sometime?"

I nodded. I wasn't surprised the new sheriff would want to try and smooth over the damage the previous one had left behind, and Dallas and Nolan were at the top of Curtis Tulley's list of victims. "I'm sure that would be fine," I said. "The sanctuary is open from eight to four on weekdays," I added.

"Good," Cam said with a nod. To Alex he said, "Should we continue?"

"Yes, sir," Alex said with a smile. Alex shook my hand and returned to the driver's seat.

"Maddox, it was a pleasure," Cam said as he shook my hand. "Ford," was all he said when he nodded at the younger man.

"Sheriff," Ford acknowledged, though it seemed to take a lot of effort to do so. He clearly wasn't comfortable around the man, but I wasn't sure if it was the man's position or something else. I couldn't say Ford seemed exactly comfortable around me either.

I watched the police car drive off, then turned to Ford. "Did you want to talk to me?"

"Yeah, um, I overheard my mom and Jimmy talking a little while ago and I don't know if this means anything, but there were a couple of guys asking about your friend... Isaac."

I automatically stiffened. "Who?"

Ford flinched at my tone. "Um, I don't know. I didn't see them. But Jimmy told them Isaac worked for your brother. I was gonna drive out there and warn you but then I saw you walking and..."

I didn't listen to the rest of Ford's words as panic seized my chest. I dug out my phone and dialed Isaac's number, but it went to voicemail after a few rings. I sent him a text telling him to call me as soon as possible. I didn't bother trying Sawyer, since he, Dallas, and Nolan were doing a rescue call on a deer that had been hit by a car and was lying injured in a field near the road a few towns over.

I waited a minute, then tried Isaac again. When there was still no answer I said to Ford, "Can you take me out there?"

He seemed surprised by my request but immediately nodded his head. The weather was growing increasingly dicey and the plan had been for Isaac to pick me up in town in an hour after I was finished with my appointment. I hadn't told him yet, but I'd started seeing a therapist about my PTSD. Today was supposed to have been my third appointment, but my concern for Isaac and Newt was overruling everything else, so I sent my therapist a quick text explaining I had a family emergency.

My therapist and I hadn't gotten into the details of everything I was dealing with, but she had offered me some ways I could make traveling in the car easier. It mostly included different breathing techniques and envisioning a place in my head where I felt safe. Not surprisingly, that place was the sanctuary and Isaac and Newt were always a part of that picture.

If Ford thought me strange for any of it as we made the drive to the sanctuary, he was kind enough not to say anything or try to engage me in conversation. By the time we pulled into the driveway, the snow was starting to fall, but it was the wind that was making things more difficult. The blowing snow was causing drifts to pile up quickly, but Ford managed the thickening snow without too much trouble.

I was out of the car before Ford even pulled to a complete stop, because through the windshield I could see some guy with his hands on Isaac and Isaac trying to get away from him. They were just outside the office and there was another man, a guy in his early sixties maybe, standing off to the side. It sounded like he was yelling, but it was hard to hear over the wind.

I reached Isaac and the guy I instinctively knew was Gary and ripped him away from Isaac so that he stumbled backward. I turned to check on Isaac and felt pure rage explode inside of me when I saw the bruise forming on his right cheek. Gary chose that moment to yell, "Hey," and grab my arm. I turned and decked him and he went flying backward. I was on him before he could even register what had happened. But I only got a few punches in before Ford and Isaac were pulling me back.

"Maddox, stop!" Isaac yelled as he got in my face.

I managed to pull in a few breaths as I tried to calm myself. Gary scrambled to his feet and stumbled back away from me.

"Get the fuck out of here!" I snapped.

The older man with Gary seemed confused as he looked between Gary and Isaac. "Let's go!" Gary called to the man as he hurried to the only other car in the parking lot besides Isaac's and Ford's. The man hesitated, then followed Gary.

I turned back to look at Isaac. I grabbed his chin and only noticed then that the knuckles on my right hand were bruised and bloody. "Are you okay?" I asked.

Isaac let out a breath and nodded. His eyes stayed on Gary's car until it was gone. Then they went wide. "Newt," he said. "I have to find Newt."

I stilled as I realized I hadn't noticed him anywhere.

"Was he with you when they arrived?" I asked.

"No," Isaac said as he began hurrying down the path leading toward the livestock barn. "He wanted to give the animals some carrots that Nolan left for him this morning. I told him to come back to the office when he was done. But Gary showed up and... Newt!" Isaac yelled as we hurried to the barn.

"Newt!" I called.

The concern in my chest grew when I saw Jerry standing out in the paddock rather than in the barn. The zebra was a treat hog. If Newt was in the barn giving the animals goodies, Jerry would've been there for sure.

We continued to call Newt's name until we reached the barn. Ford had followed us.

"Oh God, where is he?" Isaac cried when we found the barn empty.

"Loki," I said. "Where's Loki?"

Isaac shook his head.

"He didn't show up when Gary arrived?"

"No," Isaac said. "Newt! Loki!" Isaac screamed.

"Okay, let's split up and search the property. Isaac, you go check the house." Isaac was already running that direction when I told Ford where to look and where to meet back up. With the wind whipping up like it was, visibility was difficult. Five minutes later, we met back at the livestock barn. When Isaac saw that Ford and I were both alone, he began to panic.

"Oh God, Maddox, what if he saw Gary and got scared? What if Gary got him somehow? What if—"

"Enough," I said as I grabbed him by the shoulders and gave him a gentle shake. "He's here somewhere. We just need to find him." The words came out much more calmly than I was feeling. I willed myself to think. "If he saw Gary, what would he do?" I asked.

"Run," Isaac whispered. "He's scared to death of Gary. He... he used to have nightmares about him finding us. He'd wake up screaming and telling me we had to run and hide."

"Then that's what he's doing," I said. To Ford I said, "Can you check the east side of the property for any tracks and call me if you find *anything*?"

"Yeah," Ford said with a vigorous nod, then he was off and running in that direction. "Listen," I said to Isaac. "If we don't find any sign of him in the next few minutes, we need to call for help."

"I don't care," Isaac said. "Just find him. Please, Maddox."

I could tell he was on the verge of a full-on panic attack. I grabbed his face and said, "We're going to find him, Isaac. Just take deep breaths." I took his hand in mine and led him to the back of the property. There was a large, open field that led to a more densely populated wooded area. My gut was telling me if Newt had been headed up toward the parking lot and had overheard Gary yelling at Isaac, he would have turned around and run back the direction he'd come. So I focused on the swath of land just behind the livestock barn. We worked our way north looking for any tracks.

"There," I said after a few minutes when I saw both a set of human and canine tracks on the far side of the barn. We followed the trail to the end of the dog enclosure, which was the last pen on the property before it opened up into the field. But the blowing wind covered the tracks within a matter of minutes, so by the time we reached the middle of the field, there was no way to know which direction Newt had gone. We screamed for Newt over and over, but there was only the howling wind to answer us.

"Where would he go?" I asked myself.

"Maddox," Isaac whispered, completely terrified. I pulled him against me and searched out my phone. We couldn't risk waiting any longer. With the wind blowing like it was, the wind chill could turn deadly in no time. I suspected Newt had his parka, snow pants, and gloves on, but those would only protect him for so long. I was about to dial 911 when something caught my attention.

A sound on the wind.

But not the sound of a child.

"Listen," I said as I grabbed Isaac's arm.

Neither of us moved and that was when I heard it again.

It was a howling sound.

But definitely not the wind this time.

"Loki," I breathed as I began striding forward. It was hard to tell where the sound was coming from, but as we got closer to the woods, I instinctively knew.

"He's trying to get to me," I said to Isaac.

"What?"

"Newt knows I walk home this way sometimes. I told him about it. He's trying to get to my house!"

I'd only told Newt that I lived far away when I'd pointed at the line of trees on the northwest side of the field, but to a four-year-old, that wouldn't have really meant anything. And to a terrified four-year-old…?

I began running through the snow and felt a mix of relief and fear as the howling continued. We were getting closer, but Loki wasn't coming to us. He just kept howling. What if Newt had had another seizure?

I pulled out my phone and said, "Isaac, we need to call the paramedics just in case."

Isaac looked stricken but nodded. I dialed 911 and told the operator we needed an ambulance and gave them the sanctuary's address. By the time we reached the tree line, I'd hung up the phone. Loki's howls were louder now that the wind was broken up by the trees. It took just minutes to find the pair.

"Newt," Isaac yelled when he saw Newt's blue parka. The little boy was lying on the ground, but not flat like when he'd been having the seizure. He was curled in a ball against a fallen tree and Loki was lying half on top of him. Newt's head was on Loki's front paws and the wolf hybrid was resting his own head on top of Newt's. The animal's fluffy tail was draped over Newt's legs.

"Newt," I called when I reached the pair. Loki immediately moved when I got to them and frantically began licking Newt's face. The move woke Newt up.

"Isaac?"

"I'm here, buddy," Isaac cried as he fell to his knees next to Newt. I helped Newt sit up. His moves were stiff, but he seemed alert.

"I'm cold," he said, his teeth chattering.

"I know you are," Isaac said as he began rubbing Newt's face with his ungloved hands. "Let's get you back home."

Isaac's words sent Newt into a panic. "No! *He's* there!" Newt threw himself at me. "Mad, you gotta stop him. You spit on it! Don't let him take me and Isaac away!"

I wrapped my arms around him and climbed to my feet, taking him with me. "I won't, Newt. It's okay. You're safe. You and Isaac are both safe, I swear it." The little boy began to cry. He was shaking. To Isaac I said, "My coat. Can you unzip it?"

Isaac unzipped my parka and helped me get Newt beneath it. Fortunately, the child was slight enough that I could wrap the lapels of the coat around him. I couldn't zip it closed, but I was able to hold it shut with my fingers. My hope was that my body heat would help warm him more quickly.

Isaac walked next to me, reassuring Newt with every step that everything was going to be okay and that Gary was gone and wasn't coming back. Ford met us near the barn where we'd originally separated.

"Is he okay?" Ford asked.

"Yeah, I think so," I said. I could hear sirens, so I knew the paramedics were close. I didn't think Newt was in any immediate danger, but I still wanted to hear the paramedics assure me of that. He'd only been missing for about twenty to thirty minutes and between his winter gear and Loki keeping him warm, I was hopeful he hadn't experienced any kind of hypothermia or frostbite.

The ambulance was rolling to a stop as soon as we reached the parking lot. The EMTs took Newt from me and sat him in the back of the ambulance. Isaac climbed in with them and held onto Newt as they began checking him over.

"I'm not seeing any cause for concern," the female paramedic said. "But we should take him in to be checked over, just in case. They'll probably want to give him some fluids and maybe keep him overnight."

Isaac sighed in relief and hugged Newt tight. "Okay," he said softly, his voice cracking.

"I'm sorry, Isaac. I wanted to find Mad so he'd keep us safe."

Isaac kissed the top of Newt's head. The paramedic had removed his helmet during her examination.

"It's okay, buddy. Just… just don't do that ever again, okay?"

"Okay," Newt said in a small voice.

The sound of a car engine had me turning to look down the driveway and I felt my pulse speed up at the sight of the two police cruisers heading toward us.

I knew it was bad when a grim-faced Alex got out of the first car. I automatically stepped in front of the open ambulance. I glanced over my shoulder at Isaac who'd gone even paler. He was hanging onto Newt as if he expected someone to rip him from his arms.

Cam approached me, his face pulled into a mask of seriousness. The friendly man from earlier was gone.

"Sheriff," I said in greeting, because I knew he wasn't there for the informal visit he'd talked about.

"Lieutenant Kent," he responded.

Yeah, this was bad. No other reason to use my title otherwise.

Cam looked past me into the ambulance. "Everyone okay?" he asked.

The female paramedic nodded. "We're going to transport the boy to the hospital in Greenville just to get checked out, but he should be okay. Not seeing any signs of hypothermia or frostbite."

"Good," Cam said. His eyes went to Isaac. "Are you Isaac Foster?" he asked.

Isaac dropped his eyes to the floor of the ambulance. His expression broke me, and I couldn't stop myself from stepping between Cam and the vehicle. "Sheriff, you aren't—"

"Maddox," Isaac cut in. "Don't," he said firmly. He leaned down to whisper something to Newt.

"No, Isaac!" the little boy cried and clung to him harder. "No, you promised!"

Isaac kept trying to talk softly to Newt, but the child wouldn't hear him out. I couldn't blame him. Newt knew what was happening. Isaac stood and lifted Newt into his arms, making sure not to bump their heads on the ceiling of the ambulance in the process. He walked to the back. Newt was sobbing and begging Isaac not to leave him.

I held Isaac's elbow when he stepped out of the ambulance. He faced me and put his hand over Newt's head. He waited until Newt had quieted enough to hear him. "Newt, I need you to listen to me, okay?"

Newt pulled back a little. His fingers were wrapped around the chain of my dog tags which were around Isaac's neck. He'd been wearing them ever since the night I'd given them to him.

"I need you to stay here with Maddox while I go take care of some things."

Newt began shaking his head. "No," he croaked.

"You remember how you and Maddox spit on it?" Isaac asked. "The night you and I were going to leave and you asked him to spit on it and so that's what you guys did after dinner. Do you remember that?"

Newt nodded. "Yeah," he whispered.

"What did you spit on?" Isaac asked.

"That Mad would watch out for us and keep us safe and never let anyone hurt us again."

"Do you think Mad would ever break a promise you guys spit on?" Isaac asked. His eyes shifted to me and I knew he was talking to me as much as to himself. It was his way of reminding me of the promise I'd made to him the night he'd told me about his past.

No matter what, don't let Gary get Newt.

"No," Newt said sadly.

"So I need you to stay here with Maddox so he can keep his promise, okay?"

I could tell Newt wanted to say no. Fuck, *I* wanted to tell Isaac no too. I wanted to punch Cam and Alex and everyone who tried to take Isaac from me. But I had to put Newt first.

Newt finally nodded, then Isaac gave him a hug. "Love you, Newt," he said softly.

"Love you," Newt returned, then he began to cry again.

Isaac was barely holding it together as he handed Newt to me. The little boy clung to me like a vine as Isaac leaned in to kiss me. "I'll be okay," he whispered to me.

"Isaac," I said in what sounded like a strangled moan. I couldn't believe I was letting this happen. It was like I was back on that dirt road crawling between the bodies of my fallen comrades trying to make sense of why they were dead and I wasn't.

There was no sense to be made of it, though.

Isaac kissed me again. "I love you." Then he turned to Cam and said, "Yes, I'm Isaac Foster."

Cam hesitated for a moment, his eyes shifting between me and

Isaac and Newt. His face fell as he said, "Isaac Foster, you're under arrest for the kidnapping of Newton Foster-Willis. I'll need you to come with me."

I wanted to rip Cam's arm off when he closed his fingers around Isaac's upper am and led him toward the patrol car Alex was still standing in front of. I made sure Newt couldn't see as he told Isaac to put his hands out in front of him and proceeded to cuff him, then search him. I rubbed my hand over Newt's back as I watched Cam put Isaac in Alex's car. Isaac didn't look at me as the cruiser turned around in the driveway and then began making its way down the driveway. I stiffened when Cam approached me again.

"I've got a man named Gary Willis down at the station claiming you assaulted him." Cam's gaze fell to the hand I was rubbing along Newt's back. The hand with the bruised knuckles.

Before I could respond, Ford said, "It was me. I hit that guy."

Cam and I both looked at Ford, me in surprise and Cam in… well, I didn't know what to make of the look Cam sent him. I was about to protest when Newt hugged me tighter and I realized what it would mean if I was arrested too.

Newt would be alone.

But the idea of letting Ford take the fall for me was like a sour taste in my mouth.

Cam was speaking before I could figure out what to do. "I guess I should question Mr. Willis again," he said quietly. "Seems like there might be more to his story."

Something about the way he said that last part gave me a little bit of hope.

"Lieutenant, might I make a suggestion?"

I had no clue what he could offer that would undo the fact that he'd just put the love of my life in fucking handcuffs, so I didn't say anything at all.

"Get the kid a lawyer," he said as he pointed at Newt. "Protocol says I have to call family services to pick him up, but seeing as how I'm new in town, it might take me a while to find their number. If this one," –he actually touched Newt's back gently for the briefest of moments– "has a lawyer to speak for him, it might make things a bit easier on him."

The sheriff turned his attention to Ford. "I'm hearing some interesting things about your family, Mr. Cornell. You should keep that in mind the next time you lie to me."

With that, the man turned and went to his car.

"Sheriff," I called.

He turned. "I'm getting lawyers for *both* of them. Isaac's invoking his right not to talk to you," I said. "And if you know anything about *my* family, you know I can get the best lawyers money can buy."

Cam actually smiled and turned back toward his car. "I expect I'll see you at the station real soon, Lieutenant," he called over his shoulder.

"Damn straight you will," I muttered.

"You said a bad word," Newt whispered tiredly against my neck.

"I know I did. And I'm going to get Isaac back here just as soon as possible so he can tell me what my punishment is, okay?"

Newt sighed and nodded. "'Cause you spit on it."

"Because I spit on it," I agreed. "But you want to know why else?" I asked him as I climbed into the ambulance and sat down on the gurney with him. I ignored the chill that went through me at being in the vehicle.

"Why?" Newt asked.

"Because you and Isaac are my family now and I always take care of my family."

"So we don't gotta spit on things anymore 'cause we're family?"

"No, we don't."

"'Kay... but what if I like spittin'?"

I smiled against his little body and said, "Then spitting it is."

I glanced at Ford who was standing outside the ambulance with Loki by his side. "My brother will be home soon. Can you stay and tell him what happened?" I asked.

Ford nodded. "Sure. Bye, Newt. I'll see you soon, okay?"

Newt nodded. As the ambulance doors closed, Newt whispered, "You're gonna get Isaac back, right, Mad?"

"Yes, I am," I said without hesitation. I couldn't help but smile when Newt began horking up what would probably be a pretty good-sized glob of spit.

Newt and I shook on it and then I was reaching for my phone, wet palm and all, to start making the calls that would get me my family back.

For good.

CHAPTER TWENTY-TWO

ISAAC

"Here."

I looked up from where I was sitting on the cot in the jail cell and saw a cup being thrust at me. It was from one of Pelican Bay's only coffee shops that served espresso.

"Oh, um, I'm not a big fan of coffee," I said.

"It's hot chocolate," the sheriff said as he handed me the cup. He sat down next to me on the cot and dropped a bag onto the thin mattress. "It's a burger… from that little diner over on Third Street," he said as he motioned to it.

I was sitting with my knees drawn up to my chest, so I slowly dropped them and eyed the bag. The door to the cell was wide open. There were only two cells in the small building and they were in the same room where the sheriff and his deputy's desks were.

"What time is it?" I asked.

"Just after seven," he said. "At night," he added.

"Is Newt okay?" I asked. "Are you allowed to tell me that?"

"He's fine. They didn't even keep him at the hospital for observation."

Relief coursed through my body. "Where… where is he?" I was too afraid to ask if Gary had him. The lawyer Maddox had hired for me hadn't known anything about what was going on with Newt, or even my case for that matter. She'd breezed into the jail within an hour of me being arrested and promptly told me not to talk to anyone but her. She and I had talked for a couple of hours in a private interview room, and now I was just waiting to be arraigned in the morning so I could plead not guilty and hopefully make bail. I'd only been in jail for a handful of hours, but I was scared to death that I hadn't heard anything about Newt.

"I suspect he's with your man still, since he hasn't come storming in here to threaten me some more."

"He threatened you?" I asked. Oh God, if Maddox got himself tossed in jail...

"Relax," the man said. "He was just sending me a message." The sheriff seemed unfazed by the whole thing. "I'm Cam, by the way," he said as he held out his hand.

I almost laughed. Was he for real?

Since he didn't retract his hand, I figured he was. "Isaac," I said. "But you know that already."

He shrugged, then pulled a box of playing cards from his shirt pocket. "You know how to play Rummy, Isaac?" he asked.

"Um, no?"

"I'll teach you," was all he said as he began dealing out the cards. I tried to listen as he explained the rules, but I couldn't make sense of what was happening. When I said as much, he looked up at me. But he didn't answer my question. Instead he said, "How'd you get that bruise on your face?"

"I can't tell you, remember?" I said.

"Yeah," he responded with a nod. He drew a card from the pile and studied it before discarding it. When I realized he was really expecting me to play the game, I picked up a card. I was in the process of discarding a different card when he said, "My dad used to knock me around when I was a kid." He glanced at my discarded card, then grabbed it and tossed off a different one. "I never told anyone. Figured it was my fault. Figured there was just something about me that ticked him off. Never found out what it was, though," he said almost casually. "Wasn't till I joined the force that the truth hit me."

When he didn't continue, I found myself saying, "What truth?"

"That fuckers like him didn't need a reason. Your turn."

I looked down at the cards and absently played my turn. Cam was such an intimidating guy, it was hard to imagine him as ever being someone who'd been on the receiving end of a heavy hand. "Did he ever pay for what he did to you?" I asked.

Cam shook his head. "Nope. But you can be sure that a lot of people paid *because* of him."

"What do you mean?"

"I learned that silence doesn't mean a person's got nothing to say. Just means sometimes you have to listen harder to what they aren't saying." He played his turn before adding, "And then you've got people like that Gary fella who do a whole lot of talking and not much else."

As badly as I wanted to ask him what he meant by that, I couldn't risk it. This man wasn't my friend. His only job was to make sure I ended up in a cell like this permanently. Cam didn't seem surprised at my lack of response. We were still playing when the door to the building slammed open. Cam glanced at his watch as Maddox came barreling through the door. "Hmmm, thought I had a few more minutes. I almost had a winning hand," he said as he flashed me his cards, then began cleaning them up.

"Lieutenant," Cam said as he motioned to a frantic-looking Maddox. We both stood as Maddox stopped outside the cell, his eyes locked on mine. I could feel myself on the verge of falling apart at the sight of him. Cam moved past Maddox and gave him a gentle pat on the shoulder. "Go on in, Lieutenant. He's been waiting for you."

It was all the permission Maddox needed. I let out a harsh cry when his arms closed around me.

"I've got you, Isaac," he said as I began sobbing uncontrollably. I'd managed to hold it together up until that point... from being handcuffed, to going through the booking process where my picture had been taken and my fingerprints scanned into a computer, to being placed in the jail cell and the door locking behind me. But now I couldn't even manage to pull it together long enough to get a few words out. Maddox didn't seem to mind because he was holding onto me and answering questions he knew I wanted to ask.

"Newt's fine. There was no frostbite or hypothermia. They gave him fluids and discharged him. He's with Dallas and Nolan. I got him a lawyer and the first thing he did was file a protective order against Gary."

I pulled back and wiped at my face. "A protective order? What does that mean?"

"Gary's not allowed to go anywhere near Newt or anywhere that he is. The sheriff has already served him with the order."

I looked up at where Cam was sitting at his desk. He shifted his gaze to me briefly, then gave me a little nod.

I didn't know what to make of the guy.

"Isaac," Maddox said softly to get my attention. "Newt's lawyer thinks Gary is going to file a protective order against you… to keep you from seeing Newt."

"What?" I whispered.

"It's all part of Gary's strategy. Even if we get you out of the kidnapping charges, he's probably going to fight to get Newt back. He's going to use whatever ammunition he can against you."

"How did he even find us?" I asked as I sat down on the cot.

"It looks like Trey might have had a hand in it," Maddox said.

"What?" I asked, completely stunned.

"Trey hired a PI to try and find you… probably so he could get back at you for turning him in for the thing with the violin. If Trey noticed you'd taken Nolan's old violin, he probably figured you might try to return it to Nolan at some point. It would have been easy for his PI to find you here."

"So what, he called Gary? How did he even know about him?"

"You said all you had to do was google Newt's and your names, right? Did Trey know Newt's name?"

I felt my stomach drop out. I nodded. "I told him once." I shook my head. "God, I'm so stupid. I even told him about the Isaac Newton thing."

Maddox sat down next to me and ran his fingers over my hair.

"So Gary came up here to check if it really was me and Newt?" I said.

"Yeah. Jimmy Cornell recognized your picture and sent Gary out to the sanctuary."

"Who was the guy with him?"

"We're not sure," Cam said. I looked up to see him standing outside the jail cell. "When Gary came here to tell us where you were and that there was a warrant out on you, the guy hung back, like he didn't want anything to do with it. Since he wasn't the one filing the complaint, we had no reason to ask him who he was. When I served the protective order against Gary earlier tonight, the man wasn't with him." He paused and looked at Maddox before saying, "The arraignment's tomorrow at nine."

Maddox put his arm around me. "Can I... can I stay with him?"

Cam seemed to think about it a moment, then gave Maddox a quick nod. "I've got some calls to make. I'll need to lock you in," he said as he motioned to the door.

"That's fine," Maddox responded. "Thank you."

I couldn't help but jump when the door slid shut with a heavy clang. I suspected it wasn't exactly within the rules for Maddox to be in the cell with me, much less stay the whole night, but I certainly wasn't going to complain about it. I leaned into his side as the exhaustion began to overtake me. Newt was safe. That was all that mattered.

"Come here, baby," Maddox said as he lay down on the cot and pulled me up against him so I was lying with my back to his front. "Get some rest."

I could feel the tears threatening to start all over again as the uncertainty of it all hit me. "I really can't see him?" I asked.

"No, Isaac, I'm sorry, you can't. But hopefully it'll just be for a few days until we get this all straightened out."

"But he's okay," I murmured.

"He's missing you and he's worried, but Dallas and Nolan will take good care of him."

"Will he have to go into foster care?" I asked. It was one of my biggest fears for Newt besides Gary getting him back. Tears leaked from my eyes at even the thought.

"His lawyer is going to fight for Dallas and Nolan to get temporary custody. Not only does Newt know them, they're familiar with his medical condition, so the lawyer thinks that will sway the judge. Family Services might not even fight the placement, and with the protective order in place, Gary doesn't have a leg to stand on. But, Isaac," Maddox said as he turned me over so I was facing him. "If there's a custody hearing, you're going to need to tell everyone what Gary did to you. And if you end up going on trial for kidnapping Newt—"

"I know," I said with a nod. "I'm ready. Even if they don't believe me, I'm ready to say it out loud. He didn't have the right to do what he did to me. Makeup, girly clothes, liking boys… none of that gave him the right to ever lay even a finger on me."

Maddox carded his fingers through my hair. "No, it didn't." He used his free hand to wipe at the dampness of my cheeks.

My chest felt tight as I whispered, "I'm scared, Maddox."

"I know you are, baby. I am too." He leaned in to kiss my forehead. "But you're not alone anymore, okay?"

I sighed and snuggled against his chest. He held me and kept pressing kisses to my head and urging me to sleep for a bit.

Which was exactly what I did.

CHAPTER TWENTY-THREE

MADDOX

While the arraignment had been a simple process that had literally taken a few minutes, everything else was just a fucking mess.

After pleading not guilty to the charges, Isaac's lawyer had fought for bail and the prosecutor had argued, but not much. In the end, Isaac had been granted bail and I'd paid it and had him out of jail within an hour and taken him back to my house. He'd been devastated to learn that the protective order that had been issued against him meant he couldn't even talk to Newt on the phone or via video chat, but he'd managed to keep it together. He'd insisted I go to see Newt and give him a message saying how much he loved him and everything would be okay. Newt had given me a similar message to share with Isaac. The little boy was doing okay with Nolan and Dallas, but it was clear to everyone he just wanted his brother back.

With me dealing with Isaac's situation and Nolan and Dallas trying to care for a broken-hearted Newt, I'd been worried about the work piling up at the sanctuary, but I'd been surprised to learn that Ford had volunteered to help out until things got back to normal and that Dallas had actually accepted. I figured Dallas saw what I did–that Ford wasn't anything like his brother. The fact that Ford had tried to help Isaac and Newt, first by warning me about Gary being in town and again by helping in the search for Newt, was evidence enough that he had a good heart. Between him and Sawyer, they were able to keep the sanctuary going without too much trouble.

Isaac had spent the last few days just lying on our bed in front of the fireplace and when I hadn't been visiting Newt, I'd just held Isaac and let him alternate between sleeping, crying, and utter silence. His lawyer had stopped by several times to ask Isaac questions and to give us updates on things, but it'd been hard to hear that the prosecutor in Massachusetts was extraditing Isaac to face charges there, since that was where the kidnapping had actually occurred. Isaac's lawyer was fighting it, but the whole thing was inevitable, since the investigator who worked for Isaac's lawyer was still gathering evidence. The lawyer's goal was to delay the extradition as long as possible.

We were back in court for another hearing. The judge had been going through the evidence presented and was considering whether or not he wanted to meet with Newt. Dallas and Nolan were with Newt in another room within the courthouse, which was especially hard on Isaac because he was desperate to see his brother. To know he was so close but still couldn't see him was akin to torture for him.

As the judge took a brief recess, we were milling around the courtroom waiting for him to return and let us know if he'd made his decision about meeting with Newt or whether he wanted to hear more evidence. There was a slim chance he could even rule on the extradition then and there. Sawyer was there for moral support and to communicate what was happening to Dallas and Nolan.

Unfortunately, Gary was also in the courtroom and that was stressing Isaac out even more. While Isaac hadn't testified during the hearing, his affidavits claiming abuse were in the judge's hands. As were Gary's claims of innocence. Each side was hoping their argument would sway the judge one way or the other.

"All rise."

"Love you," I whispered to Isaac before giving him a quick kiss and returning with Sawyer to the seats just behind the defendant's table. We waited until the judge was seated and the bailiff gave the all clear to sit down. Isaac cast me a glance over his shoulder and offered me a wobbly smile, but I could see the fear in his eyes.

"Okay, folks," the judge began, but then paused when his clerk suddenly got up and handed him a note. He read it, then called the bailiff over and spoke to him. The bailiff went to a side door and opened it. I stiffened when I saw the old man who'd been at the sanctuary the day Gary had attacked Isaac. No one had seen or heard from him since then. Gary had been mum about who he was when Cam had questioned him, and since there'd been no evidence the man's identity was pertinent to the case, the sheriff had been forced to let it go.

The older man entered along with a middle-aged woman dressed in an expensive-looking suit. The man looked at Isaac and I once again saw the same expression I'd seen that day at the sanctuary.

It almost looked like longing.

But that didn't make sense.

He and Isaac didn't know each other.

"Would you introduce yourself to the court?" the judge asked the woman.

"My name is Karina Sumner. I'm a managing partner at Sumner, Horst and Winehouse. My firm is based in Houston. My client is Mr. A.R. Sheridan and he has a personal interest in this case that the court should be aware of, Your Honor."

"How so?" the judge asked.

"Mr. Sheridan was contacted by Mr. Willis" –the lawyer motioned to Gary– "a few months ago. Mr. Willis claimed to know the whereabouts of Mr. Sheridan's daughter, Jillian."

I heard Isaac stifle a gasp.

"As well as Jillian's two sons," the lawyer continued.

I stiffened at that. The older man once again looked at Isaac and it hit me all at once who he was.

"I'm afraid I don't understand," the judge said. "How is that connected to this case?"

"Because Mr. Foster," –the lawyer pointed at Isaac– "is one of those sons."

"May I speak, Your Honor?" the man, Sheridan, asked.

"You may," the judge said.

"When Mr. Willis called me, he told me my daughter had died in a car accident two years ago, but that she had left behind two sons, Isaac and Newton." The man glanced at Isaac again before continuing. Isaac seemed completely lost in shock.

"Mr. Willis told me that Isaac had kidnapped Newton because he wanted some money my daughter had left Newton in a trust and was hoping to blackmail Mr. Willis by offering to return Newton to him in exchange for the money in the trust."

I glanced at Gary in disbelief.

"I'm sorry to say that I believed him at first. He said a lot of things about Isaac that I've come to realize aren't true. I was desperate to meet my youngest grandson and wanted to, what I thought was rescue him at the time, so I agreed to come with Mr. Willis to confirm it really was Isaac and Newton." Sheridan pulled in a breath and said, "When I saw Mr. Willis punch my grandson–Isaac–without any kind of provocation, I knew he'd lied to me." The man suddenly turned toward Isaac. "I'm so sorry, Isaac. I should have tried to stop him but it all just happened so fast and I—"

"Mr. Sheridan, you need to address your comments to the court," the judge interjected.

"Yes, I'm sorry," he murmured. "After I realized Mr. Willis had lied, I had Karina see what she could find out about him. I just… I wish I'd done it sooner, but I was so desperate for word on my daughter, and then on my grandchildren." The man shook his head sadly. He looked completely broken.

His lawyer handed the bailiff three identical envelopes. The man took one to the judge and handed the other two to both Isaac's lawyer and the prosecutor. "This is the evidence our firm has amassed against Mr. Willis so far, Your Honor. One of our investigators was able to match fingerprints lifted from a beer can Mr. Willis had been drinking from to a man named Gary Halloran. Mr. Halloran," –she motioned to Gary– "has an extensive criminal record including domestic violence and battery charges. He spent time in prison for putting his girlfriend's twelve-year-old-daughter into a coma after pushing her into a wall."

"That's a lie!" Gary yelled as he jumped to his feet. One of the court officers immediately went to him and ordered him to sit down.

The judge skimmed through the file, as did the other two lawyers. Isaac looked at me, completely shocked. I mouthed the words, *it'll be okay* to him, and he nodded. I could see that he was tapping his foot incessantly beneath the table.

"There's also proof in there that Mr. Foster has been acting as Newton's primary caregiver since his birth. There are affidavits from former neighbors and friends as well as medical records that prove Isaac took him to all his wellness exams from the time he was born. There's also proof from a pharmacy that Isaac was the one who got Newton's anti-seizure medication filled. Additionally, the ER doctor who treated Newton has agreed that it is very possible the seizures Newton is still experiencing could be from a head injury caused by having his head slammed into a wall. I would urge this court to ask the child himself about what happened that day—"

"That won't be necessary," the judge said as he skimmed the documents. To the prosecutor he said, "Mr. Lewis, I take it you want some time to do your own investigation?"

The prosecutor nodded as he glanced from the paperwork in his hand to Gary. The lawyer looked pissed and Gary actually squirmed a bit in his seat.

"You have twenty-four hours," the judge said. "But unless you find something concrete, I'm going to be ruling in Mr. Foster's favor and denying extradition. I suggest you look a little closer to home if you want someone to put behind bars," he added as his eyes settled on Gary.

"Your Honor," Isaac's lawyer called. "In light of this evidence, we ask that you remove the protective order against my client. I believe it's clear to everyone in this room that Isaac isn't a threat to his brother and that he's only acted in Newton's best interest."

"Granted," the judge said, then he was banging his gavel. I automatically jumped, but fortunately he just slammed it down once, then he was up and leaving the bench. Sawyer slapped me on the back and pulled out his phone.

"I'll tell Dallas and Nolan," he said, then he was walking out of the courtroom.

"Is that it?" Isaac quietly asked his lawyer. I got up and went to him. He leaned into me when I put my arm around him.

"You're officially still charged," the woman said. "But my guess is the charges will be dropped within a matter of hours." She held up the folder. "This is some pretty damning stuff, and the prosecutor is going to look like a fool for not having done his homework before filing the charges."

"And I can see Newt?" he asked hopefully.

"Absolutely," she said. "And the protective order against Gary is still in place so he can't come anywhere near Newt. My next stop is to file one against him on your behalf."

I glanced over and saw Gary being ushered out of the courtroom by the prosecutor.

Isaac let out a rush of air and then he was hugging me. I shook the lawyer's hand and then wrapped both my arms around Isaac as she left. My eyes caught on Sheridan's face. His lawyer was talking to him on one side of the courtroom, but he didn't seem to really be listening to her. When Isaac made eye contact with him, the man said something to his lawyer, then came toward us.

Isaac tensed a bit and straightened. His hand dropped down to search out mine.

"Hi, Isaac," the man said. "My name is Aaron Sheridan." He hesitated, then stuck out his hand.

But I figured Isaac was caught on the same thing as me.

Aaron.

As in Isaac's middle name.

"She named me after you," he whispered. "I mean, Isaac Newton *and* you," he corrected.

"She did?" Sheridan asked.

"My middle name is Aaron. Newt's is too."

Sheridan laughed and then let out what sounded like the smallest of whimpers. He discreetly dashed at his eyes. "She was the oddest girl," he murmured.

"She was," Isaac agreed. Both men had made the comment with the same level of affection. "She never talked about you," Isaac said. "She never even told me your name."

Sheridan nodded and smiled sadly. "That doesn't surprise me. She was very stubborn. Once she made up her mind about something, it was hard to change it."

"She said you kicked her out when she got pregnant with me," Isaac accused.

The older man sighed. "I said some terrible things to her when she told me she was pregnant," he admitted. "Her mother died when she was six, so it had only been her and me for the longest time. When she started showing signs of being sick, I foolishly thought if she just had structure and goals, it would help keep her on track. I didn't really understand her disease–that was something her mother had always been good at, but not me. Jilly naturally rebelled, but when she was off her meds, she was impossible to get through to. When she said she was pregnant, I just saw her entire life, all the plans we made, get derailed and I said some things to her that I shouldn't have and that I regretted."

Sheridan wiped at his head as if he had a headache and I had no doubt bringing up his daughter and the way they'd parted must have been hard on him.

"She was gone the next morning. I thought she would come back. When she didn't, I tried to find her. But it was like she'd disappeared into thin air. Then nearly twenty-two years later I get this call out of the blue from this complete stranger telling me he had information about her. He... he didn't even tell me she was dead until I went to Boston to meet him."

"How did he even know how to find you?" I asked.

"Jilly told him about me. He made it sound like he needed my help to get Newton back, but looking back, I realized he had a bigger goal in mind."

"What?" I asked.

"The same thing that drove him from the moment he met my daughter. Money." He looked at Isaac and said, "I've been very successful in the oil industry in Texas. That's where I'm from… Houston. All Gary would have had to do was check my name on the internet and he would have seen how much I was worth. Your mother may have left Newton a good deal of money, but it would have seemed like nothing compared to the inheritance he would have gotten from me. He figured out pretty quickly how desperate I was to be a part of my grandson's life because he even offered to move to Houston with Newton after he got him back." He paused and said, "I'm sorry, Isaac. I shouldn't have believed him but when he called, it was like Jillian herself was reaching out to me and I finally had the chance to make things right."

The ache in the man's voice was clear and his regret was profound and honest.

"Are you… are you going to try to take Newt from me?" Isaac asked softly, his voice racked with fear.

Sheridan quickly shook his head. "No, no, absolutely not. You've been an amazing big brother, Isaac. I can see that just by all the things you did for him when he was born. You were and are the father he should have had from the beginning. I'm just sorry it had to fall on your young shoulders. I'm thinking life with Jillian meant you didn't have much of a childhood yourself."

Before Isaac could respond, the courtroom doors swung open.

"Isaac!" Newt yelled and then he was running. Isaac met him at the spot where there was a small swing door leading to the front part of the courtroom. He caught him up and held him.

"Oh God, I've missed you," Isaac said softly.

"Are you coming home now?" Newt asked. He looked like he was on the verge of tears.

"I'm absolutely coming home, Newt," Isaac said, then he kissed his temple. I glanced up to see Nolan, Dallas, and Sawyer standing by the main doors. Dallas's gaze caught mine and he smiled warmly. I had a million things I wanted to say to him in that moment, but they'd keep until we were home.

Because there was no doubt I was going home too.

But not to the big ugly house on the water that hadn't ever really been home. I was going wherever Isaac was going, and I knew in my gut that place included my brother and the man he now called family.

"Spit on it," Newt demanded, then he was horking into his palm. Isaac automatically looked at me with a *you gotta be kidding me* look. I shrugged my shoulders. His look promised retribution and then he was spitting into his hand and shaking Newt's.

"I promise I'm coming home," he said.

"And we get to stay with Nolan and Dallas and Loki and Sawyer and Gentry and Snotrod and Mad?"

"I'm last?" I called out to Newt. "I'm last on your list? Behind Snot?"

Newt giggled and shrugged.

"Yes, we get to stay with Nolan and Dallas and Loki and Sawyer and Gentry and Snot and, most definitely, Mad," Isaac said as he flashed me a smile. I felt my insides go impossibly warm.

Isaac's eyes fell on Sheridan, who was looking at both him and Newt with blatant want. But the man continued to hang back. It was Isaac who returned to us. When he was once again pressed up against my side, Newt still in his arms, he said, "Newt, I want you to meet someone. This is Aaron."

"Like our name?" Newt asked, and Isaac nodded.

"Hello," Newt said, then he stuck out his hand.

The spit-covered one.

Sheridan didn't even hesitate to take it. "Hi, Newt," he said, his voice cracking just a little.

Isaac put out his hand next... also his spit-covered one. "I'm Isaac, Aaron. It's very nice to meet you."

The man nearly crumpled in relief. His eyes looked watery as he said, "It's so very nice to finally meet you both."

I put my arm around Isaac's shoulders and then leaned down to kiss his temple. He put his free arm around my back. "Aaron, this is my boyfriend, Maddox."

Aaron and I shook hands.

The older man couldn't seem to stop looking at his grandsons, but he seemed to catch himself because he fished around in his pocket and pulled out a business card and handed it to Isaac. "Um, I know it's too soon after all that's happened, but if you ever want to talk or need anything, anything at all, would you…would you call me, please?"

Isaac took the card. Aaron stared at him for a long beat, then Newt. He quickly patted Newt on the knee before saying, "Well, I should leave you to it." He turned to go.

Isaac glanced at me, and I quickly pulled his hand up to my lips and kissed the back of his knuckles. "Go get him, baby," I said softly. He nodded, then he was handing me Newt and hurrying after Aaron. He stopped him about halfway between the front of the courtroom and the exit. I only overheard a little bit of their conversation, but it was the most important part.

The part where he invited Aaron to come have dinner with his family.

I looked at Newt. "You ready to go, buddy?" I asked as I gave him a squeeze.

He nodded and then grinned at me.

It was a bit of an evil grin.

"What?" I asked.

"You still gotta get punished," he said slyly.

"For what?" I asked as I squinted my eyes at him.

"You said a bad word."

I smiled when I remembered the moment right before I'd carried Newt into the ambulance when I'd said the word *damn* and he'd called me on it. We'd both agreed my punishment could wait until Isaac was home.

"I gotta tell Isaac."

"Hmmm," I said as I began carrying him toward Isaac. "Any chance you can forget that happened?"

Newt slowly shook his head. "No, 'cause I've got a big memory," he said as he pointed at his head. He was wearing his soft-padded helmet, but I loved that he didn't even seem to notice.

"Okay, what about a deal?" I asked. "What do you want for your silence?"

He thought about it for a long time.

Too long.

I saw the moment he came up with his evil plan because his eyes went bright and he grinned.

"Oh no, what? I don't have to go near Jerry, do I?" I asked.

Newt shook his head. Then he leaned down and whispered in my ear. I was laughing by the time he was done.

"What are you two whispering about?" Isaac asked as he came up to me. He held his hand out to me and I immediately took it.

"Oh, nothing," I murmured.

He eyed me suspiciously. "Okay, then. Aaron's going to come over for dinner," he said as he motioned to where Aaron was talking to Nolan, Sawyer, and Dallas.

"Good."

"I thought we could invite Ford. Cam too, maybe."

I eyed him. I'd told Isaac the day before about the weird friction between the good-looking sheriff and the troubled younger man. "Yeah, not sure that's a good idea," I said.

Isaac gave my hand a squeeze. "You and I didn't seem like a good idea, either. And look at how well that turned out," he said.

"Touché."

Newt began wiggling in my arms as we neared Nolan and Dallas and I quickly put him down and watched as he ran up to my brother. He motioned them along with Sawyer down to his level, then began whispering in their ears. All three laughed as soon as he finished talking.

The little traitor.

"What is all that about?" Isaac asked.

Since I knew my secret was going to get out anyway, I pulled Isaac to a stop and then tugged him close enough so I could brush my mouth over his. "Are you wearing them today?" I asked.

Ever since Christmas, Isaac had taken to wearing his pretty underwear every day. He blushed prettily at my question.

Which was answer enough.

"Which ones?" I asked so only he could hear.

"Maddox," he groused under his breath.

"Fine, just tell me the color. The rest can be a surprise for when we're alone tonight."

With that, his cheeks heated for a whole other reason. "The bright pink ones... with the white flowers."

My dick immediately responded because those were a personal favorite of mine. Oh hell, who was I kidding. Anything the man wore on his person was a favorite. I kissed him softly, then called to Newt, "Newt, I know what color I want. Bright pink... with white polka dots!"

"Okay, Mad!" Newt called, then he was following the guys out of the courtroom.

Isaac laughed. "*What* was that all about?"

I took his hand in mine to lead him from the room. "Oh nothing, I just have an appointment at Newt's Nifty Nails tonight, that's all."

Isaac pulled me to a stop and eyed me. "What did you do?" he asked.

I tugged him forward and wrapped my arms around him. "I got smart and fell in love with you, for starters," I said, then I kissed him until we were both breathless and he completely forgot what we were talking about.

So did I, for that matter.

"Take me home, Maddox," he murmured against my mouth. Then he pulled the dog tags out from beneath his shirt and began rubbing them between his fingers as he put his free hand in mine.

I pulled his hand up to my mouth for one final kiss and then did exactly that.

EPILOGUE

ISAAC

Six months later

"Okay, I'll call you every day from the road. Make sure you do everything Dallas and Nolan and Grandpa tell you, okay?" I said.

"'Kay," Newt said dutifully. He spit in his hand before I could stop him. "Spit on it."

"Maddox," I growled.

Maddox appeared from where he'd been putting our bags in the back of the SUV. He kissed my temple and said, "It's Dallas's fault."

"Hey!" Dallas called in his raspy voice. He flipped Maddox the bird when Newt wasn't looking. Nolan laughed and patted his fiancé's stomach.

Newt was still waiting expectantly, so I spit on my hand and shook his. And immediately vowed to google alternative pact-making methods. After the shake, Newt threw his arms around me. I got down to his level and tugged him into my arms. He was wearing his helmet, so I kissed his cheek. "Be good," I said as I put some distance between us so I could look him in the eye.

"I will," he responded, then he put his arms around me for an extended squeeze. Loki's big tongue lapped over both our faces and while I sputtered to get the doggie spit out of my mouth, Newt laughed and hugged Loki's neck.

"Have fun with Justin and Emily today," I said.

"I will," he said again.

"And make sure to clean Snot's litter box every day."

"I will."

"And no riding your bike past the sign in the driveway."

"I will."

I frowned at him and he smiled. "Oops. I mean, I won't."

"Go say goodbye to Maddox," I said.

Newt hurried around the car and I wasn't the least bit surprised to hear spitting sounds. I shook my head as I went up the walkway to say my goodbyes to Nolan and Dallas. The couple had only recently gotten engaged and were planning to marry once Maddox and I got back from Oklahoma.

The call had come in the previous day that Jett's grandmother had taken a turn for the worse and wasn't expected to last more than a week. It'd been the woman herself who'd called Maddox a couple of weeks earlier and begged him to look out for Jett once she was gone. The man had continued his decline over the months and both Maddox and Jett's grandmother feared what he'd do after his last reason for living was gone. Maddox had told me I didn't need to go with him, especially since I'd only recently started up with some online college courses, but I'd quickly disabused him of the notion by yelling a couple of non-Newt-friendly words at him for the ridiculous suggestion. Fortunately, Newt hadn't been around to hear me and buying Maddox's silence had been incredibly easy… and pleasurable. I was seriously considering tossing the occasional swear word out there now and again when only Maddox was within hearing range to see what it could get me.

Neither Maddox nor I expected Jett to come easily, but he also wasn't going to get much of a choice in the matter. Between his grandmother making it her dying wish that he return to Pelican Bay with us and Maddox planning to blackmail the man by threatening to have him declared unfit to make his own decisions, we were sure we'd manage to get Jett to agree. However, once we got him here, it was a different ballgame.

The plan was to have him stay with us in the house we'd only just finished building on some of the vacant land that bordered Dallas and Nolan's property. Our houses were so close that Maddox and I were fine with Newt walking the short path between the two homes on his own. We'd made sure to build a house that was wheelchair accessible on the off chance Jett would be coming to stay with us at some point in the future. Dallas and Maddox had also started paving some of the trails around the sanctuary so it would be easier for Jett to use his wheelchair, since the man hadn't made use of the prosthetics the military had offered to fit him for. That was on our to-do list too, but our biggest concern was just getting him somewhere that he could hopefully start the healing process.

We'd ended up living in the apartment above the garage while our house was being built because Maddox had sold the house his parents had once owned to my grandfather. Newt and I had taken things with Aaron slowly. It'd been almost two months before I'd even told Newt that the man was our mother's father. He'd been confused at first, and had had a lot of questions, but he'd eventually gotten excited about the idea that he had even a bigger family than before. Aaron had initially gone back to Texas, but he'd been coming up to see us every other weekend in the beginning, then every weekend. After a while, he just hadn't gone home again. He'd retired a few years before Gary had found him, so there'd been nothing tying him to Houston. His company was run by other people and Aaron just collected the substantial profits.

Profits he'd tried to share with Newt and me on numerous occasions. It had taken him a while to accept that we really just wanted him and not his money. After Gary had been arrested and prosecuted for assaulting Newt and me, I'd been named the trustee for the money our mother had left Newt. But Maddox and I had decided to leave it all in the trust for Newt when he was old enough to decide what he wanted to do with it. Maddox hadn't been kidding when he'd said he had more money than he knew what to do with. I hadn't liked the idea of him supporting us, but since we were both still helping out at the sanctuary, he didn't see it that way. In fact, we'd bought into the business with Nolan and Dallas so we could split the costs with the other couple, since there were no actual profits to be made. It had literally become a family business that made no money whatsoever, but that brought us so much more than dividends.

While Maddox and I had been setting up house together, my grandfather had been redesigning the mansion overlooking the town of Pelican Bay. When he wasn't dealing with the renovations, he was working on various volunteer projects around town. And he spent several nights a week having dinner with us, either at our house or Dallas and Nolan's house.

I gave Dallas and Nolan a hug and reminded them not to get married without us, then hurried back to the car. I saw Maddox was holding Newt in his arms and saying his final goodbyes on the other side of the SUV. When he put Newt down, my brother came running toward me, Loki on his heels. He gave me a final squeeze around my lower body.

"Love you, Isaac."

"I love you, too, Newt," I said as I lifted his chin so he'd be forced to look at me. I knew for all his show, it was hard for him to watch me go. We hadn't ever been apart more than the few days after Gary had shown up and I'd been arrested. All those charges had been dropped and my record had been cleared. Right after that, I'd gotten legal custody of Newt. Maddox and I were looking into adopting him once we were married.

I couldn't help but glance down at the dog tags around my neck. Maddox had asked me to marry him the night of my birthday a couple of weeks earlier, and while he'd gotten me a ring that I loved and was currently wearing on my left hand, it was the dog tags that I saw as the proof of our commitment to one another and our desire to spend the rest of our lives together.

"I'll be back soon, okay?"

Newt nodded. I leaned down and gave him one last kiss on his cheek, then sent him up the walkway. Nolan and Dallas embraced him and then he was turning and leaning back against them as Maddox and I got in the car. Maddox had only recently started driving again and it had taken a lot of work on his part to get that far. He was still meeting with his therapist every week, and while he had the occasional episode that was linked to either loud sounds or when he had a nightmare, they were happening further and further apart.

Maddox got the car started and in gear, then his hand was searching out mine. I waved to Newt until we were out of sight. Maddox looked a little tense behind the wheel, but I knew he'd relax eventually. But I also didn't mind helping him along.

"I spy with my little eye…"

Maddox smiled and looked at me.

"…something black."

Maddox glanced around the interior of the car and began guessing things.

"I spy with my little eye something that's sheer."

A grin tugged at his mouth as heat filled his eyes. "Babe, I think you're kind of breaking the rules."

"No, I'm not," I said.

He looked pointedly at my pants, since he was assuming I was talking about my underwear, which wasn't visible. Of course, my body reacted.

"Fine," he said and began guessing again. Ridiculous guesses that had me smiling. He finally gave up and asked for another hint.

"I spy with my little eye something you might have seen on the internet one day, but they didn't have it in my size."

Maddox jerked the wheel just a bit before he caught himself. "No," he said in disbelief.

I glanced down at my arm where my sleeve was pulled up just a bit. There was a tiny bit of sheer black material peeking out.

"Got an email a few days ago that they had it in my size," I said with a wink.

"Show me."

I shook my head. "Nope, sorry, can't. Wouldn't want you to be a distracted driver."

He eyed me, then suddenly he was veering off onto a side road. "What are you doing?" I asked with a laugh.

He didn't answer as he pulled the SUV beneath a line of trees bordering a field and jammed it into park. "Show me," he demanded.

"Someone might see," I said coyly.

"The windows are tinted and you know we own this land," he said impatiently. "Now off."

I eyed him and then reached for the door handle and stepped outside. The weather was still on the cool side, but it was a sunny day. The line of trees provided enough privacy that we wouldn't be seen unless someone was practically on top of us.

Maddox had picked well.

I went to the front of the SUV and he met me there. I turned around so he could see the best part of my surprise when I took my shirt off. I heard him groan as I revealed the nearly see-through, snug tunic that was scooped low in the back. So low it revealed most of my shoulders. I took my time getting my pants undone and as soon as they cleared my hips and fell into a pool at my feet, Maddox whispered, "Oh, fuck."

I'd only had a little time to look at myself in the mirror the night before when I'd tried the ensemble on while Maddox had been out locking up the sanctuary, but it'd been enough to see it fit me perfectly. The top piece was see-through material that hugged my body and ended at my waist like a normal top. The sleeves were long and went to just above my wrists. The sheer material meant Maddox could see the high-waisted panties that exposed most of my ass to him. But the best part were the long, thin garter straps that tied the bottom of body-hugging tunic to the tops of the thigh-high stockings. The stockings had lace bands at the top but the rest of the fabric was a sexy fishnet material.

I put my hands just slightly behind me so it would cause the muscles in my upper back to flex. I knew Maddox loved that and it had been part of the appeal of the outfit when we'd been looking through a lingerie webpage. We'd both fallen in love with the elegant piece but had been disappointed when they hadn't had it in my size. As I felt Maddox press up against my back, the bulge of his cock riding my ass, I was glad I'd paid for rush shipping.

Maddox nuzzled my neck.

"You look gorgeous."

I *felt* gorgeous and that was what Maddox loved more than anything. And that was only one of the many reasons I loved him. He turned me around and let his eyes roam over my front. "I know I should wait until tonight," he said with a shake of his head, then his hands were on my outer thighs, playing with the garter straps. "But that's just not going to happen."

He kissed me deeply, then took his time sliding my panties off, which I'd had enough sense to put on over the garter straps, meaning he didn't have to undo them at all. Maddox left my top on, as well as the stockings. He kept toying with the attached garters for the longest time before reaching into his pocket for his wallet. He removed a packet of lube and put it on the hood of the car, then he was freeing his dick and pushing his pants down. I put my hands on the car so that my body was splayed out for him like some kind of offering. The hunger was hot in his eyes as he lubed up his bare dick, then he was lifting me and swiping the rest of the lube over my opening. Maddox used one arm to brace my back as I wrapped my legs around his waist. He used his free hand to place his cock at my hole and begin to push inside of me.

I was so turned on that I grabbed his face with one hand and said, "Hard, okay?"

He nodded, seemingly unable to speak. He sealed his mouth over mine and shoved into me deep. I cried out into his mouth as the pain and burn mixed. He was balls-deep within a couple of thrusts and then he was pounding into me. I was reliant on him not to let me fall because I had nothing on the car that I could hold onto. But I knew Maddox wouldn't let me go.

It just wasn't in his nature.

Not in any sense of the word.

His free hand kept stroking all over my body as he fucked me. Sometimes my skin, sometimes the softness of the material that hugged my body. It didn't matter. I felt his touch no matter what.

Maddox supported my ass with one hand as the other pressed my upper body back onto the hood. He fucked me ruthlessly and I couldn't stop crying out from the sheer pleasure of it all. I came hard and fast and without any kind of warning. My cum hit his chest and mine, as well as my chin. It looked bright against the black material. Maddox kept fucking me as he leaned down to lick the fluid off my skin and the lingerie. My ass was rippling around his pulsing cock and semen kept spewing from the head of my dick as aftershocks rocked my body. It wasn't until my body seemed like it had been sucked dry that Maddox came deep inside me, roaring in satisfaction as he did so. I reveled in the heat of his cum as he filled me up. I clung to his neck as I tried to jam my hips down on him to prolong both his pleasure and mine.

When we were both spent, I collapsed against him and he used the car to help support me. He kissed my neck, then my mouth and I tasted myself on him. I could feel the mess we'd created, but I didn't care. We could easily change clothes.

"I love you, Isaac. So very much."

"I love you too," I said as I ran my fingers over his hair. The dog tags shifted between us and we both looked down at them. They weren't stained with cum, but my pretty outfit was.

And that made me incredibly happy.

Besides, it would be easy to clean for the next round.

"I guess I need to change," I said. "Any requests, soldier?"

He smiled and whispered into my ear which panties he wanted me to wear, and I couldn't help but nod against his neck.

I nuzzled his skin for a moment, then kissed his ear. He'd made an excellent choice and when I told him as much, he merely looked me up and down and agreed with me that he had, and I knew he wasn't just talking about the panties.

He wasn't the only one who'd chosen well.

And so I told him that too, and then I told him we should get going so we could go bring his friend home.

Because there would always be room in our family for one more lost soul… or a few.

The End

ABOUT THE AUTHOR

Dear Reader,

I hope you enjoyed Maddox and Isaac's story. They and Newt will be back, along with the whole gang, for the next book in the series which will be Ford and Cam's story.

    As an independent author, I am always grateful for feedback so if you have the time and desire, please leave a review, good or bad, so I can continue to find out what my readers like and don't like. You can also send me feedback via email at sloane@sloanekennedy.com

Join my Facebook Fan Group: Sloane's Secret Sinners

Connect with me:
www.sloanekennedy.com
sloane@sloanekennedy.com

ALSO BY SLOANE KENNEDY

(Note: Not all titles will be available on all retail sites)

The Escort Series
Gabriel's Rule (M/F)
Shane's Fall (M/F)
Logan's Need (M/M)

Barretti Security Series
Loving Vin (M/F)
Redeeming Rafe (M/M)
Saving Ren (M/M/M)
Freeing Zane (M/M)

Finding Series
Finding Home (M/M/M)
Finding Trust (M/M)
Finding Peace (M/M)
Finding Forgiveness (M/M)
Finding Hope (M/M/M)

Pelican Bay Series
Locked in Silence (M/M)
Sanctuary Found (M/M)

The Protectors
Absolution (M/M/M)

Salvation (M/M)

Retribution (M/M)

Forsaken (M/M)

Vengeance (M/M/M)

A Protectors Family Christmas

Atonement (M/M)

Revelation (M/M)

Redemption (M/M)

Defiance (M/M)

Unexpected (M/M/M)

Shattered (M/M)

Protecting Elliot: A Protectors Novella (M/M)

Discovering Daisy: A Protectors Novella (M/M/F)

Non-Series

Letting Go (M/F)

Twist of Fate Series (co-writing with Lucy Lennox)

Lost and Found (M/M)

Safe and Sound (M/M)

Body and Soul (M/M)

The following titles are available in audiobook format with more on the way:

Locked in Silence

Absolution

Salvation

Retribution

Lost and Found

Safe and Sound

Body and Soul

Made in the USA
San Bernardino, CA
04 May 2018